MW01110256

Also by Peter McCabe

City of Lies: A Novel
Apple to the Core: The Story of the Beatles Breakup
Bad News at Black Rock: The Sell-Out of CBS News

I wish to thank Det. Mike McDonagh of the L.A.P.D. for
his guidance on police procedure, and an old friend,
George Sibley, for his thoughts about the American West.
Once again, I am grateful to my agent, Loretta Barrett,
and my editor, Lisa Drew.

Wasteland

1

A few weeks ago, on a warm spring afternoon, I sat in the office of a psychiatrist, Dr. Donald Weiss, sifting through all that had happened to me in the past year and examining my options. I wasn't seeing him on any lark, believe me. After what I'd gone through I didn't have much choice but to seek professional help—my past year was the kind of year nobody should have, and I trust I'll never have another like it. Still, in the wake of it, I was utterly depressed. Feelings of futility hung over me, and like the summer smogs above the city, these never seemed to disperse.

I'd seen Weiss once before with Caroline, but I'll get to that. On this particular day, I told him I was thinking of leaving Los Angeles, for good. After a moment he asked me why I came to L.A. in the first place. I said, "Same reasons as everyone else, I guess. Fame, money, tanned women."

He smiled. "So what's so different now?"

I started to think about what I'd said in response to his first question. It was 1983, and I could still see myself, a fresh-faced kid, getting off the United flight at LAX, with a couple of grand in my wallet. I saw myself leaving bars on Melrose, going back to the apartments of young women in Westwood. I saw myself, a few months down the line, sitting opposite John Clem in his Century City office, praying he would hire me and wondering what this guy had, that he could come from nowhere and be as rich as Croesus by age thirty-three. And as I sat there, I wondered whether I'd brought any moral armor with me from Chicago, and if so, how quickly it had tarnished in the land of the sun.

But then, what did I know? What had I had until then? Three years of school in Evanston. Two years of working at my father's staple-manufacturing plant in Elmhurst. Watching my mother grow old, and more alone, and resentful about the one thing my father did spend money on—his mistress. The truth was, until I moved to Los Angeles, my life seemed bounded—by snow, by cold, by grit, by the staples I was forever picking out of my hair, by the Bears' prospects . . . and by my father. To him, it seemed like the natural order of things that I should take over his business, until that cold day in January, when I announced I was going to live in Los Angeles.

He blew his stack. He told me I could get along without him from then on. And so I landed in Los Angeles a week later with my savings, and the pressure of pride, knowing I could not go back.

I'd told Weiss all this—and as I sat thinking about it, it took a moment before I realized he was still waiting for an answer to his second question.

I said, "So what's different? . . . The difference is I can't feel anything for this place after what happened."

Weiss sat quietly for a moment. Then he said, "You mentioned some dreams a while back. Do you want to talk about those?"

I shifted on the couch. The sun was filtering through the blinds into my eyes. Then I told him I had two dreams that occurred back-to-back.

"I'm at a ribbon-cutting ceremony in the first one," I said. "It's the inaugural for the Pike Mountain project."

He'd heard about Pike Mountain. It was out in the middle of nowhere, on the edge of the Mojave, an industrial site near a big hole in the ground, with lots of heavy equipment. In this dream, politicians from L.A. were gathered around my boss, John Clem. Helicopters and limos were waiting. TV cameras rolled.

Weiss asked, "Is Caroline there?"

Caroline's my wife. We had just been talking about her. I said she was not in the first dream, but she was in the second one—in fact, she was central to it.

Weiss nodded and asked to me go on.

"Well, the ribbon is cut. Applause breaks out. And after a while, I go up to Clem to congratulate him. I stick out my hand, but he makes no attempt to take it. He gives me this ice-cold stare and says, 'Save it, Will.' Then he walks off."

"Is this anything that actually happened?"

"No . . . I mean, the ribbon-cutting ceremony happened. Only I wasn't there."

Weiss scratched his chin and nodded slowly. Then he asked, "What's the other dream about, Will?"

"Well, it's the same day . . . only later. We're on a hotel lawn, waiters are bringing drinks. I'm with this group of politicians, then I look across the lawn, and I see Caroline chatting to several guys. Only the thing is . . . she's in her underwear. I can see guys eyeing her, kind of smirking . . . and I want to go over to her . . . take a cape or something . . . wrap it around her and escort her out of there . . . only I don't do it."

"Why not?"

"Because she's having a good time. She won't appreciate me going over to her."

Weiss nodded slowly. Then he asked, "How do you feel about that?"

"Sad . . . sad because she doesn't get it."

"How about *you* not getting it? She knows how you feel, doesn't she?"

I nodded.

Weiss rocked forward and folded his hands in his lap.

"Will," he said, "don't you see the connection between these two dreams?"

I didn't.

"What about the parallels in terms of your own childhood?"

I stared at him, and eventually he asked, "How did your father react when you told him you didn't want to be part of his business?"

"Like I'd betrayed him. . . . "

"Clem's a lot like your father. Maybe in your heart, you feel that's how he feels. . . ."

I'd never seen it this way until then. I sat thinking about it. Then Weiss said, "How did your mother react when you told her that you wanted to leave Chicago?"

"She thought I should do what my father wanted—take over his business."

"So, when you needed her support, she sold you out."

I didn't say anything. Then he said softly, "Caroline thought you should stay with Clem, right?"

I felt a little dizzy from the impact of the revelation. Weiss was quiet for a few moments; then he said, "Did you ever get any support from her?"

"From Caroline?"

"No, from your mother."

"Well, not in that instance . . . "

"Well, when did you get it?"

I felt a void open up inside me, a big hole, like that hole in the ground on Pike Mountain. Weiss lowered his eyes for a moment. Then he looked at me directly and said, "You never got it from your mother, Will. You never got it from Caroline."

I sat thinking of all the excuses I'd made for my mother—she was acting in my interest, thinking of my security. She wasn't. She took the easy way out, siding with my father because she lived with my father.

Weiss cleared his throat and said, "Don't you see the parallels, Will? Caroline . . . your mother . . . they're not thinking of you, they're thinking of themselves."

I suddenly realized I was staring at him. He hitched his shoulders and said, "Maybe because of your mother, you never expected much. After all, you married someone a lot like her, someone who couldn't give support."

I was silent for a moment. Then I said, "Well, you know what happened. . . ."

"Sure . . . she's a lot like your mother."

I could feel something welling up inside me. And for a while we just faced each other. Then he said maybe now I could recognize some things more easily. He offered a wan smile and asked if I was all right.

I nodded. Then he turned the clock around, and I saw we had overrun by twenty minutes.

I got up. So did he. He squeezed my shoulder, and I returned his grasp. Then I walked out and sat down on a low wall in the sunshine, gazing up the hill at the billboards on Sunset, and as I sat there thinking about the discussion, I was suddenly aware that my eyes had filled with tears. . . .

2

There were tears streaming down my face almost nine months before that day, but they weren't tears of regret. They were tears caused by sand, driven by a gusting Santa Ana wind. Clem and I and a photographer from *Business Week* were riding in an open Jeep up Pike Mountain, so the photographer could get some shots of Clem above that pit. Every so often, as we made our way between the rock outcrops, the wind would pick up and rake the Jeep with another fiery blast, and each time Clem would snap me a look, as if I controlled the elements.

Finally, we reached the crest and began to descend on the leeward side, and suddenly the wind dropped. The mountain, or what was left of it, had become our protector. Clem turned around, grinning. The photographer offered some remark about the excellence of the light. Then Clem parked the Jeep in what he considered the most advantageous spot and marched down the slope through three inches of sand toward the lip of the pit.

At times, he reminded me of the roughnecks I knew in Chicago—the guys with the big shoulders. He, himself, wasn't big, even if he acted big, but he had the manner of a guy who always knew what he wanted, always knew where he was going. Sheer drive had gotten him to where he was, and when he cranked it up, he acted as if nothing could stand in his way. It was infectious—I'll admit. To many people at Clem Resources—Caroline included—he was an inspiration, a mentor even. She admired his style even when he was at his most tiresome. Myself, I'd grown a little tired of the act by then, having witnessed it for eight years.

I sat down on a rock and gazed out at the vast pit. It had taken fifty years to make this dent in the earth, an entire plateau and half a mountain stripped away. I'd referred to it in press releases as an "ugly scar," but the truth was, it never offended me. I saw it as a testament to diligence—the pursuit of ore—maybe that's absurdly romantic, but I'd sooner have left the thing as it was than make it the biggest garbage dump in the West, which was what Clem had in mind for it.

My opinion, of course, didn't matter. I worked for Clem, and I'd learned long ago to keep my personal views under wraps. Nor did it bother me to be thinking one way and talking another—that's a time-honored rule in business and the price one pays these days for an inflated, six-figure salary. But a few things were bothering me at that time—not the least of them my role at the company. In the past several years, I'd gone from being a PR man to a lobbyist to a bagman. That's right—among my various functions at the company, I now doled out bribes.

How did I get into this?

The first time for me was when a county supervisor's aide intimated that there might be a way to speed up approval of one of the company's developments if a site inspector could be persuaded to see the light. When I mentioned this to Clem, he asked me to find out what the supervisor's aide had in mind. I went back to the guy and he said five thousand in cash ought to cover it, and when I told Clem, he nodded slowly and asked me how I felt about handling this. I said, "I guess I could handle it," and that's how it began—on a small scale, with a very practical reason to justify it—a bit like tipping a maître d' to ensure a good table. I paid the aide off at a taco stand on Third and Western. He slipped the envelope into his jacket pocket and went on his way. It was that simple.

So where was my resistance, my conscience, if you will? I can't say I didn't have one—at some level I felt a distaste for what I did. I guess it was on leave, or subjugated by youth and ambition, or by the promise of potential rewards from the company—bear in mind, I was still trying to prove to my father that I could get along without him. In any event, I went along with it, rather than buck the system, and over the next few years I went along with it more and more. I was the son of a businessman, and I was familiar with the hidden costs of doing business, and I also figured nobody was getting hurt by what I did—and when these things are done on the corporate ledger, there is always the tendency to see oneself as merely the intermediary.

And yet I was profiting by it. There were raises—big raises—leading to an improving life-style that needed to be maintained.

There was a mortgage, and car payments, and a child, and Caroline's ever-increasing demands, and a growing awareness that others did business this way, so why not? Clem was careful of course. The payments were almost always in cash, and if not, they could be made to look like campaign contribution oversights. In fact, it surprises me at times that I eventually began to chafe against what I did. But that's the God's honest truth—I did. And for reasons quite apart from the illegality and the risks entailed.

Why? I don't know, exactly. Maybe I'd gotten nauseated or a little older, smarter. Shades of mortality, maybe. Without getting too philosophical, I'd come to realize that this town was full of grubby men like me, whose lives would probably never amount to much. Part of the reason, I know, was self-interest, a desire to quit while I was ahead, but in truth, it was all mixed up. Some of it had to do with me, some of it had to do with Caroline and me, some of it had to do with the way things were between us, and some of it had to do with our working life together at Clem Resources. I like to think that I was looking toward higher ground—maybe I was—but the more I think about it, the more I think I was just sick of it . . . maybe a little bored with it. . . . I just didn't want to fucking do it anymore.

Off to one side, the photographer was talking to Clem about the background for his picture. Clem concerned himself greatly with how he was photographed, and that morning he had affected an executive-on-the-move look, right down to the binoculars he was holding. As I glanced over at him, he handed the binoculars to me, having decided that he didn't want to be photographed with them, after all. I sat holding the things, and after a while, since I was a fifth wheel here anyway, I took off the lens caps.

The lenses were powerful. I trained them across the pit, and as I scanned the site offices on the far side, I could see Sam Gilmore, in corduroy shirt and L. L. Bean slacks, standing among a group of men in hard hats, giving orders. The Pike Mountain project was his brainchild.

Three years ago, Gilmore had asked himself whether the answer to the city's burgeoning garbage crisis might be to haul the stuff east, where it could be buried in some remote spot in the desert. He had gone to Clem with the idea, and Clem, a developer with interests in resources, had agreed to bankroll the project. Feasibility studies were done. Pike Mountain rose to the top of the list as the ideal site, and after lease option arrangements were made for the land, Clem presented his proposal to the Los Angeles and Riverside County councils. The truth was, Los Angeles didn't have much choice but to seek a solution, and the city was fortunate, as ever, to have as its neighbor a whore with an empty backyard. Riverside County was to be bought, with fees per ton of waste hauled, and if the deal went through, Sam Gilmore would become a rich man, and John Clem, already a rich man, would become even richer.

That's where I came in. My job was to sell the idea—to everyone. To the Bureau of Land Management, to the press, but above all, to the councils. I was Mr. Fixit. In any other city but Los Angeles, I'd have spent my days in smoke-filled back rooms, but in L.A., of course, there are no smoke-filled back rooms, so my bases of operation were the county supervisors' offices, the council chamber, and of course, the West Side restaurants like Orso and Morton's, where things really got done in this town.

I'd come a long way toward understanding politics since my early days working for Clem, and certainly since my dabblings in student politics at Northwestern. I'd also come far enough to realize that Los Angeles was unlike any other city in the United States. For one thing, it had never had a Tammany Hall—at least not a full-blown one—so there were no agendas set forth by a coalition of traditional Democrats that had to be taken into account, and in the rough ground between business and politics, the players more or less made up the rules as they went along. The mayor's office had no power—that's why the real powers kept a weak man in office—because the power lay where it had always resided, where the money was. Or it gravitated to new money—to men such as John Clem.

He was now making broad sweeps of his arm, running down the benefits of the site for the photographer—a case of overkill, I thought, since the guy was here only to take pictures—and while this went on, I swung the binoculars across the site and focused on a group of people that included Caroline. It occurs to me that the image of her I evoked for Weiss in his office that day derives from this one. She was dressed in boots and a work shirt, rather than in one of her Armani suits, and she was the only woman in a group of men, and I could see she was having a good time, enjoying being the center of attention. There were men all around her, and I wondered what needs she might be feeling, living as we did in Los Angeles, the city of too many exposed body parts, with its long, hot summers, the dry heat, the need for escape. We hadn't had sex in about two months, and our relationship had reached a point where too much was going unsaid—and yet I'd let things slide. To do otherwise, it seemed to me, would have made the situation even more precarious.

By then we'd been married five years. We had met at work, after Clem hired her to be in charge of planning at one of his resort projects—an old-style office romance is what we were. Well, sort of. We'd noticed each other right away, and the first night we went out for drinks, any constraints we might have had about working for the same company, and dating, slipped their moorings. That night, as I pulled up outside her building, she hesitated before getting out of the car. Then she said, "You know what I like about you?"

I said, "What do you like about me?"

"I feel at ease with you. I don't get the feeling you're judging me."

I asked if other people judged her, and she said, "Sometimes." Then she smiled and said, "You're sexy, too."

She started to get out of the car, and I caught her arm and asked if she'd like to have dinner the following evening. She said, "Of course." And that's how that started.

It was months before I attached any significance to her comment about me not being judgmental. But in the meantime, Caroline brought to an end an era in my life. After we met, I was far less interested in the party life and in stray encounters with assortments of women. I wasn't judging her because I'd found one woman whose intelligence I respected, with whom I had a rapport, and with whom I could get all my thrills and kicks. Caroline was my friend, but she was also wild, sensual, provocative—my very own "sexual terrorist." She would come into my office, lock the door, strip down to her underwear, and ask whether I wanted it on the couch or the desk or against the metal file cabinet, which sang a beautiful tune to the rhythm of her bare ass. For five months, it went on this way, each of us barely able to keep our hands off the other. Then, passion exacted its price. Caroline got pregnant.

We talked for days about what to do, but in the end it came down to one thing. If we planned to stay together, we'd probably want to get married and have kids, so why not then? Why risk the anguish of an abortion? And so we bit the bullet and plunged into marriage and parenthood—and from then on, a lot of things changed.

For one thing, our sex life came to an abrupt halt. Caroline could not understand how I could possibly be interested in sex with a pregnant woman—this when she hadn't gained an ounce and was feeling virtually no morning sickness. After a while, I was concerned enough that I got her to a counselor—which was how we met Weiss—and during those conversations a number of things came out. I discovered just how abusive her father had been toward her—she may have gotten her artistic talent from him, but during her childhood she had taken her share of welts. Her mother, she felt, had allowed the abuse, because deep down she considered Caroline a rival, because she was pretty.

And during one session something else emerged. Caroline announced she had been married briefly to a man who had masqueraded as wealthy but who had turned out not to be. When I asked her why she had never told me, she said she felt it wasn't that important because she had promptly cut her losses and divorced the guy. Weiss then asked her, "Do you think maybe Will had a right to know?" She shrugged and said, "Not really."

Then, one day, at the height of my concern, I spoke to Weiss alone. I was looking for insights, and he volunteered a couple of observations. He felt Caroline didn't have much of a sense of identity in part because of her childhood. I remember his words exactly. "She has an image of herself," he said, "and she has the weapons, yes . . . but does she have the armor?" What he was describing was a woman who presented herself to the world as talented and capable, but underneath it all was vulnerable.

I bore this in mind, and somehow we got through the pregnancy. Caroline went back to work a month after our daughter, Katia, was born. And within weeks of her return, Clem promoted her to be head of planning for the entire firm.

She threw herself into the job with new intensity, and whether it was the added stress of new responsibilities or hormonal fluctuations in the aftermath of her pregnancy, I wasn't sure—but there were signs of strain, and by then even our conversations didn't seem to sparkle as they once had. At the same time, Caroline began to attach great importance to maintaining high visibility in Clem's eyes, as if she wanted him to know there was nothing she couldn't pull off. She was also becoming increasingly acquisitive. Her material visions were far more grandiose than mine—I guess I looked at money in terms of what it could buy me, then and there—Caroline, on the other hand, like Clem, viewed her entire self-worth in terms of what she possessed. If she could demonstrate to the world that she possessed enough, the world would be forced to reckon with her. And to this end, I began to realize, John Clem was her passport, and I was not.

So what was I? Some ornament? A sideshow? I began to get a little sullen. Our arguments grew more frequent, and it began to get harder to forge reconciliations when we seemed to be diverging. Slowly, I began to ask myself, What were *my* goals? And on the heels of this came a second question: Would I have stayed with Clem as long as I had if it had not been for Caroline?

Like everyone else in L.A., I'd begun to dabble with a screenplay. I'd mentioned it to Caroline once or twice, but she had reacted negatively, as if I were distracting myself from the main business at hand—Pike Mountain. I'd said, albeit half-jokingly, that I didn't think it was so bad to make one's living as a writer, but she had looked at me as if I were about to steal from her all the visions she had conjured for herself. And so I dropped the subject, things mired down between us, and it had been this way for a while. I wanted to quit, but I wasn't sure what kind of furor would ensue if I did, and so I hung in there, debating with myself. And I was still debating with myself as I sat on that rock that day, on Pike Mountain.

Suddenly, I was aware that the photo shoot was already under way. Clem was standing on a pile of stones, sticking his chin out like some commemorative statue of Karl Marx—meanwhile, the photographer shifted around him, suggesting this and that, and after a while I sensed Clem beginning to get the urge to take charge. We'd come all the way up here so the photographer could get some pictures that might inspire the *Business Week* editors to put Clem on the cover, and the photographer kept remarking that he wished there were some way he could get higher up, above Clem, so he could really capture the extent and depth of that huge hole in the mountain. But there was no way to get the Jeep down to here, and the only point of elevation was a single boulder with a cone-shaped top, nothing the photographer could stand on—or so he maintained. And it was then I saw that look come over Clem's face—a look I'd seen many times before.

He barked over to me, "Will . . . is there a rope in that Jeep?" I waited a moment too long. He was already marching by me toward the Jeep, and sure enough, there was a rope—a tow rope. He checked it out cursorily, marched back with it, then wrapped it around the boulder a couple of times, and called out again, "Will! Get over here!"

I guessed what he had in mind.

I got up and walked over to him. He grinned and handed me the mid-part of the rope; then he wrapped the other end around his waist and began backing up slowly toward the sheer five-hundred-foot drop. The photographer caught on, and his mouth flapped.

He asked me, "Is he serious?"

I said, "Believe it."

Clem aimed a look at the photographer and said, "Hey, Annie Leibovitz . . . I'm not doing this twice."

The photographer shot me another look; then he scrambled to focus his camera, and when he was ready, Clem braced his legs and eased over the cliff, working himself down a few feet or so. I knew the boulder would hold him if the rope didn't fray—still, I had hold of the thing—and suddenly I felt a huge strain. Clem—or so I saw later in the photo—had leaned back horizontally and extended an arm in a gesture of pride.

The photographer was on his belly, snapping shots—then there was a ferocious tug, and the photographer spun toward me with a look of panic and yelled, "Get him up!"

Clem's footing had slipped. He was now dangling five hundred feet above the pit floor. I began hauling him up, using every ounce of strength, feeling only dead weight at first; then the weight eased as Clem got his feet braced, and with the photographer directing and me hauling, we got him back up to the edge. It probably took all of thirty seconds, but it seemed like an eternity.

The photographer hauled him in to safety. Clem lay on his back for a moment, catching his breath. Then he uttered a guffaw, looked up at the photographer, and said, "Did you get it?"

The photographer nodded and mopped his brow. Clem got up, dusted off his clothes, and walked over to me. He clapped me on the shoulder and said, "What's up, Will? Did you think I was going down?"

I said, "No such luck."

He laughed uproariously; then he glanced at the photographer and said, "Get him to print one up. Maybe you can show it to Romero tomorrow."

Then he went off to take a leak in the sand, and the photographer wandered over to me, shaking his head. After a moment he asked, "Why would a guy . . . worth millions . . . risk his life like that? . . . For *garbage*!"

He was staring at me, his logic confounded in a way I've grown to expect of Easterners faced with the anomalies of the West.

I said, "For the future, friend."

3

I told Caroline about Clem's heroics on the way to lunch. She could believe it, she said, but she was impressed, nonetheless. We were driving in one of the site Jeeps south to Interstate 10, where there was a Mexican restaurant, a quarter mile or so from a Holiday Inn. Clem had begged off, saying he wanted to bone up for a press conference scheduled for later that afternoon at the site, and so Caroline and I were due to meet Sam Gilmore, his wife, Cynthia, and Greg Stannert, the site engineer, at the restaurant.

Caroline seemed in a cheerful enough mood. She had changed into a blouse and skirt, and as I glanced over at her, I saw that the lower button of her skirt had come loose, and I was tempted for a moment even then to reach over, ease my hand between her thighs, and ask her how that felt. But she had been so unapproachable lately, and I figured she'd probably ask if I'd been drinking, or something like that—so I held off. Indifference I could live with, I wasn't sure about outright rejection.

I drove on. We took the interstate west for five miles past scrub and cactus, until the Holiday Inn sign glistened on the horizon. I turned off the highway then and drove by the hotel to the restaurant. It wasn't fancy—one of those places with dark wood and studded tables. But the food was good, and when we walked in, Gilmore, Cynthia, and Greg Stannert were already seated and were well into the nachos.

I ordered a margarita, and at Caroline's instigation I again had to tell the story of Clem's daring. Greg let out a couple of raucous laughs and kept making expressions of disbelief. Gilmore, on the other hand, smiled only briefly, and at the end of the account he shook his head in a studied sort of way, as if he couldn't approve of such blatant exhibitionism. There was always the potential for conflict between Gilmore and Clem—in part because of clashing styles. Clem knew how to talk a great game, but at heart he was a developer. Gilmore, on the other hand, was a geologist, Stanford-educated, ecology-minded. He knew his way to a dollar, but he downplayed the stakes very effectively. If Clem was streetwise, Gilmore was urbane—impressive in a way. He was young, handsome, erudite, smart—and I'd sat in on enough meetings with him at the Bureau of Land Management and the EPA to see him work his charm with bureaucrats and officials. Yet there was something about the guy I hadn't figured out. A restlessness, maybe, or some dissatisfaction, or something about himself he hadn't come to grips with. He was like a man who'd gone to a lot of classes and yet along the way had missed a vital lesson.

The conversation broke up after I'd told the Clem story. Gilmore and Greg finalized some details about an upcoming meeting with the Bureau, which was supposed to sign off on Pike Mountain that week. Caroline and Cynthia Gilmore comparison-shopped through several clothing stores on Robertson, a game that occasionally threatened to turn into one-upmanship, then retreated into reserved politeness. I'd seen Caroline studying Cynthia Gilmore in the past, not knowing what to make of her. Six months ago, the Gilmores had invited us to dinner at their home in Montecito, and on the drive back Caroline had said enough to me to suggest that a part of her envied Cynthia Gilmore's life-style.

Envied it, and at the same time, scorned it. Cynthia Gilmore didn't work. As Caroline had said, "What does she do—other than ride?" But at the same time, Caroline couldn't write Cynthia Gilmore off entirely, because the woman was smart, conversant, educated at Stanford with Gilmore—and she was pretty, in a willowy-blonde sort of way. She also knew her way around art and design—in fact, their home in Montecito was as tasteful as any in California I'd ever set foot in—a low-slung hacienda, modernized in the Frank Lloyd Wright style—very cool, airy, and spacious. But if Cynthia Gilmore did nothing herself in terms of earning a living, she sure took an interest in what her husband did. Even as she sat talking to Caroline, I noticed that one shoulder was nudged toward Sam as she kept abreast of his discussion with Greg.

I was silent throughout most of their talk. I was still a little preoccupied with what I'd been thinking about earlier. Then Cynthia

Gilmore turned to me abruptly and said, "So, Will, where do we stand with the council?"

I told her I'd know more next week, and that was all I wanted to say. There wasn't any overt animosity between us, but in the past she had acted as if I'd rubbed her the wrong way, and I wasn't about to start currying favor with her now just to satisfy her curiosity.

She persisted.

"But they're leaning in favor, aren't they?"

I hesitated. Then I said, "There's a couple of people haven't taken positions yet."

I could understand her wanting to know. After all, the fate of the project hung on the council vote. But I knew, the less said at this stage, the better. I'd learned recently about an alternative plan that was due to be put before the council. I was pretty sure it wouldn't amount to anything, but its rumored existence had caused some council members to postpone making up their minds about Pike. I'd told Clem about it, and I'd seen him grow uneasy, and to have mentioned it in this group would have been to set off a panic. I could see Gilmore hastily convening meetings, wanting to know how to attack the thing head-on, when by far the best policy was to sit quietly and let it fade into oblivion—sometimes it didn't pay to draw attention to others' plans. I had additional reasons besides for keeping my dealings to myself. As I say, there were things I'd done on behalf of Clem Resources I didn't even want Caroline to know about, and I sure as hell wasn't going to say anything in front of Cynthia Gilmore. I'd made it a policy for years not to talk about this stuff with anyone except Clem.

I saw Gilmore gesture with his fork, indicating for his wife to back off. She changed the subject—then Gilmore asked me who would be at the press briefing. I told him the major California papers, the *Wall Street Journal*, several TV stations, a couple of business journals. I said it might be helpful if both he and Greg were on hand throughout, so that Clem could deflect any technical inquiries. They understood, and then the conversation switched gears. Greg started to talk about a wilderness resort in Alaska he planned to visit once the deal was done, a safe-enough subject.

Ten minutes later, we were on our way out of the restaurant. I was already out the door—Gilmore was paying the tab, Caroline was still in the ladies' room, and Greg was helping himself to toothpicks when Cynthia Gilmore came out and collared me.

"Will, I don't mean to push . . . but I think sometimes you enjoy keeping us in the dark. I don't know why. . . ." She had picked her moment to make her point, and suddenly I was annoyed.

I said, "You think this is some kind of power play?"

She planted her hands on her hips. "Well, why can't you be more forthcoming? Sam's worked so hard on this, and you make it all seem like some state secret. . . ."

Greg came out of the restaurant and walked toward us, and I wasn't about to let her off scot-free.

I said, "Get off my case, Cynthia."

I saw Greg roll his eyes, and that was the end of the conversation. Gilmore came out of the restaurant with Caroline. Greg said he wanted to stop by the Holiday Inn and pick up some magazines, and five minutes later, when I was alone with him at the newsstand, I asked him, "What's her problem?" I knew he and Gilmore went back a long way—Greg had been the engineer on a dam project Gilmore had worked on.

Greg laughed. As he paid for his magazines, he said, "She likes to be informed, Will. Maybe Sam doesn't talk to her enough."

I mumbled something about people making my job even harder. Greg seemed faintly amused. Then we walked out into the hot afternoon.

I got back into the Jeep with Caroline, and we drove back to the site, and on the way I brought up the subject of Cynthia Gilmore. Caroline didn't seem to want to talk about her. She was leaning back in her seat, letting the desert wind catch her hair, and she sat this way throughout most of the drive, until the air began to get a little thick with the site dust. Then she sat forward and took cover behind the windshield, and a few minutes later we drove in through the site's main gate.

I dropped Caroline at her office and drove across the rail line and beyond the freight tippers to find Clem. He was with his assistant, Al Premerlani, and they were both reading over my press release. Clem set his copy aside without a word; then he suggested we hold the press briefing up at the edge of the pit. Premerlani wasn't sure this was a good idea—too much dust—but Clem wasn't budging.

"We flew these guys in here. Fuck it, let 'em get a feel for the place."

He looked at me. I suggested we hold it next to the recycling plant. There was no actual construction going on that day. There would be less dust. The reporters could still get a good look at the site. Clem agreed. Premerlani took a batch of press releases and went off to set up mikes and tables. I wandered over to the office next to Greg's, which had been set up for the press to assemble in.

When I walked in, Greg was pinning up the engineer's diagrams. I helped myself to coffee and sat with him—I had a few minutes before the reporters were due to show up. There was a travel magazine on his desk, open at an article about the resort he'd been talking about over lunch, and as I glanced through it, he said, "Not to get in your craw, Will . . . but when do you think the council might vote?"

"Couple of weeks . . . if all goes well."

He raised an eyebrow; then he grinned and said he wouldn't mention it to Cynthia.

I'd gotten to know Greg pretty well. I saw no harm in letting him know. I turned the magazine page and looked at the rates for the resort he was planning to go to. Four hundred and fifty bucks a night.

I said, "What do they throw in for this?"

"Forty-mile views of the Bering Straits, salmon fishing, river rafting . . ."

He said he planned to make the trip just as soon as the deal went through. "May set me back a few bucks, but if the deal gets done, I won't be complaining."

"You bought a few Clem shares, huh?"

"Ages ago."

"You and a few other people."

I tossed the magazine down and asked if he was taking along the pretty, young designer I'd seen him with one night, about six months ago. He gave me the thumbs down, and before he could say any more, the outer office door opened and a couple of reporters walked in.

I went out to meet them. One was from the *Orange County Register*, the other from the *Desert Sun*.

Over the next half hour, the TV crews arrived, and finally Premerlani showed up with a dozen site vehicles and drivers, so the press could all be driven to the rim of the pit together. Premerlani was still griping about the threat of dust. He was worried that if the wind kicked up, the press might wind up writing about dermal abrasion. But the wind stayed down, and when the reporters arrived at the makeshift podium, Clem was waiting for them. Behind him a crane lowered bales of trash into the pit, and Clem made his speech, pointing out all the assets of the site—the recycling plant, the rail access, and, of course, the capacity—"Enough to accommodate the needs of Los Angeles for the next fifty years!"

It was then question time, and Clem had done his homework. Gilmore and Greg were at the podium with him, but he answered almost everything himself. He introduced Greg and Gilmore as the guys who deserved the credit *if* the council voted in favor and the deal went through. Then he deferred a question to Gilmore about feasibility studies. Eventually, a reporter asked whether Pike Mountain was, in fact, a long-term solution to the city's garbage crisis. Clem got back on his horse and launched into an impassioned speech.

I was standing off to one side, smoking a cigarette and half-listening when a reporter, Mike Grady, drifted over to me. I'd known Grady several years and I asked him if he'd gotten everything he needed. He said, "Yeah, Will . . . thanks." He glanced back at

Clem, who was still in the middle of his speech, and after a moment he glanced at me again and said, "Do you have a minute, Will?"

We moved away from the main body of reporters. I said, "What's up?"

His expression grew serious. "Listen, Will, you've done me a few favors. . . ." He glanced around to make sure nobody was listening; then he said, "Bernie Kurman's been talking to someone about you."

I felt ice start to flow in my veins. I said, "About what?"

Grady shifted a bit. "I heard him tossing your name about the newsroom. I think he's got a source for a story."

Again, I felt the trickle of ice. Bernie Kurman was one of the best investigative reporters in the city and about the last guy I wanted to be talking about me to anyone.

I realized my apprehensions might be showing, and I didn't want Grady to see I was concerned, even though he'd been decent enough to tip me off. I said, "Bernie talks to everyone, Mike. Sooner or later, my name was bound to come up. . . ."

"You know Bernie. He doesn't fuck around."

"Well, let him call me if he wants. I've got nothing to hide."

"I just thought you ought to know, Will."

It occurred to me, a little belatedly, to thank him. I didn't want him to think I was ungrateful. He nodded; then he headed back to the press group, and I stood looking on, sweating a little, and wondering who the hell might be talking to Kurman about me. Some politician's disgruntled aide? That was all I could think of.

The press briefing was starting to wind down. I left ahead of the reporters and drove one of the site vehicles back to the office and sat thinking that if ever I'd heard a warning, this was it. Maybe what I'd been thinking about earlier that day wasn't a matter of conscience but a matter of survival.

I knew I had a meeting the next day. There was really no way to drop that ball on that . . . but afterward? Yeah, afterward . . . or at the very latest, as soon as the deal was done. I didn't give a shit how Caroline might react.

4

Around three o'clock the next afternoon, I was in downtown Los Angeles, a few blocks from city hall, killing time before my meeting at Councilman Romero's office. Downtown was really my Los Angeles—not the clubs, not the entertainment scene—although lately I'd taken interest in the latter, since I'd been dabbling with the screenplay. But what I knew best was the Los Angeles that doesn't get as much attention as the other stuff that makes the tabloid headlines. I'm talking about the low, fetid ground where political deals were made, agendas set, understandings arrived at.

Coming from Chicago, I wasn't surprised by political corruption, but in truth, Chicago could have prepared me for Los Angeles. Here, corruption had been elevated to an art form and passed into law. County supervisors paid themselves more money than U.S. senators and were chauffeured around town in bulletproof limousines, having classified the work they did as dangerous. Their lavish suites outdid those of most corporate executives—I remember once sitting down in one suite with Clem, and Clem being blown away by the polished granite, the Persian rugs, the mahogany furniture. The political establishment here was more grasping, more rapacious, than in any other city in the country, and the reason was simple. The politicians here could get away with it.

They made off like bandits for a variety of reasons: the enormous rate of growth of the city, the sheer diversity and opportunity. There were multifold layers of government and subbureaucracies, and none of these were subject to any serious policing, except for brief periods following flurries of outrage when some egregious excess would come to light. That's how it was—that's how it still is—and it was in this pond scum that I floated.

I can't say with a straight face that it seduced me, or that I didn't have a choice. I could have quit, but until then I'd chosen not to, and I simply operated within the vaguely recognized guidelines. I worked for Clem as his liaison with the politicians, and when people needed to be paid for things to get done, I was the guy with the bag. The political establishment was like a vast burrow of gophers or gerbils, harboring secret stores and accounts that needed to be serviced from time to time. And so, between my other work, I serviced them.

And yet, that afternoon, as I wandered around the palm-ringed government buildings, which look out onto broad avenues running north, south, and west, I stood gazing at the many-tiered departments, now hopelessly understaffed and underrun, and I had to admit: Maybe there was a vision here at one time, a sense of building for the future, and I guess one could still have looked at it and said, "What a beginning!" So what went wrong? As the Faustian soul would say, "Did we lose the faith?" I don't know . . . but I remember thinking that day how it might be best if this city were to quietly implode, out of boredom or excess, so that we might begin again—on a more modest scale.

But then I had my meeting to go to.

I walked over to the council offices on North Spring and rode the elevator up to the office of Paul Romero. I was a couple of minutes early, and as I sat in Romero's anteroom with the door ajar, I noticed that a disproportionate number of the female staffers were middle-aged. Discretion had won out in Romero's place of work. A year ago, he had been hit with a sexual harassment suit, and although he had defended himself vigorously, and the suit had been dropped, there was never any doubt about the veracity of the charge. I'd seen Romero at parties. His modus operandi was to hit on every woman who crossed his path, knowing that from time to time one would say yes.

After ten minutes or so, one of his aides came in and collected me, and when I walked in, Romero was on the phone. He was an overweight man of about fifty, whose hair was now darker than it had been ten years ago—not that this did much for his looks. He had protruding lips and sagging jowls, and the lower part of his neck was beginning to merge with his shoulders. I took a seat, and as he talked on the phone he indicated his liquor cabinet and told me to help myself to a drink. Then he interrupted his conversation to tell his aide there was no reason for him to stay. I took this as a good omen. The aide left, and I sat quietly, glancing at Romero from time to time as he rolled his eyes, despairing of ever getting rid of his caller.

Finally, he hung up with a look of relief and extended a fleshy palm toward me. Then he buzzed his secretary and told her to hold all his calls, and again I saw this as a positive sign. He knew I was here to put some cards on the table.

We spent a few minutes on informalities. Then he dug in his desk drawer and took out a summary copy of the Pike Mountain report that I'd sent him two days ago. It was a three-page document, a digest of more than 180 pages, setting forth the arguments for the site. He asked for a minute to look the thing over; then he looked up and said, "You guys want to double the sanitation charge?"

He knew this as well as I did. But I played along with his look of surprise.

"Thirty cents a day, Paul . . . to clean up the Santa Monica Bay. Thirty cents won't even buy you a swizzle stick."

He glanced at me; then he read on, meantime doing a quick calculation on his stubby fingers. "Hundred bucks a year, Will. Lot of money in my district." He glanced up. "Out in Indian territory we don't give a shit about Santa Monica."

"The bay's a communal resource, Councilman."

"Sure, Will."

He put the report aside. "So . . . ?"

I said, "So . . . can you vote for this?"

He tilted his chair back, cracked his knuckles, and said, "I can vote for it, but it's going to cost me."

"Cost you what?"

"Come on, Will. I'm in a tight race. Why do you think I haven't endorsed the thing?" His brow knotted a little; then he said, "Will . . . this isn't like the rezoning project. That created jobs. How do I sell this to my constituents? What's the benefit?"

I said, "You don't give 'em enough credit, Paul."

"Credit's one thing they understand."

He laughed at his own joke. Then he said, "What's the vote breakdown?" Like he didn't know already.

I said, "Six for, six against . . ."

"McAlister undecided, Braddock leaning in favor, and me—right?"

I had to hand it to him.

He rocked back in his chair; then he eased himself up, went to the window, and gazed out at the downtown traffic. He turned to me and said, "How much does John Clem have riding on this?"

"Twenty million dollars."

He whistled softly. Then he came back to his desk and sat down, and I decided we'd danced around enough.

I said, "Clem'll help out. You know that."

He nodded. Then we sat for a while in silence, and finally he said, "We're talking a substantial contribution here, Will."

"John understands."

"You make sure he does."

"That's my job, Paul."

We sat in silence again. Then he nodded and said, "Okay, I'll vote for the damn thing."

I forced a smile and got up, and I was halfway to the door when he called after me. "I mean *substantial*, Will . . . and we should do it right away."

I aimed a look back in the room and said I'd speak to Clem. Then I left, closing the door behind me.

I went to the men's room and washed up—I was always sweating after these encounters. I stood at the turn-of-the-century sinks, gazing at my face in the mirror, and I remember thinking, This might mark the last time I ever set foot in this place. Then I rode the elevator down to the lobby and stepped out into the searing heat of the afternoon.

I walked west past the panhandlers and the orange vendors, and I was on the third floor of a parking lot, juggling my car keys, when a woman's voice, calling my name, echoed through the concrete enclave. I didn't see who it was for a moment; then I saw Nadine Jarmon getting out of her car. She closed the door and walked over to me, and we faced each other, a little awkwardly at first, as we generally did when we ran into each other.

Seven years ago, we had been an item. I'd run into her half a dozen times since then. The first time had been about five years ago—and on that occasion I was stunned to learn what she was doing. When we'd dated, she was studying law at USC, but after graduating she had decided not to practice. She was now working at the office of the Drug Enforcement Administration, a block from here—as an agent.

I stood looking at her. She was wearing a smart gray suit, and her hair was cut a little shorter than when I'd last seen her, but other than that she looked the same—the same keen blue eyes, with a fleck of green at the iris, the same ready, slightly ironic grin. I asked if she had time for a drink, and she said, "Sure . . . it beats sitting on the freeway." She grinned and went back to her car to get her briefcase, and I stood looking at her . . . looking at the neat curve of her body . . . and given the way things had been lately with Caroline and me, I decided that in the best of all possible worlds, the two of us would wind up in a hotel room together. It was a careless notion, I'll admit, but I thought about it.

We walked out of the parking lot. I took her arm as we crossed the street, and as we walked through the rush-hour crowd, I imagined we looked a bit like that couple in the American Express ads—where the guy is a little older and a little more jaded. We walked into the Hyatt and took the escalator up to the Gold Room, or whatever the place was called, and we wound up sitting at the bar because the tables were all occupied by conventioneers from Atlanta.

Nadine ordered a Perrier and helped herself to a handful of nuts. Then she slid off her jacket and swung around to face me, and I could see a couple of conventioneers checking out her profile. I told her it was nice to see her and asked if she'd moved from her apartment in Venice—she was thinking of buying a place the last time I'd run into her. She shook her head and told me she was still looking. Then she said, "Actually, I was thinking of you the other day. I was up near Carrillo Beach, looking at a few places. . . ."

This sparked a few memories.

She took another handful of nuts and asked, "Do you still go there?"

"Not much," I said.

"Too busy, huh?"

I smiled slightly. Then she said, "Don't tell me, Will . . . too many memories?" Her tone was ironic.

I said, "Of course." Then I told her we had some friends with a beach place near La Jolla.

She didn't offer any comment, and I switched gears and told her I'd taught Katia how to swim that summer. She asked, "How old is she now?"

"She'll be four in a couple of months."

I took out a picture and showed it to her. She looked at it; then she studied me closely and finally she said, "She's got your eyes . . . not much else."

She handed me back the photo. Then she started to tell me about the job and about an escapade she'd been involved in, a week earlier, when she had gone to arrest a coke dealer with a team of agents. Apparently, the dealer had fired off a couple of shots and made a run for it.

"So we're following this asshole. All of a sudden he starts slinging money out onto Sepulveda . . . to cause a diversion. When we caught up with him, he claimed he thought he was being mugged."

She laughed. Then I guess she saw how I was looking at her. She grinned and said, "Go ahead, ask me."

"Ask you what?"

"What you always ask . . . why do I do this? Isn't that what you always end up asking?"

"Nadine . . . it's hard enough to stay alive in this city as it is."

Her smile broadened. "I told you, it beats poring over law books. Anyway you always told me I took life too seriously."

I could remember saying that, but in a different context. I said, "I'm glad you're having a good time." Then I told her I was writing a screenplay.

"You mean you're getting fed up working for Clem?"

"No . . ." I was a little defensive. "It's just something to do. It makes a change."

She grinned. "Am I in it?"

"Sure . . . Annie Oakley . . ."

She laughed. Then she shook her head a little wistfully.

I said, "What?"

"I find it interesting, that's all."

"Why?"

She didn't answer, and I gave her a nudge. She took a sip of her drink, and for a moment she appeared to back off from what she was about to say. Then she said, "Well, I think there was always something going on in you. But you were so dead set about sticking to what you did. I thought you'd be happier doing something else, but we'd get into fights about that—remember?"

We were silent for a moment. I had no reason to think the conversation was going to get heavy—our encounters were usually the same, a quick drink, a quick catch-up conversation.

She said, "Are you offended?"

"No . . . no . . ."

I was thinking about what she had said. It had actually fortified me a little. I said, "You're right," but she reacted then as if I were being patronizing, which I wasn't.

She changed the subject, and for a while we played catch-up about the few friends we still had in common, and ten minutes later, she said she had to leave, and by then I didn't feel like getting into it again.

We walked back to the parking lot, and she wished me luck with the screenplay, and I told her I'd send her a copy when it was finished. She drove off, and I nudged my way through the downtown traffic toward the Santa Monica Freeway, and in the midst of the evening crawl, I began to think about what she had said.

I remembered the general tenor of our arguments. She was cause-oriented. I was selfish, or at least opportunistic, and after a while I had convinced myself we were a mismatch. Yet there was something special about Nadine. She was always concerned I was selling myself short to Clem, for money. And in a sense I had bulldozed her aside because I felt she would stand in my way. But while we were together, there was some glue. And maybe she was right—maybe there had been something going on in me all along, some buried conflict.

I turned off the freeway at Motor Avenue and headed north, and I started to think about Caroline. It seemed to be my fate, to be with particular women at the wrong time in my life, in circumstances when they would urge me to be other than who I wanted to be.

When I got home, I drove Katia over to the playground, and I sat on a bench for an hour and thought again about what Nadine had said. Then Katia and I headed home, and I desanded her sneakers and read to her for a while before turning her over to Fran, our nanny.

Caroline got home a little after seven. She spent an hour or so with Katia. Then she came downstairs and asked if I'd order in some food while she showered and changed. This was our routine at least a couple of nights a week, and half an hour later, we were sitting in the dining room, picking Chinese food out of containers. Katia was in bed, Caroline was glancing at the paper, and I decided this was as good a time as any. I said, "I need to talk to you . . . about a number of things."

She dabbed at her mouth with a napkin, and I had the feeling she thought I was going to talk about our relationship. Then I said, "I'm getting word that Bernard Kurman may be writing something about me."

She stared at me. "About what?"

"What would you think?"

She knew about the bribes, even if she didn't know about the extent of them. Then, in a halting way, she said, "How do you know this?"

"From a reporter at the press briefing. He told me someone's talking to Kurman about me."

She put her fork down and didn't say anything for a moment. Then she said, "Can he prove anything?"

I shrugged.

"What could he have?" she asked.

I told her there wasn't anything I could think of, and she looked a little relieved. Then she asked me if I had any idea who Kurman might have been talking to. I laid out my disgruntled-aide scenario, saying if this were the case, it could lead to an allegation. The danger, I said, was if someone was indicted and wanted to make a deal . . . but again, Clem and I had gone out of our way to make sure the bribes could be construed as campaign contributions, so if anything did come to light, we could insist this was what the money was for.

Caroline seemed relieved. She said she hoped it wouldn't come to that. I was thinking, she had not once asked how I felt about this.

Then she asked, "Does John know about this?"

"Not yet."

"You *are* going to tell him?"

"I wanted to talk to you first. . . ."

She looked at me, realizing I was about to say something else. I said, "I've decided to quit Clem Resources just as soon as this deal goes through."

Her mouth tightened. Then her jaw set, and she made no effort to conceal how she felt. Finally, she said harshly, "Is that why you brought this up?"

I looked at her, thinking it might have been a mistake to downplay the worst-case scenario vis-à-vis Kurman. But I wanted her to see the whole picture.

I said, "That's part of the reason."

"Or are you using this as an excuse?"

Her tone was accusing, and I felt myself getting angry. I said, "I don't need an excuse, Caroline."

I gazed at her, still feeling anger over her lack of empathy. Then she said, "It's not the reason you're quitting."

"It's part of the reason. It's not the entire reason. I just don't want to do it anymore."

Her mouth flickered. "Terrific."

She gazed at me, her resentment all too apparent, and as I looked at her, I felt like getting into a host of other issues. But I held off. I'd laid a bombshell on her, and I could see she was having trouble dealing with it.

After a while she said, "I don't believe this. . . ."

I didn't say anything for a moment; then I said, "I want out of the slime. It's different for you, you're running planning."

She laughed scornfully. "Welcome to the real world. Wasn't that what you said?"

She was turning the tables on me. Serving my own words back at me. Then she said, "So when are you going to tell John?"

"When I'm ready."

She laughed a little sarcastically.

"Nice of you."

With that, she got up and left the room.

I hadn't expected a sympathetic response—still, I was saddened by her reaction. Were we strictly a business partnership? I could hear her moving about upstairs, and I decided I'd give her some time to absorb this—Caroline's reactions tended to be swift and abrasive, and I knew how goal-oriented she was. I was hoping that, given time, she might come to see this as something other than her "business partner" letting her down. At the same time, I was feeling some satisfaction from having done what I wanted to do.

An hour later, I went upstairs. Caroline was sitting on the bed brushing her hair. After a moment I sat next to her, but when I reached over and tried to drape an arm across her shoulders, she said, "No, Will . . ."

I said, "It's been 'no' a lot lately."

She faced me. Then she said, rather emphatically, "No."

She got up and put her brush back on the dresser. Then she turned on the TV and got into bed. I sat on the edge of the bed, looking at her, and after a moment, she said, "What?"

I said, "You tell me."

She flicked through several channels; then she said, "You know how I feel."

We were getting nowhere, and I saw no point in getting into another argument now. I told her I was going out to have a drink somewhere. She didn't respond, or, rather, she did—through a total lack of response—and after a while I got up and left the bedroom.

I watched the tail end of a meaningless ball game and then I went downstairs, got in the car, and drove. I drove west on the Santa Monica Freeway, then north on the 405, then I made a loop and drove east on Sunset. It didn't matter where I was going. I just felt like driving, taking some small pleasure in the smooth handling of the car. But when I crossed Doheny, the traffic gummed up outside one of the clubs, and I found myself sitting in the fumes, glaring at the billboards and the tanning parlors, and at a guy in an Infiniti M-30 coupe talking on his car phone and running a tiny comb through his toupee—one more absurdity in the city of the absurd. I started thinking how much easier it might have been for Caroline and me if we'd gotten away from all this.

Finally, the traffic shunted forward, and I turned south off Sunset and headed down the hill on La Cienaga to Chaya Brasserie, where there was always a bar crowd. I nursed back a couple of drinks and considered getting into conversations just for the hell of seeing where they might lead. But some inertia had hold of me.

After an hour I walked out and handed the valet my ticket. There was a woman in front of me wearing a skimpy dress and black "fuck me" pumps, and as she got into her Alfa, she smiled at me, and in her careless grin I saw the vague promise of some kind of future if ever Caroline and I got divorced. But this wasn't what I wanted. I didn't want to go back to casual dalliances with strangers, replete with necessary safeguards. I wanted to be home with Caroline, see her approach me in the bedroom with an expectant smile, as it had been in the past. But there was little hope of that tonight.

When I got back, I checked in on Katia. Then I groped through the dark and into bed, to find Caroline's back firmly planted toward me. I wasn't sure if she was asleep, but it didn't matter.

I lay awake for a while, thinking she wasn't always as hard as she was now. Not when she was Caroline Bryant, five years out of design school, the woman who had once told me that she liked it that I didn't judge her, and who had also said that she didn't think there was anything I couldn't turn my hand to.

5

In the morning I put in an hour on my script, until Caroline called downstairs and asked if I'd drop Katia at her preschool. She said she had a meeting at nine o'clock. I had the feeling there was to be no further discussion between us that morning, and I wasn't sure when we'd talk about it next—Caroline could brood with the best of them, and in the game of silence she could always outlast me. Still, there wasn't much else I could say at this stage, and so I resisted an impulse to suggest we have lunch. I dropped Katia at school, came home, showered, and dressed. Then I drove to the office—a high rise in Century City—and on the way I decided I'd lock down the council vote first, then tell Clem I was quitting.

When I walked in that morning, my secretary said Clem wanted to see me right away. I had a momentary panic thinking Caroline might already have told him I planned to quit, but then I decided, no, she wouldn't pull a stunt like that. I walked down to his office, realizing he was probably eager to know how things had gone with Romero. But when I walked in, I saw that any discussion of this would have to wait. Gilmore, Greg, and Al Premerlani were already in the office, and from the look of Greg's downcast eyes, I sensed that the discussion between Clem and Gilmore had been heated. Clem seemed relieved I was there, and I guessed what had happened. Sure enough, Gilmore had found out about the alternate plan that was due to be put before the council, and he had blown his stack.

He'd gotten more incensed when he discovered that Clem already knew about it, and he had worked himself into a snit, demanding to know why he hadn't been told. In a sense he was lending support to our decision not to tell him, by the panicked reaction he was now having. I wasn't sure what Clem had said so far. He was trying to assure Gilmore that no deviousness was intended. But since Clem didn't know the ins and outs of the alternate plan, he'd been unable to be convincing. He quickly turned the floor over to me, saying, "Will can give you chapter and verse." Then he leaned back and shook his head, like he really needed this brouhaha over nothing.

I said, "There's nothing to get worked up about, Sam. The other thing's going nowhere."

Gilmore studied me a moment. Then he asked, "How do you know that?"

"Because Kern County's too late into the game."

Gilmore looked at Greg. Greg shrugged. Gilmore's temperature came down a few degrees. He looked at Clem and me in turn; then he said, "Why the hell aren't I told about these things?"

Clem said, "Don't blame Will. This was my call."

I said, "Riverside wants the project, Sam. There's no reason for us to undermine the other one, because the Riverside County supervisors will take care of that. The reason John and I didn't bring it up is the less people talk about it, the better."

Gilmore seemed somewhat appeased in the face of this. He said, "So you're saying this other thing's bullshit?"

"These guys haven't completed a feasibility study. All they've done is submit a proposal with competitive fees."

"How did the council react to that?"

"Well . . . some members want to make it seem like they're playing hardball to get the charges down. But it's a pretty weak bargaining chip."

I sensed what was really bothering him. The fact that another company had dared to copy his brainchild. His ego was all tied in with this thing.

Then I said, "This may all be moot in a day or two."

Gilmore looked puzzled, but Clem played it beautifully. Without missing a beat, he asked, "Why's that, Will?" As if his money had never bought anybody.

I said, "Romero came on board."

A silence fell over the room. Then they all started talking at once, tossing out suggestions, discussing final meetings with the various agencies. Clem suggested inviting council members to his house one evening, at the same time avoiding the appearance of a premature victory celebration. There was a sense of anticipation in the air.

I stayed on the perimeter for the rest of the conversation. Clem eyed me as he got up, and I understood that he wanted me to stay. The others left, and he asked me how things had gone with Romero. I told him. He wanted to know when I could make the arrangements to pay Romero. I said I'd take care of it that day.

Clem's secretary brought him some coffee, and when she left, I said, "It's not all good news." I told him what I'd learned about Bernie Kurman.

Clem seemed to retreat within himself for a minute. Then he asked the same questions Caroline had asked—could Kurman possibly have any proof? I said the chances seemed remote, but there was always the possibility. He and I shopped around awhile, considering who Kurman might have been talking to. We couldn't come up with anyone, but obviously Clem was bothered by the news.

After a while he shook his head and said, "Maybe we're doing a Gilmore—getting bent out of shape over nothing?"

I nodded.

"I'll tell you one thing," he said. "If that son of a bitch does write anything, we'll claim this is a blatant attempt to sabotage Pike Mountain. It might even win us some points."

He wanted to know what I'd do if Kurman called me. I said, "Hold him off until the council's vote."

He was silent a moment. Then he asked which council member we should go after to clinch it.

"Braddock," I said.

"You're the expert."

He told me he was flying up to San Francisco that afternoon for another project. He said if anything came up, I should let it wait. Gilmore would be using his office for a meeting with the Bureau of Land Management. "That's the trouble with partners, Will," he said. "You take one on, pretty soon, you're moving out of your digs."

I thought about telling him of my decision to quit right then. It just seemed like an opportune moment. Then I decided, no—I'd at least get the deal set. I went back to my office and made a call to Beth Braddock's aide. And an hour later, the aide called back and said Beth Braddock would see me at four.

In the meantime, I collected the cash from Clem, called Romero, and took care of the payoff by simply handing over a briefcase in Pan Pacific Park. I knew it wouldn't be that simple with Beth Braddock. I'd told Clem she could not be bought. She was in her mid-thirties, conscientious, and independent-minded. Her husband was a wealthy attorney. Clem's lawyer, Martin Borchiver, knew George Braddock fairly well and had suggested at one point that Clem and he have a friendly lunch. I'd argued against it. My sense was Beth Braddock would have an adverse reaction to any approach initiated through her husband. I felt the best plan was to simply go in, low-key it, and talk about the plan's merits.

And that's what I did that afternoon. I spent nearly an hour with Beth Braddock, going through the advantages of the project, point by point, even mentioning the downsides, rather than have her find out about them and come back at me. She listened attentively, asking the odd question from time to time, and when I was done, I said, "Beth, there may be a magic solution to the garbage problem one day—but until then we're at least sending the stuff to a thinly populated area that's already spoiled. And millions of people in this city will benefit from a cleaner environment."

She nodded slowly. Then she said, "It's not perfect, I guess, but it's the best we've got."

"Exactly."

She was silent for a moment. I held my breath.

"I like the guaranteed rates of haulage. . . ." She smiled. "All right, Will. I'll vote for it."

I called Clem, and they paged him in the San Francisco airport. He told me later he had tossed his briefcase in the air when he heard. I told Caroline that evening.

"Congratulations," she said.

Her tone was dry, but she couldn't entirely conceal her satisfaction about the thing going through—she'd been working on it two years. Then she asked, "Did you tell John you were quitting?"

"Not yet."

She sat looking at me. I was still looking for an opening, and I thought there might be one, especially when she said she felt like making dinner. But during the meal she again raised the issue of what I planned to do, and when I said I was tired of PR and lobbying, and wanted to do something entirely different, she became very quiet.

We didn't make love that night. But the improvement in mood was a small step in the right direction. As I dozed off that night, I was thinking things might improve once we were each bringing something separate to the marriage, but what I could not have foreseen was that my plans would blow up in my face before I even got started.

It began innocently enough.

Two evenings later, we were driving up Sunset Plaza Drive to John Clem's place for a party to celebrate his birthday, though this was probably the least of the reasons for the gathering. It had simply occurred to Clem to put his birthday to use, to bring under his roof the people who had backed him on Pike.

It was a weekday evening, and as we drove up the hill, Caroline seemed in a good mood. She hadn't even brought up the issue of wanting to move to the hills, which she'd been harping on ever since the riots, a few months back. As we drove, I glanced over at her, and she actually seemed content. She looked nice, too, in her black Chanel suit.

We drove along Mulholland, gazing down at the vast plain of jeweled light below. Then we pulled into Clem's walled retreat and turned the car over to the valets. When we walked in, there was already a crowd of about a hundred, the sleek and the wealthy, politicians, attorneys, key employees, and a sprinkling of celebrities, who were there not to flaunt themselves but to shed their mantle of ego temporarily and lend their support to an environmentally sound project.

I slipped into my usual glad-handing ways—I knew most of the politicians, and they knew my stripes, and they needed no icebreakers with me. I circulated briefly with Caroline, and we maintained all the appearances of a busy L.A. couple, whose only problem was a lack of free time. Then Caroline went off to charm a couple of heavy hitters from Pru-Bache, and Clem buttonholed me and wanted to be reminded of Councilman Stephens's wife's name. I told him. He glanced across the room and saw Stephens talking to Romero. Then he turned to me and said, "With those two on board, it'll be hard for anyone to carve out middle ground."

He touched his glass to mine and said, "To Project Sandlot."

It was my label—the name I'd first given the project when Gilmore had come to Clem with his vision.

Clem went off to talk to one of the mayor's aides, and for a while I talked to a state assemblyman. Then I joined a group of people at the bar that included Clem's attorney, Borchiver, Romero, and Greg Stannert. After a while Borchiver wanted to introduce Romero to his partner, and I wound up talking to Greg alone. He gazed around the room, took it all in. Then he said, "So, this is the power structure?" He shook his head slightly. "Amazing what you've got to do to get a vote passed."

I said, "You want to get to heaven, Greg, you need friends from hell."

He glanced around the room again. Then he said, "Okay, whose ass do I kiss?"

I suggested he meet Walt Gallagher, a Riverside County supervisor, and we walked over to the group where Gallagher was holding court. As I introduced Greg, Al Premerlani tapped me on the shoulder and drew me aside.

"Will, talk to John. He's got some crazy idea about having his photo taken with Stephens and Romero."

I didn't need this. It was a victory getting the two of them in the same room. Clem might consider it a savvy ploy to be photographed with opposite ends of the political spectrum, but I knew they'd hate it.

I said, "Shit, where is he?"

"Upstairs . . . making a call."

I cut through the crowd and up the broad circular staircase, and as I crossed the mansion's first-floor landing, I called out, "John!" The place had been remodeled recently, and I wasn't sure which was Clem's study.

His voice came back from a room at the far end of the hallway. "I'm on the phone, Will!"

I walked to a window and waited. There was a faint mist settling in the canyon opposite, and a crescent moon rose above the downtown skyline. Then I heard the murmur of voices from the veranda below, and as I glanced down, a couple of people stepped out from behind a planter, and suddenly my blood ran cold.

It was like a movie sequence . . . fingers interlaced, fingers playing. Then a woman's hip entered the frame, and a man's hand moved across it, caressing it, and even before the woman turned, I recognized the Chanel suit as Caroline's.

The hand on her hip was Sam Gilmore's.

I felt my face turn clammy as I looked on. They were on the veranda alone, away from the main body of the party, and they must have assumed nobody would be afforded a view of their hand game. Neither saw me. Caroline smiled and moved away from Gilmore, and the two of them drifted to the far side of the veranda.

I took a breath. Then I started downstairs.

I put my drink down in the main room, and I walked out the far side and came around to the veranda where they were. Another couple was out there by then. Gilmore saw me coming, and he didn't seem to think anything was amiss. He smiled, tugged at one end of his natty bow tie, and said, "How's it going, Will?"

I said, "Not as well as for you, I guess."

Caroline caught the ire in my voice, even if Gilmore didn't. She looked alarmed. Then I told Gilmore he had three seconds to get off the terrace or I'd kick his ass all the way to Sunset.

There was a silence. He looked at Caroline, then at me, then he said nervously, "What's this about?"

I said, "I mean it, Sam."

I took hold of Caroline's arm and started to lead her aside, and when I glanced back, Gilmore was still standing there affecting blank amazement. I took a step away, and he said, "You got nice manners, Will."

I turned back to him. "What did you say?"

He was silent. Then, as I half-turned away, he said, "Maybe you oughta go learn some."

I guess a lot of repressed anger welled up in me, because I hit him hard, once, in the stomach. He doubled up, and when he raised his eyes, his face was white—for a second I thought he was going to throw up. Caroline's face was something else. I think at that moment she felt I was capable of anything. Then her face grew dark, and before she could say anything, I walked away from both of them and into the house.

I made my way to the bar and ordered a drink, and I already sensed that some people in the main room had seen what I'd done. But the first hard evidence was when Greg Stannert came over to me and grabbed my arm. "Will, what the hell's going on?"

Greg was looking at me in disbelief. I took down a good portion of my drink. After a moment, I said, "He was feeling up Caroline."

"Oh, man . . . "

I saw Greg glance over my shoulder. He looked nervous. "Will, come on . . . take a walk. Let's go outside."

I said I didn't want to go outside.

"Will, please . . . just cool down."

I breathed hard. Then, without turning, I walked out the front door ahead of him.

We walked off into the grounds, and I lit a cigarette, and we just stood there next to each other. Finally I said, "Fuck, what else was I gonna do?"

Greg shook his head. "Jesus, Will . . ."

It had been so sudden. I was still in shock. Then the heat began to drain from my face, and after a moment I asked, "Did a lot of people see it?"

Greg nodded slowly. I didn't say anything. Then he eyed me warily and said, "Was Caroline going along with it?"

I nodded, and he shifted his feet for a moment. I tossed my cigarette into a flower bed and Greg sighed. Then he stuffed his hands into his pockets and said, "We really need this. . . ." We stood in silence for a long time then, and finally he said, "Do you want me to go get Caroline?"

I looked back at the house, but nobody else had come out, and eventually I said, "Just tell her where I am."

He nodded and patted my arm. Then he went back inside the house.

I walked to the edge of the grounds and stood gazing along Mulholland Drive at the walls of ivy, at the soft lights of multimillion-dollar homes. And as I stood there, I began to understand that this explained a lot in terms of Caroline and me lately. I'd been wondering what the hell was going on. Now I knew, and I guess some time went by before I even asked myself whether hitting Gilmore was the appropriate response.

I could hear the hard Chicago accent of my father telling me it was justified. I could even hear Clem saying it. But some inner voice was already telling me this was a no-no, even though I planned to quit, even though I didn't give a shit about Gilmore. And yet, at the same time, I felt a certain satisfaction from having given the whole California-cool way of being one round slap in the face.

I heard heels on the gravel, and when I turned, Caroline was walking toward me. She stopped three paces away from me and folded her arms.

She said, "Are you proud of yourself?"

I said, "Don't play Miss Self-Righteous with me."

She started to say something, but I talked over her. I said, "I'm leaving. You can leave with me or stay here. It's up to you."

She didn't say anything for a moment. Then she sighed and started walking toward the valets. I handed the ticket to one guy, and I didn't look at Caroline while he was getting the car. Then he returned with it, and we got in and I drove out to Mulholland.

I saw no point playing games. As I made the turn onto Coldwater, I asked how long it had been going on. Without looking at me, she said, "Three months."

I said. "You've got a lot of class."

She uttered a little sardonic laugh, and I glared at her. Then neither of us said a word until we were driving through the gilded glens of Beverly Hills.

"Why?" I said, finally.

"Let's talk about it when we get home."

We were talking in even voices. We could have been discussing the traffic or some item on the news. I almost had to remind myself what we were discussing here—my wife getting into bed, naked, with someone else, doing the very same things with another person's body that were once reserved for ours. I'd already decided where it had gone on. Caroline had been making frequent trips to Riverside County for the project and staying overnight. Between the Holiday Inn in Palm Desert and an occasional soiree in L.A., I figured she'd had plenty of opportunity.

We were silent as we drove down Doheny. After a while, I said, "You think I like being duped?"

"Let's talk about it when we get home."

Her tone was insistent. Then we were silent again, and I said, "Suit yourself," and I said nothing from then on until we were pulling into our driveway. I turned off the engine and said, "Let's talk downstairs."

She glanced at me as I got out of the car. I walked into the house ahead of her, and she went straight upstairs. Then she came down, having changed, and we faced each other in grim silence.

I said, "You expect this to work when you're fucking another guy?"

My voice was tight. It didn't even sound like mine. She looked at me a long time. Then she rested her head back on the sofa and finally she said, "I don't expect you to believe this, but this has really nothing to do with us."

"What?"

She sighed. "Unless you're determined to make a big deal out of it."

"I'd call a three-month affair a big deal!" My voice had risen.

"Maybe we should talk about us . . . instead of that."

"Talk? I've been trying to talk to you for the past year." I glared at her. "How would you feel if I went off and fucked someone?"

She didn't say anything for a while. Then she said, "I guess I wouldn't have been surprised."

"What?"

"No."

I was holding a lot in. I still wasn't sure whether at any moment I might let rip.

Then she said, "I'm sorry you found out about this. . . ." She lowered her eyes. "I'm sorry, period." Then she looked up. "But I feel a lot of ambivalence about this marriage, at least that's what I've been feeling lately."

I said, "So do I!"

At the same time I felt something growl in my gut. I waited. She didn't say anything for a moment, and in those few short seconds, I thought, People did get divorced. People grew apart and split up—even people with kids—it didn't necessarily mean the end of the world.

Then she said, "This isn't all me, Will. I don't even think you realize that."

"Realize what?"

"What you've been like. You've changed."

She started to add something, but I jumped in. "Maybe you haven't, Caroline . . . did you ever think about that?"

She rolled her eyes; then she said, "What am I supposed to do, Will, adapt to cynicism?"

"What?"

"That's the only way I can describe it."

"I'm cynical about what?"

"Everything . . . work . . . You denigrate everything you come in contact with. You don't have ambitions anymore."

So that was it. I shook my head.

Then she said, "I see you walking away from a lot of things."

She looked at me for a long time and didn't say anything. Then she got up and went into the kitchen. I wasn't sure if the conversation was over at that juncture. Then she came back in and stood holding a glass of ice water, and eventually she said, "Why the hell did you have to hit him?"

I said, "Fuck you. And your modern manners."

I got up and marched down to the spare room.

I spent the night there, too. For a while I thought of going upstairs and continuing this, but I was dug in by then. I'd heard one muted apology and a lot of justifications, and I was royally pissed. I felt the next move was hers.

It took me a long time to get to sleep. I sat up and smoked cigarettes and thought about a lot of things, and I had a couple of savage attacks of jealousy. At one point I decided I didn't regret hitting the son of a bitch, not for a moment. I hoped his wife heard about it. Then unease stole up on me again. The recognition of having acted out. There was only one word to describe what I'd done—it was *stupid*.

I'd crossed a boundary, and I knew it.

6

The fallout began early the next morning. Around seven-thirty, Clem called.

"Mr. Fisticuffs," he said, "I hear you throw a hard, short right."

I wasn't quite sure of his attitude. Or mine, for that matter. I'd woken up feeling uneasy, jarred, still angry. After a moment I said, "Did it make the late news?"

"It made an impression on a few people–I can tell you that." Then his voice grew serious. "Al told me about it."

He told me he had sensed an odd mood at the party when he came downstairs, and when he had asked Premerlani where I was, he had learned about what had happened. I asked if he'd gotten the whole picture. He said, "Pretty much." Then he said, "We don't need this, Will. I spoke to Gilmore. . . . I told him to straighten it out with you, one way or another."

I felt maybe it was his place to intercede, since this could impact on his company at a rather critical time. He told me I'd be hearing from Gilmore. Then he said, "Tell Caroline from me, she must have her head up her ass. . . ." He also told me to take the day off, let it blow over, and when he hung up, I felt he'd been pretty decent about it. He had not taken my head off, and here I was, about to quit on him.

I collected the newspaper and some coffee and went out into the yard with Katia. She had been asking me to let her ride her bike. It was an overcast morning, and a heavy fog had rolled in from the ocean, and the lawn was covered in a thick dew. I wiped off the glider and sat and read the paper as Katia rode, but after a while I found myself glaring at the same headline.

After fifteen minutes or so, Caroline came outside, dressed for work. She stared at me from the back door. Then she walked over to me, and we faced each other, and I felt the conversation could go any number of ways. Finally she said, "Can we get into this tonight? I'm late."

"Sure."

She asked who had called.

"Clem."

"What did he say?"

"He told me to take the day off."

She rolled her eyes. "What did he say, Will?"

"He told me to take the day off."

I looked at her narrowly. I still had the feeling I could erupt, even with Katia out in the yard. Then Caroline said, "Let's talk tonight." She kissed Katia and went to her car, and I watched her drive off. She did not look back. I let Katia play for another ten minutes; then I drove her to school.

When I got back to the house, I went to the room downstairs I used as an office, deciding to make use of the time and work on my script. But I'd been at the computer only ten minutes when the phone rang. It was Greg, calling to check in, and I was probably a little more forthcoming than I might have been had he not been with me the previous night.

He asked how things were, and I told him things were okay. Then he ran on for a while about what had happened after Caroline and I had left. He said there had been a little buzz for a while, but that it had abated by the time Cynthia Gilmore arrived, so she was none the wiser. I said maybe she should be. I told Greg I really didn't give a shit.

He asked me if I was coming in, and I said Clem had told me to take the day off. He said, "It really doesn't matter, Will. Sam went out to the site."

I told him I knew a gift horse when I saw one—I'd take advantage of a free day. Then we hung up and I got on with my work.

By ten-thirty, I was into it. Outside, the fog lifted, and the morning sun streamed into the room, and there were no further distractions. The only sound in the house was Fran going about her housework. I was on a roll, and I resisted getting up for coffee. Since I'd decided to quit Clem Resources, this was no longer something I could treat as a lark.

Then shortly before noon, the phone rang again, and for a

moment or two I was tempted not to pick up. Then I did, and when I said hello, the voice on the other end was Sam Gilmore's.

He said, "Will, you and I need to talk, in person."

"No, we don't," I said.

He started to say something, but I talked over him.

I said, "Sam, I've got one thing to say to you. I catch you looking cross-eyed at Caroline again—"

"Wait a minute! Wait a minute, Will!" It was his turn to shout over me. "You haven't heard my side of this!"

"I don't need to—"

"Yes, you do. Look, Will, I'm sorry about what happened, and I want us to straighten this out. So does John. We have to work together."

I backed off a little in the face of his apology. I said, "It isn't necessary." I sure as hell didn't want to see him.

"Well, I think it is. You and I are gonna be in a lot of meetings, Will."

Less than he knew. But at the same time I was thinking I owed it to Clem not to let this get out of hand. I didn't say anything, and eventually he said, "Why don't we meet at my place in town. I don't want to come over there, obviously."

We went back and forth for a while. Him insisting. Me maintaining it wasn't necessary. Then he said, "Look, there's some things you don't understand, and I'd like to explain them in person."

Again I told him I didn't want to hear it. But he kept going at it. Then he invoked Clem's concerns again, and finally, out of exasperation, I said, "All right . . . when?"

"How about eight o'clock?"

I said I'd be there; then I hung up.

After a while I went and lay down on the sofa. My first thought was that Gilmore might be facing a crisis of his own. Maybe he was worried Cynthia would find out. Either that or he just wanted to make a clean breast of it—in order to make himself feel better.

I got off the sofa and got some coffee. Then I tried to get back to work, but the rhythm was gone by then, and after a few false starts I decided I might as well go out and grab a bite of lunch. I asked Fran if she'd pick up Katia from school. Then I saved what I'd written and left.

I drove to Delmonico's on Pico, sat in a booth, and read the paper until my food arrived. As I ate, I started thinking again about what Gilmore had said on the phone. I was also beginning to feel a shift in my attitude toward Clem and his pragmatic response to all this. He'd been through the marriage wars. When I'd first started to work for him, he was married to an attractive woman from New Orleans who had wandered into his life at a business convention. But within eighteen months he was going through a vicious divorce.

Constance was her name, and she wanted a return on her investment. Fifty percent of the pie, including half of Clem's shares in the company. He fought it. At one point he told me he'd give away a million a day, rather than give it to her, and in the end, Constance settled for five million dollars, which, as Clem said, "should hold her until the next guy."

I sat thinking he might have demonstrated a little more understanding for me, knowing what I was going through. Then I began to entertain a few scenarios about what might happen between Caroline and me if things did get rough. She made a good living, and I doubted I'd get carved up, and I was sure she would agree to joint custody of Katia. Still, I didn't want it to come to divorce. I wanted to leave the single life safely packed away in the past.

I paid the waitress and drove home, took Katia out, and spent the afternoon with her. We drove over to Santa Monica, played at the arcades on the pier for a while, and then we had a bite to eat. When we got home, I let her watch *Lady and the Tramp* for the five hundredth time. Then I went downstairs to check my phone messages. There was one, from my secretary, but when I called her back, it was five-forty, and she'd taken advantage of my absence and left. I called Caroline's office, but her secretary was gone, too, and I figured this was probably just as well. I wasn't sure how she'd react to me talking to Gilmore.

Around seven-fifteen, I left the house and drove east on Olympic. The traffic was light, and by the time I turned north on Fairfax, it was still only seven-thirty. I didn't want to be early, so I spent a few minutes at a newsstand on Oakwood; then I got back in the car and drove north on Fairfax again, killing time by making a loop along Melrose to La Brea and driving back west on Sunset, and as I drove, I began to think about Caroline driving over here to see Gilmore, and before I knew it, I was in the grip of another jealousy attack.

After a while I pulled over. What the fuck was I doing, going to see this guy?

I fought off the attack and tried not to think about Caroline. And as I sat there, I began to think that maybe I was out of sync with the way things were in the circles I moved in. Maybe it was the mark of civilized people not to give a shit.

I looked at my watch. It was nearly eight. I figured I might as well get this over with, and I started the car and drove north on Genessee.

Gilmore's street, Courtney Avenue, was a block east of Nichols Canyon Road, which runs down from Mulholland through the east end of the Hollywood Hills. Both streets give out where the hills meet the flats, on a stretch of Hollywood Boulevard about a mile west of the seedy commercial section. Along Hollywood itself, there are mostly cheap apartments and rooming houses, but on the hill streets to the north are some of the finest old Hollywood homes—Spanish and Mediterranean styles with mission tile and ironwork.

Still, it wasn't the safest neighborhood. Neighborhood watch signs proliferated throughout the area, and during the riots I'd seen news clips of the local residents standing guard—armed, too—ready to ward off looters who might venture north from the Hollywood streets. I assumed Gilmore kept a place here because it was to his or his wife's taste, or because it was a convenience to him, of one sort or another. At least he could explain to his wife that he could get out to the site more easily from here than from Montecito.

I turned onto his street as the daylight was fading and checked out the house numbers by the porch lights. His place was barely a half-mile north of Hollywood. It was one of the older homes—Spanish and walled. I parked out front, feeling the same reservations I'd felt earlier, only more so. There was something really unseemly about going to see him. It was like being in a bad French movie, and I was half-tempted even then to turn around and cut out. I halted on the pathway, thinking about it; then I decided I'd keep it short, tell him I didn't want to hear about his problems. If he raised anything about my future attitude in meetings, I'd let him know I'd be cool so long as he stayed away from Caroline.

I walked to an oak door, rang the bell, and waited. After a minute or so, when there was still no answer, I began to feel the first flush of irritation that the son of a bitch had gone out, even knowing I was coming.

I rang again. Still no answer. Then I stepped back from the house and saw a yard light out back and a BMW parked in the driveway. He was home. I started around the side of the house to a patio and an open French window, and I could hear classical music from within. I didn't see anyone as I glanced in, and so I continued on to the rear of the house, where the real charm of the place was concealed—an oval pool with a stone facade, and beyond the pool, avocado trees laden with pears. I still didn't see Gilmore, and so I turned back along the path to the French window.

As I approached, the classical movement on the stereo ended, and a steady stream of audience applause followed. In the brief pause before the announcer's voice broke in, I stuck my head in the French window and called out, "Gilmore!"

I figured he must be in the shower, so I went in, turned down the stereo, and called out his name again. There was still no answer, so I decided I'd wait on his patio rather than have him come downstairs and find me in his living room. Then, as I started back to the French window, I heard the rear screen door close. So he had been in the yard after all.

I called out, "Sam!"

No answer.

What was he doing? Walking around with headphones on?

I started across the room, and as I headed into the darkened dining room, I tripped. And at that moment, the ordinary life of yours truly—William K. Dunbar—came to an end, and the nightmare that was to be the next year began. It started with a searing pain as the blood began to hammer at my temples.

Strange how the mind works. First impulse—denial. And yet something had drifted up to my nostrils as I looked down, and as the stench caught in my throat, I knew I hadn't tripped on any folded rug. I staggered. I don't know what took over, but I groped for a light switch and turned it on, and as I looked down, the hammering in my brain rose several decibels. There was a feeling of having been nailed by my feet as I continued to look. Gilmore lay on his back, his eyes open, his expression frozen . . . in a death stare.

They say shock has many symptoms. The pulse weakens, the pupils may dilate, the blood rushes from the extremities to protect the brain—I guess this accounted for the hammering at my temples. Then the hammering began to recede, and something like a wave washed over me, and as I stared at Gilmore, I saw he'd been shot twice—once in the head, once at the base of the throat. God, was he a sight! His mouth had foamed up. A part of his scalp lay detached from his head. He'd been *butchered*. I don't know why there should have been a qualitative difference from a man who might have fallen, struck his head, collapsed, or suffered a hemorrhage—but there was.

I don't know how long I stood there. But suddenly I froze. The back door had just closed. I sprang back, wondering if I should bolt out of there, screaming like a banshee, and to this day, I don't know why I didn't. Maybe it was a fear reflex more powerful than anything I could imagine until then, but in any event, I just stood there, listening, hearing nothing. I saw no movement, no shadow. And finally, I leaned forward and took a step by the body and glanced into the kitchen. Nobody was there.

I darted forward and flung open the rear screen door. I saw nothing at first; then I heard a rustling from the far side of the yard. A man slipped from behind the pool house, ran a few steps to the wall, and hauled himself over. I didn't see his face. It was pitch-dark back there, but I formed a vague impression that the guy was agile and compact. I yelled something—I don't know what—then things seemed to go into motion of their own accord. I tore after him, hauling myself over the wall, just as he had done, and landed hard on the far side. He had already disappeared, and all I heard was the distant sound of his sneakers on the tarmac. Then I heard a car coming down Nichols Canyon.

I turned and stood in the road, and waved frantically. There was a couple in it, and the driver slowed, and I saw him look at me nervously. Then he made up his mind to keep going, veered around me, and speeded up, and as he drove on I saw the woman staring back at me. The car's taillights disappeared around a bend, and the street fell quiet again, eerily quiet.

I climbed back over the wall, tore my jacket on the top, and stood a moment getting my breath back. Then I went back inside the house, and when I looked at Gilmore again, my stomach started to churn. I checked his pulse—God knows why, there was nothing I could do for him. And after fighting off another wave of nausea, I went into the main room, found a phone, and dialed 911.

The emergency operator came on, and I babbled that there had been a murder at 3069 Courtney Avenue. The operator asked for my name, and I gave it to her. Then she asked me to repeat the information, and I gave it to her again, and she told me to stay where I was. She said the police would be right there.

Then I hung up.

Suddenly, I felt confused. I can't remember the exact progression of my thoughts after that. I know at one point I decided I'd wait out front rather than risk a run-in with nervous cops in the house. So I went out by the French window and stood outside the front gate, and I started to shake a little—I guess by then I'd begun to emerge from the shock. Then, as the seconds went by, other thoughts leaped to mind. Images, really. Caroline. The cops. Questions. More questions . . . There *was* a fleeting moment when I recognized how this might look.

But I dismissed it. I was still trying to deal with the nausea that kept welling up in me, and I leaned over the wall as a precaution against staining my clothes. I managed to choke back the bile, to fight it down. But in the midst of this, I asked myself a question. Why was I here?

I do remember that I asked myself that question—right then—as I hung over that wall.

7

A few minutes went by. There were no cars on the street. For a while the only sound was the insolent chatter of blue jays. Then a dog began to bark, and a moment later, I heard sirens. They grew louder; then two black-and-whites swung around the bend toward me, their dome lights transforming this quiet street into ugly, urban Los Angeles.

The first of the cars pulled up alongside me, and two Hispanic cops got out. The driver yelled, "You the guy called this in?"

I nodded.

Then a second car pulled up and two white cops got out, one a Gates-era sergeant with a broad jaw and a brush cut. He let fly with a barrage of questions:

"Where's the dead guy?"

I told him.

"You sure he's dead?"

I nodded.

"You know who did it?"

I told the sergeant I'd caught a glimpse of the guy as he took off. I said I didn't see his face.

Another cop came alongside me holding a notepad.

"Black, white?"

I said I didn't see. "He was wearing sneakers. . . ." They looked at me blankly, and I said, "I heard him running down Nichols."

The other officer went to his car and picked up the radio. The sergeant turned to me.

"What's your name?"

"Will Dunbar."

"Okay, Will. Show me where he is."

He shoved open the gate, and I followed him up the front path. He asked, "Does the dead guy live here?"

I nodded.

"What's his name?"

"Sam Gilmore."

We started around the side of the house, with two other officers following, and as we reached the French window, the sergeant said, "Where?"

"Off to the left, in the dining room."

He took a flashlight from one of the officers, drew his service revolver and went inside.

I waited outside with the other officers, hearing other cars pull up. Vehicle doors were now opening and closing, dogs were barking throughout the neighborhood, and I could hear the high-pitched wail of an ambulance somewhere close. Then more cops came around the side of the house, their radios crackling. They appeared in a group, three of them, one carrying yellow police tape. He asked where the sergeant was, and another said, "Inside." Then the first cop called out, "Vern!"

There was a short silence. The sergeant emerged a few moments later, nodded grimly, and told one cop to start putting tape out front, others to begin door-knocking.

"And get license plates! Two blocks' radius!"

Then he got on his radio and called for detectives and a forensic team.

I sat down on a stone bench and lit a cigarette. I was still thinking that at any moment I might wake up.

After a while the sergeant put the radio back on his belt. A Hispanic cop stepped toward him, and as the guy was about to rest his hand on the window jamb, the sergeant's arm went up like a semaphore signal. The Hispanic cop jumped back. The sergeant rolled his eyes; then he told the cop to go get license plates, too, and in the absence of anyone else to show his scorn to, he rolled his eyes at me.

After a moment, he said, "This window was open?"

I nodded.

"You went in this way?"

He broke off as two paramedics came around the house, and after a moment's discussion with them, he got on his radio again and asked to be put through to the detective who'd been summoned. Over the radio I heard the dispatcher say Detective Lowndes was on his way. The sergeant asked to be patched through, and when the detective came on, the sergeant said, "Mike . . . you want the medics to go in?"

"Fuck, no. I don't want those dumb bastards getting prints everywhere."

The sergeant looked at the medics and shrugged. Then he said, "They're standing right here, Mike." He got no response. The sergeant said, "I got a witness here. You want him brought down to the station?"

"No. I'm on La Brea and Fountain."

The sergeant snapped off his radio, looked at me, and said, "They'll need you down at the station sometime tonight."

I started to tell him what had happened, but he cut me off and said there was no point my getting into it, I'd only have to go through it again for the detectives. After that, he spoke only to the paramedics, and I sat down on the stone bench, lit another cigarette, and tried to resign myself to being detained here several hours.

A few minutes went by. Then the detective showed up. He was a guy of about forty, a little over six feet, with sandy hair. He huddled with the sergeant for a moment; then he turned to me and asked how I was doing, and I said I was okay. Then another uniformed officer walked along the path toward us, and the sergeant asked him to wait outside with me, while he, the detective, and the medics went inside. The cop took up sentry duty at the window, and the others went in.

They turned a light on, and they were inside awhile, and as I sat waiting, a police photographer arrived, and a few minutes later, another detective showed up. Then the first detective appeared in the main room talking to the sergeant, and after a while he came outside and walked toward me.

"Will, right?"

"Will Dunbar."

"Detective Lowndes . . . You've been inside, Will?"

"I found him there."

"What time was that?"

"About twenty minutes ago."

"The sergeant says you saw a guy leaving."

"Yeah, I saw him go over the wall out back. I didn't see his face."

He nodded slowly. Then he said, "You called it in from here?"

"Yeah."

"I guess you touched a few things inside? Do you remember what?"

I took a moment to think about this. Then I said, "The back door . . . the kitchen door . . . the dining room light switch . . . maybe the table in the dining room . . . the phone . . . and the stereo, I turned it down."

"Why'd you do that?"

"I was calling out to see where he was."

He took out a notepad and jotted down some notes.

"Anything else?"

"I tripped over him when I walked in. I also checked his pulse."

I started to run through everything that had happened, but he was still scribbling what I'd just told him, and after a moment, he asked me to hold up. Then he said, "All right, Will. Start at the top."

I went through it all. I said I rang the doorbell, got no answer, so I walked around to this window, looked in and saw nobody, so I continued around back. "I saw nobody in the yard, so I came back here, went in, turned the stereo down, and called out his name. . . . Then I heard a door close out back."

He stopped me there. "Wait a minute, you're saying the perp was still in the house?"

"I thought it was Gilmore."

"Go on."

"So I called out to him. He didn't answer—I thought he might be walking around with headphones on. So I was going toward the back when I tripped over him."

Lowndes asked me to hold up again as he scribbled fast. Then he said, "Okay, then what?"

"Well, I'd heard the back door close . . . but I didn't hear anything else, so I went through the kitchen, opened the back door, and saw this guy go over the wall."

"Do you remember anything about him?"

"Uh-uh. It's dark back there. I went after him, but by the time I got over the wall, he was gone."

He was looking at me.

"When I got over the wall," I said, "I tried to flag down a car, but it didn't stop. So I came back here and called it in."

He studied me thoughtfully. Then he put away his notebook and asked me to show him where this guy went over the wall. We walked back along the path and down the steps, past the pool, and I pointed to the stretch of torn vine where the perp and I had gone over. He studied it; then he took out his notepad again and scribbled something else in it. Then he indicated the house and asked me, "So, who was this guy?"

"He's a geologist . . . *was* a geologist."

"Friend of yours?"

Somehow I knew he was going to ask me this. I said, "He's the partner of the guy I work for."

"You'd been here before, then?"

This question caught me by surprise. I said, "No. He called today . . . about getting together tonight."

Right then I felt a little uncomfortable. And I knew if he asked why, it would probably serve me to put my cards on the table, and tell him the truth about why I'd come to see Gilmore. But he didn't ask why. He asked me how I was holding up.

I said I was okay, a little shaken.

He nodded and glanced back at the house. Then he walked to the wall and studied it again, and in that interval I figured I should hold off saying anything. If I told him about punching Gilmore, he would be sure to look at me in a whole different light, and I didn't want to be here all night.

He turned back to me and asked me my full name, address, and phone number. I gave them to him. Then he flipped his notepad closed and said, "Okay, Will, here's what I want you to do. Wait on that patio by the French window. Don't wander around because I don't want you going anywhere you haven't been. Soon as the coroner arrives, I'll take you down to the station and you can give us a statement. Okay?"

I nodded and looked at my watch. It was nine twenty-five, but it felt more like midnight. I asked him how long we'd be, and he said it might take a while. He asked if I needed to call anyone, and I said I might need to call my wife if we ran late. Then we walked back to the patio, and a few minutes later, the coroner showed up.

Lowndes was inside with him awhile; then he came out with another detective, a young black guy with a mustache. He said, "Let's go, Will," and we walked back along the path and around to the front of the house, where a slew of police vehicles was now parked at random. Beyond the police tape, a group of neighbors had gathered, and they were shaking their heads and talking in low voices. Lowndes said I could ride with him. He told me he would be coming back here anyway, and I could pick up my car then. We got in his car, which smelled of air freshener, squared the block, and drove down Nichols Canyon Road to Hollywood Boulevard, and as we waited for the light at Hollywood, he asked me what I did for a living. I said I did PR for a company called Clem Resources.

He nodded quietly and didn't ask any more, and I wasn't sure where I stood with him at that moment, but I felt a little uneasy. From the moment he'd first spoken to me, I was sure he was sounding me out, taking stock of me. He could expect me to be a little shaken, but I wasn't sure if he was taking this into account, or if he was looking beyond it.

We drove east on Hollywood and turned south onto Wilcox, and pulled into his parking space at the Hollywood Division station. As we got out, he hit a small button on the dashboard. There was a slight hissing sound, and suddenly the car filled with the scent of pine air freshener. I tried not to read too much into the gesture.

We walked in past the complaints desk and made a left through the detectives' section, where there were actually movie posters hanging in the waiting area. At the desk, some fracas was going on between a detective and two black couples over the impounding of a vehicle, and it was still going on as we went into the main room, which was laid out like a newsroom, with an assortment of desks shoved together, and signs above reading: "Robbery. Burglary. Juvenile. Sex. Homicide." Lowndes walked to the far corner, and I told him I needed to use the men's room. We had reached his desk, and he said, "Before you do, Will, turn out your pockets."

I reacted with surprise.

"When you're a witness to a homicide, Will, there's things we need to do to eliminate you as a suspect."

Despite the assurance, I got an uneasy feeling again. I felt he was still estimating me, applying an instinct honed over the years, and trusting in it as much as anything else.

I pulled batches of stuff from my pockets—keys, wallet, business cards, a couple of clippings. Then he asked me to raise my arms, and he patted down my sides and checked my pockets.

"Okay, Will. Go ahead."

I figured there had probably been a few guys who lingered at murder scenes and claimed a thief did it.

When I got back, he got us both some coffee, then he asked me if I needed to call home. I asked him how long we were likely to be, and when he said an hour, maybe two, I said I wasn't sure if my wife would be home yet, but I'd just as soon tell her about this in person, rather than on the phone. The truth was, I didn't want to get into any of this on the phone with Caroline, not in front of Lowndes.

Then he said they needed to get some prints—"to match against what you touched in the house. We'll get a Polaroid shot of you, too, in case a neighbor saw you."

The young black detective walked in, and Lowndes asked him to get the camera, and while he was gone, Lowndes took down various details from my ID—credit cards, driver's license number. The young black detective came back with the camera, and Lowndes took two photos of me.

When this was done, the young detective, whose name was Tremaine, escorted me over to the fingerprints section, and one of the uniformed officers fingerprinted me, all the while chatting about the Lakers' draft choices. Then I was escorted back to the main room, and I sat at Lowndes's desk while an interrogation room was set up. I looked at the stuff from my pockets. It was in a different order than when I'd last seen it, and I imagined Lowndes had taken a good look through it all.

Lowndes came back and said I could pick up my stuff. He was ready to take the statement. We walked toward an interrogation room, and on the way he asked me, "What kind of PR work do you do, Will?"

"Political work, mostly."

"You've got a few friends downtown, huh?"

"A few," I said.

I decided it wouldn't hurt to let him know.

The tape recorder was set up when we walked in. Lowndes closed the door, and we sat down. Then Lowndes pressed the "record" button and said this statement was being taken at 10:25 P.M. at the Hollywood Division station, and that present in the room with me were Detectives Michael Lowndes and Anthony Tremaine of the Hollywood Division. Then he paused the tape and said, "All right, Will, take us through it again, in your own words."

I went through it all once more, trying to make sure I'd left nothing out. Once or twice Lowndes asked for clarification, and again he asked me what I'd touched in the house and whether I'd been anywhere else aside from the locations I'd mentioned. I said I'd been nowhere else. Then they asked me if I'd touched the body, and I said I'd tripped over Gilmore when I found him, and that I'd checked his pulse after chasing the perp.

Tremaine looked puzzled. He said, "You checked his pulse *after* you chased the perp?"

I nodded. "It was just a reflex, to make sure. . . ."

There was a knock on the door, and another detective looked in and beckoned to Lowndes.

Lowndes got up and went out. Tremaine and I sat in silence for a few moments. Then Tremaine asked me if I wanted to say anything else. I asked him if he wanted me to go on, and he said it was up to me. I asked him if he'd rather wait until Lowndes got back.

He seemed undecided whether to stop the tape or not. I said I could just as easily wait, and after a while he hit the "pause" button. But in that uneasy silence, I realized something. No matter what Lowndes had said about standard procedure, they had definitely not eliminated me as a suspect. In fact, the way I saw it, they were being very careful.

I felt a little apprehensive. I knew I'd already made a mistake by not volunteering to Lowndes earlier why I'd been meeting with Gilmore. If he and Tremaine asked other people about me, they were going to learn about what had happened at Clem's party—and I could guess what they might decide to draw from that. But then I figured they were bound to find plenty of evidence of an intruder by then—stuff disturbed, stuff missing. My guess was the intruder had come in the same way I had. Gilmore hadn't heard him with the stereo on. He'd surprised the guy . . . the guy had panicked.

Lowndes came back in. His finger hovered over the "pause" button; then he started the tape and asked me, "How far behind the perp would you say you were, Will . . . ballpark?"

"Maybe half a minute. . . . But he got over the wall a lot easier than I did."

Lowndes looked at me steadily. "Weren't you a little scared, going after the guy?"

"Sure . . . but it was an impulse."

I looked at both of them. Then Tremaine said, almost offhandedly, "You weren't carrying a weapon or anything, were you, Will?"

I guess my mouth wavered a little. Then I said, "If I was, I'd have said so."

I realized I sounded a little hostile, but what the hell was I supposed to say to a question like that? I looked at Tremaine and said, "What the fuck is that supposed to mean?"

Tremaine shrugged. "A lot of people are packing these days, Will."

"Yeah, but if I was, I'd have a weapon on me." I glared at him. "Wouldn't I?"

He shrugged.

Lowndes said, "Take it easy. . . ."

"Well, what the fuck . . . "

"We're just doing our job, Will."

I calmed down a bit and lit a cigarette. Lowndes drummed his fingers on the table. Then he said, "All the same, Will . . . you've got to admit, the way you describe it . . . it's a little strange." His voice was even, but I heard an undertone in it.

"Why?" I said, finally.

"You rang the front bell. If I'm the perp, I split right then, right? Go out the back?"

"It didn't happen that way."

I was staring at them and being met by blank expressions. Things seemed to have come a long way these past two minutes. And right then, I decided I'd better tell them.

I said, "Look, before we go any further, there's something I want to say."

Lowndes glanced at the recorder and asked, "What's that, Will?" His tone was condescending, as if he knew all along I'd been holding something back.

I said, "Gilmore wasn't a friend. Last night I punched him out at a party, after I saw him groping my wife. That's why I went to see him tonight. . . . He called me today, said he wanted to talk things over."

There was a silence. Then Lowndes said, "What are you saying, Will, your wife was screwing this guy?"

"Maybe you should ask *her* that."

There was another silence. Then Tremaine said, "Are you playing games with us, Will?"

"No . . . I'm not playing fucking games."

I was suddenly angry. I looked at both of them, trying to get a read. Then I said, "Did you find anything at the house that backs up what I said?"

They didn't answer, and after a while I said, "Who's playing games?"

Again they didn't answer, and I said, "Look, I know I could stop this at any time and ask for an attorney, but I haven't. I've told you the truth. I didn't kill him. I've got too much to lose."

They were still studying me. I said, "For God's sake, if I killed the guy, why the hell would I call the cops?"

But the minute I said this, I realized how questionable it sounded. Calling the cops was the smart thing to do. After all, when the cops asked people if Gilmore had any enemies, my name was bound to come up. I had no alibi for the evening, and as I sat there, thinking about it, I realized it made absolute sense, if I'd been the killer, to call the cops, concoct a story, and claim an intruder had done it.

Lowndes said, "You were going to say something, Will?"

I shook my head. Eventually I said, "You guys think I did it?"

"We didn't say that, Will."

"I figured you'd sooner hear this from me."

Lowndes's mouth drooped in a sardonic smile. For the longest time nobody said anything. Then Lowndes shifted in his seat and asked if I had anything else to say. I said I'd given them everything, and I was sure they'd turn something up at the crime scene to corroborate it. They were still facing me, and eventually Lowndes cocked his head to one side and said, "You want to take a short break, Will? Have some coffee? Think about this?"

"No." I said, "That's it. Either cut me loose or charge me, but that's it for the questions."

Lowndes nodded slowly. Then he said, "Right now, you're just helping us, Will."

"Sure," I said sarcastically.

Lowndes looked over at the tape recorder, then back to me. Then he indicated for Tremaine to turn the thing off. He got up and walked out, and this time Tremaine went out, too, and the detective who had interrupted us earlier came back in and sat down and didn't say a word—I guess he was just there to make sure I didn't mess with the tape recorder. I sat in silence and took a few deep breaths.

Five minutes later, Lowndes and Tremaine came back in.

Lowndes sat down and drummed his fingers on the table. Then he glanced at Tremaine and finally turned to me and said, "Maybe we're all getting a little overwrought here."

It wasn't an apology. And I wasn't about to trust them. I said, "Do I need to call an attorney?"

Lowndes flashed a smile; then he said, "We'd like to send you home, Will. But first we need a couple of things."

"Like what?"

"Your car. You can either give us permission to impound it or wait here until we wake up a judge and get a warrant. We also need your clothes."

I stared at him. Then he said, "You can call an attorney—and be here all night. It's up to you, Will." He stood up and shrugged.

I hesitated, and Tremaine said, "We search your car, we find nothing, we have to say so . . . if it comes to that."

Lowndes pointed to my right wrist and said, "There's blood on your shirt cuff, Will."

I turned my arm over. There was a bloodstain. Lowndes smiled. "Wouldn't want you to think we put it there."

I knew there was nothing in the car that could hurt me. And I'd already told them I'd touched the body. Still, there was a part of me that wanted the advice of an attorney then and there before I gave them anything, even if it meant I had to be here all night. But I was sure they could get this stuff anyway, one way or another, and another part of me badly wanted out of there. I still had to deal with Caroline. . . .

They were waiting, and finally I agreed, not knowing if I'd done the smart thing. I said, "How long's this gonna take?"

Lowndes said he could have the paperwork ready in ten minutes.

They went out, and the other detective came back in, and I sat staring at the walls and getting up occasionally to pace. Then Lowndes and Tremaine came back in, and they put a couple of sheets of paper in front of me, and again I checked out their attitudes, trying to decide how important this was to them. Lowndes asked me to read the papers over, and I did, and when I looked up, he asked if I was ready to sign. I nodded, and he said he needed me to agree to it on tape. He turned the recorder on and went through the ritual again about where we were, and what time it was, and who was present. Then I made a brief declaration that I was signing, allowing them to impound my car and take my clothes. Then Lowndes handed me a pen, and the other detective came in and handed me an old shirt, some sneakers, and pants.

I asked if he'd gotten these from the jail. Tremaine smiled.

I signed, and as I signed, Lowndes said, "How many of those do you smoke a day, Will?"

"Too many."

He took the papers back. Then he said, "You didn't smoke in his house, did you?"

"What?"

"Did you smoke in Gilmore's house?"

"No . . . out on the patio."

Tremaine turned the recorder off. "Okay, Will. There's a car waiting to take you home."

They went out, and I changed into the scruffy clothes. Then I walked out of the tight, airless cubicle and did my best to ignore the glances of the other detectives in the main room.

Two uniformed officers escorted me in silence to the rear of the station. One held the door for me and I got in the squad car, and we drove out of the parking area, and as I sat in the rear of the car, I felt a sense of dislocation, a sense that none of this was real.

We headed south on La Brea and west on Wilshire, and the two cops up front talked between themselves. My thoughts began to drift to Gilmore's house, and to what would probably be going on there right now. I thought, They're bound to find something. Then I tried to envision the actual "event" at the house, and to guess what mistakes the perp might have made. One of the cops up front asked for directions. I gave them to him, and a few minutes later, they dropped me at my place and drove off. To my surprise, I didn't see Caroline's car in the driveway. I looked at my watch. It was past midnight.

In a sense this was a relief. At least I could get out of these clothes. For a second, it occurred to me that she might have gotten worried, but even if that were the case, where would she be, other than here? She'd also said she wanted to talk that evening.

I went in, and for a few minutes I checked around, looking for signs that she had come home and gone out. There were none. Then I went upstairs, changed out of the ratty clothes, put on a bathrobe, and checked in on Katia. She was sound asleep. I went to Fran's room and whispered to her through her door. She said she'd heard me come in, but she hadn't heard my car. I said there'd been a problem with the car, and I asked her if Caroline had come home and gone out. Fran said she hadn't. She said she'd heard the phone ring once, but she had let the machine pick up—Fran had her own line, and if Caroline needed to call her, she would call her on that.

I went downstairs and checked the machine. Caroline had left a message at eight-thirty saying that a meeting with Clem was running late. She said it couldn't be helped, and she suggested we talk tomorrow if she got in really late. I poured myself a drink, and sat on the sofa, and thought about it all again. Then, conscious of what I'd been wearing for the past hour, I went to take a shower.

I stood for a long time under the hot water, and again I tried to reconstruct how things might have unfolded in Gilmore's house. The way I saw it, the perp could have been upstairs, looking for valuables, when I rang the front bell. Maybe he'd been heading for the back door as I came around the side of the house, and held up as he saw me continue around back. I stepped out of the shower and felt a sudden chill at the thought of him watching me. Maybe I'd had a close call myself. I tossed the clothes the cops had given me in the trash and toweled off, and as I tugged on a clean shirt, I heard the front door open. Caroline was home.

I started to dress, giving some thought to how to break this to her. I felt like the meeting place for a dozen crosscurrents. Why the hell did I have the job of telling my wife that her boyfriend was dead? At this stage, I couldn't even feel bitter about the affair. I didn't know what to feel.

I came out of the bathroom and started downstairs. The living room door was open, and I could see a pool of light in the hallway. Then, to my surprise, I heard a man's voice, and a second later, I recognized it as Clem's.

There was a silence as I came down the last few stairs. Caroline was sitting on the sofa, looking ashen. Clem was seated opposite her, holding a drink, looking about as somber as I'd ever seen him. They looked up as I came in, and after a moment Clem said, "You'd better sit down, Will. Something's happened. . . ."

I looked at both of them, and it was clear they knew. I said, "I know about it. . . ."

They stared at me and then glanced at each other. Finally Clem said, "How, Will?"

I came over to the couch and sat down. I glanced at Caroline. Then I said to Clem, "You told him he should straighten things out with me?"

Clem nodded, and I said, "He called this morning. He said he wanted to see me . . . to talk about this. . . . It was me found him."

I heard Caroline suck in her breath. They both stared at me, and after a long silence, Clem said, "Holy shit."

I looked at Caroline and saw she was trembling a little. Clem was shaking his head in disbelief. Then I asked him, "How did you find out about it?"

"Greg called over there. . . . He got the police."

He started to shake his head, as if overcome by disbelief, and finally, I said, "The police know about what happened at the party."

I glanced at Caroline. She didn't seem to understand. Nor did Clem.

He said, "What?"

"I told them about it—they'd have found out anyway. They may be looking at me as a suspect."

Caroline's jaw wavered. Clem's brow knotted. Then he said, "Are you kidding me?"

I shook my head. I saw his mouth form a dozen questions, and finally he said, "Wasn't it robbery?"

"Did the cops tell Greg that?"

Clem's mouth flapped. "He didn't say. . . . I assumed—"

He broke off, and started shaking his head again. Then I told them about the guy I'd seen going over the wall.

Clem exclaimed, "So it was robbery?"

I said it looked that way.

"Well, what the fuck—?"

He broke off again and asked me how the cops had responded to my telling them about the spat with Gilmore. I said I didn't exactly get the kid-gloves treatment. "They took my clothes and the car."

Clem was still staring at me. Then he got up and started to pace. I looked at Caroline. Her face muscles had tightened, and she looked about as vulnerable as I'd ever seen her look. I reached over and took her hand, and after a moment, she spoke for the first time. She said, "I need some air—badly." Then she got up and walked out of the room.

When she came back, we went through it all again. But it was hard to talk—the conversation kept bumping up against all the incestuous knots. There was the magnitude of the event itself, and in the midst of our exchanges it would loom abruptly. Caroline lowered her eyes a couple of times when Clem made allusions to what the cops might see as motive.

After a while, there didn't seem to be anything more to say. Clem sighed and got up. I'd seen him look at both of us a couple of times, as if he wished he'd never set eyes on either one of us. He suggested we meet tomorrow at noon.

I saw him to the door, and in the hallway he told me he had driven back here with Caroline to be sure she was okay. Their meeting had been going on when they'd heard the news, and Caroline had seemed to go into a state of shock, he said. I said I appreciated it. He shook his head several times and said, "Jesus, Will . . ."

He left, and when I turned back into the living room, Caroline had left the room.

I sat down, and I could hear the faucet in the bathroom running for the longest time. Then the faucet went off, and the house seemed silent for ages. Finally, I heard Caroline's heels in the hall again. I heard the click of a hanger on the hall closet rail, and she appeared at the door.

I said, "Why don't you sit down?"

She stood facing me, her face slowly changing through degrees of pain. And it was weird, I tell you, seeing how she looked at that moment. The look on her face drove a lot of things home to me, but I didn't know how I should be reacting. I didn't know what to feel.

All this took place within seconds, though it felt like hours, as Caroline slowly eased herself into the chair, a tissue at the ready.

"Are you okay?" I said.

She didn't say anything, and I reasoned at this juncture she was probably too overcome to say much. I had no idea what she could be thinking, let alone if she could bring any perspective to this. And so I sat opposite her, and when she asked the odd question, I responded, but basically I was just giving her time to get a handle on it all.

Then, after a while, she said, "You were there . . . my God." She looked confused for a moment. Then she seemed to focus a little, and in a low voice she asked, "When did you get there?"

"Ten, fifteen minutes after he was shot, I guess."

She flinched visibly.

"The guy was still in the house," I said. "He took off just after I came in."

"Are you sure you wouldn't recognize him?"

"Positive. It was too dark."

I was silent for a moment. Then I told her a little about the grilling by the detectives. She shook her head in disbelief, and for a while we both sat in silence. Then she began to probe around the edges of what might have happened to Gilmore, but after a few questions I stopped her.

She gazed at me for a moment, and then she began to cry. Eventually, she asked if I'd leave her alone. I got up and went into the kitchen, telling myself that among the bad evenings in my life, this was probably the worst.

I puttered about awhile. Then I sat in the dining room, glanced at my watch, and saw it was almost two-thirty. I heard Caroline go out the back door, and I went upstairs to the spare room and looked out the window. She was sitting in the yard, next to the umbrella, staring at the night sky, contemplating infinity, or eternity, or whatever.

I went and sat in the living room, and after ten minutes or so, I heard Caroline come back in. She returned to the living room and sat down opposite me without saying anything, and eventually I asked her, "How serious was this?"

She stared at me a moment. Then she said, "You don't listen, do you, Will?" It wasn't said in an unkind way.

She sighed and said she needed to lie down, and she got up and went upstairs to the bedroom. I followed and lay down next to her, and over the course of the next ten minutes we both mumbled some muted apologies for the way we'd been acting toward each other lately. She got undressed and curled into a fetal position—facing me—and I held her for a while. Then she turned away from me. She said, "Let's try to get some sleep." I wanted to sleep, but I wasn't able to turn my mind off, despite how tired I was, and after a while I got up and went downstairs, and smoked a cigarette. Then I came back, and we both tossed and turned for a while. Caroline finally went to sleep, but I lay awake, I don't know for how long, trying to wipe from my mind the image of Gilmore on the floor, staring at me with those dead eyes.

8

I was awake by eight, once the sunlight hit the blinds. Caroline was already up, and there was no way I was falling back to sleep. I got up feeling jittery, as if I had a hangover, and I spent a long time in the shower, trying to shake off the effects of lack of sleep. When I came back into the bedroom, I took out some clean clothes, and the sight of my wallet, keys, and papers lying on the dresser was a vivid reminder of these objects lying on Lowndes's desk the evening before.

I went downstairs, got some coffee, and scanned the Metro section of the paper. There was nothing about Gilmore's murder, and I figured if the cops had released it, the paper had not received it until after deadline. Then Fran walked in, and I asked her where Caroline was. She said she was outside with Katia. She gave me an odd look. She seemed to have an inkling something strange was going on, and for a moment I considered telling her about it, some of it at least. Then I decided not to. I went into the den and turned the radio on and tuned it to the all-news station. But after ten minutes, I'd heard nothing about Gilmore, and then I heard Caroline come into the house, and a minute later I heard her on the phone, calling her secretary to say she'd be late.

I found myself gazing at the phone next to me, hoping it would ring. The person I really wanted to hear from was Lowndes. I wanted to hear him say they'd found a weapon with prints on it, other than mine. I even thought about calling him, but somehow I didn't feel I could make that call. If they hadn't found a weapon, it would be like reminding him of my existence—not that I imagined I'd slip his mind.

Caroline appeared at the door to the living room. She was dressed for work in a dark suit, and her eyes were a little more heavily made up than usual. I asked how she was.

"Not great, obviously."

She said she was going to drop Katia off at school. As soon as she'd done that, she said, she'd be back and we could talk, if I wanted to. I said, sure. Then she left, and in her absence I decided I ought to call an attorney. I knew plenty, but most practiced corporate law, or they were litigators, or they served as advisers to legislators. Finally, I called Leonard Ahnemann, a litigator I knew, and when he came on the line, I told him bluntly that I needed a referral to a criminal attorney. He sounded surprised and said, "Anything serious, Will?"

I said it was complicated, nothing I was losing any sleep over. He asked what it was about, but I was reluctant to tell him. He said, "Hey, Will . . . I'm three hundred dollars an hour, but this call's for free."

So I told him briefly. Then I elaborated a bit, and he told me he thought I probably should retain someone, and he gave me the names of three attorneys in order of preference. His highest recommendation was a woman named Stella Nichols. I said I wasn't sure anything was going to come of this, and I hated to waste time and money if it all blew over. He chuckled a little and said, "Time's the name of our game, Will." Then he said, "If I get another call from you, night or day, I'll be sure to take it."

I thanked him, and we hung up. I sat staring at the names he'd given me, trying to decide if I should call Stella Nichols right away or not. I was still going back and forth with it when I heard Caroline's car in the driveway.

She came in and saw the numbers on the pad next to me, and asked if there was anything new. I said I'd just gotten some names of attorneys.

She sighed and sat down, and after a moment she said, "Look, Will . . . I really don't know how to say this . . ."

She hesitated, and I said, "Say it."

"Well, I want us to start talking again. I don't want you to be holding this stuff in . . . no matter what's been going on with us, I want you to talk to me."

I said that was nice of her. She said, "Well, you never were one to ask for support."

I wasn't? What was I asking for when I said I wanted to leave Clem? Still, I saw she was making the effort, and I wasn't about to bring this up right then. She said, "I still don't believe anything's going to come of this. I can't believe the cops would be that stupid."

I said we'd probably find out soon enough.

She sat in silence for a moment and eventually she said, "I feel like I never went to sleep. I feel so drained."

We talked a bit, and I had the feeling she was trying to avoid mentioning Gilmore by name, and eventually she said, "So what are you going to do?"

I said there wasn't much I could do. I'd gotten a few references for attorneys. . . .

"No, I mean about John."

"About quitting?"

She nodded, and I said I couldn't even think about that right now.

She got up slowly and asked if I was going in to the office.

I said, "Not yet."

Then she looked at her watch and said she had to go. I stood up with her, and as she brushed by me on the way out, I took her hand and thanked her for what she'd said before. She stared at me, and we remained silent awhile. Then she lowered her eyes and gently released her hand. She said she'd see me later.

She left, and I got some more coffee and sat in my office awhile, and when I couldn't sit there any longer, I decided I'd go out for breakfast. I got halfway to the garage before I remembered I didn't have my car.

I wound up walking ten blocks to a coffee shop. I took the paper with me, and I sat and read until I found myself reading the same sentence over and over. So I put the paper down and finished my coffee and paid. I decided I'd better rent a car. I caught a cab over to the rent-a-car place, then drove back to the house, thinking about Caroline. She seemed to be handling Gilmore's death pretty well.

When I got back to the house, it was a little after eleven. There was a message on the machine, and with a few trepidations I played it back. It was from Clem, and I called him back. He asked if there'd been any developments, and I said I'd heard nothing. He was silent for a moment. Then he made a few clicking noises and finally he said, "We'd better get together and figure out what to do about this. I don't want it blowing the council vote." I asked if he still wanted to meet at noon, and he said, "No, let's make it at two. And let's not do it here. You can't believe this place . . . secretaries weeping in the hallways. . . ."

He was silent for a moment. Then he said, "I had Borchiver make a couple of calls. I hope you don't mind."

"No, that's fine," I said.

Then, with a certain grim humor, he added, "He doesn't think you did it either, Will."

I said I was grateful for that.

I asked where he wanted to meet, and he said, "Let's do it at the Beverly Wilshire at two. I had a suite reserved there for a meeting, so we might as well make use of it."

I said I'd be there. He said Borchiver was on the other line, and he'd call back if there was anything that couldn't wait. But fifteen minutes went by, and he didn't call back, so finally I went and sat in the yard.

I sat on a rattan chaise and gazed at the muted pink wall of the house, the sunlight filtering through the leaves of a magnolia. I'd thought I might actually take the time and do some yard work once I quit. There were a hundred things I'd promised myself I'd do one day, ever since we'd bought this place. But then I realized there was probably little point in that. Caroline would want to move sooner or later, and I wasn't about to argue with her over where we lived. In Los Angeles, it didn't really matter. It was all the same.

Shortly before two, I nudged my way through the lunch-hour traffic along Wilshire, turned south on El Camino, and pulled into the valet parking area of the Beverly Wilshire Hotel. I went to the main desk, asked the clerk for Clem's room number, and was told John Clem was in Suite 303. I took the elevator upstairs and walked along a corridor toward the rear of the hotel.

It was a suite one floor above the swimming pool, which was set in an outdoor area in the center of the hotel. When I walked in, Clem was there with Borchiver and Al Premerlani. Clem said he had invited Caroline to be here, but under the circumstances, she had decided to pass.

Premerlani laid a hand on my shoulder, and said, "You're having a rough week, Will?"

I said that was understating it.

Clem said, "Sit down. Anyone need a drink?"

Borchiver shook his head. Al said he'd take a soda, and Clem said he'd have whatever I was drinking, since he figured whatever I was drinking he could use right now. Borchiver offered a thin smile, and Al got the drinks. Clem asked Borchiver to start, and he intimated to me that things had moved along since we'd spoken earlier.

Borchiver settled back. He said his information came from a woman at the D.A.'s office, who just happened to be going into private practice in a few months, thanks to a reference from him. He told me that he'd asked his friend to make a call to the watch commander at the Hollywood Division station. He studied his nails a moment. Then he said, "Will . . . there isn't a cop in Los Angeles doesn't need brownie points right now."

Clem waved his hand impatiently and said, "Marty, you're being a lawyer."

Borchiver sighed and said, "Okay." Then he turned to me, and said, "They're looking at it this way, Will. You could have hiked over the wall, ditched the gun, then called it in."

I said, "What?"

"According to the watch commander, they think you might have been looking for a way to lay it off. . . ." He paused and looked at me a bit ruefully. Then he said, "I'm sorry, Will, I'm just telling you how they're looking at it."

I felt a hollow feeling inside of me. I saw Clem studying me out of the corner of his eye, and after a moment I said, "Are you telling me they haven't found any evidence of an intruder?"

Borchiver shrugged. "I guess I'd have heard if they had."

The room fell silent, and I felt anger and frustration building.

How could the house be so devoid of evidence that the cops would have to focus on me? I vaguely heard Al Premerlani say, "So how do we back these guys into a corner?"

I didn't say anything at first. I was trying to think.

Premerlani said, "Any ideas, Will?"

After a moment I said, "I don't know. That could backfire."

Clem looked at me and raised an eyebrow. "How so?"

"If the cops get a whiff they're being pressured, they could get the bit between their teeth."

Premerlani looked a bit chastened. Clem nodded and said, "Will has a point."

Borchiver eased back on the couch and said, "Will, why don't you take us through everything that happened."

I wasn't sure it would help, but I launched into it again. And as I talked, I saw each of them reacting as if it could have been one of them, caught up in this Kafkaesque situation. Then I saw them remind themselves: It wasn't them . . . it was me.

Borchiver said, "So as far as you could tell, it was a robbery? One that turned sour?"

"I guess."

Clem got up, exasperated, and started to pace. After a moment, he said, "This is fucking absurd." He turned to Borchiver. "Ferchrissakes . . . Will saw the guy. . . . How do we get these guys to do their fucking jobs?"

Nobody said anything, and after a moment Clem sat down, looking a little subdued.

I said, "Did anyone talk to Gilmore's wife yet?"

Clem said, "I did. So did Greg. He went out to Montecito to see her." He shook his head as if he didn't want to elaborate.

Premerlani said, "How is Greg?"

"He's pretty shaken up."

There was a silence. Then I said, "Did Cynthia know about Gilmore and Caroline?"

Clem seemed a bit uncomfortable. He said he didn't know, at least Greg hadn't said anything. Then he shrugged, and after a while he cleared his throat a bit unctuously. "Let's get back to how we handle this. . . . I hear what you're saying, Will. I still think we ought to do something here."

I looked at each of them, and nothing was forthcoming for a moment.

The phone rang, and Premerlani got up to get it. The call was for Borchiver. Clem got up to go to the bathroom, and I got up, too, and stepped out onto the veranda and stood leaning against the railing, looking down at the hotel pool. My thoughts drifted to the night before, when I was looking out over Gilmore's pool. Why didn't the guy take off when I got back to the French window? Why did he wait until I was inside?

"Will?"

I turned and followed Premerlani inside. Borchiver said, "That was Diane McKenzie, Will."

She was Councilman Stephens's aide.

Borchiver cleared his throat. He said, "Suppose we have Diane talk to a few people on Stephens's behalf. She can tell 'em Stephens wants this put on the back burner for a few days. No leaks to the press, at least until the council votes on Pike. . . ."

I laughed a little dryly. I said I could see how that might solve Clem's problem. It didn't necessarily solve mine.

Clem said, "Might give 'em pause to think, Will."

The phone rang, and Premerlani picked up. He listened for a while. Then he hung up and said his assistant had just watched the local news. A TV reporter had done a stand-up in front of Gilmore's house, but the reporter had said nothing about the police having a witness or a suspect.

Clem said, "So far, so good."

In the interim I'd been thinking about what Borchiver had suggested. It was a lousy suggestion by any criteria. Getting Stephens to intercede in any way wasn't going to solve anyone's problems.

I turned to Clem. I said, "You guys do what you think best, but if I were you, I'd forget about Stephens."

Clem asked why, and if I'd been alone with him, I'd have told him that Borchiver's suggestion was a corporate lawyer's—light on judgment, as lawyers' suggestions often were, because the more complicated situations became, the more profitable it was for them. But Borchiver was sitting here, and so I said, "First, I'm not even sure Stephens would do it. Nobody wants to meddle in a homicide case. Second, if I do get implicated in any way Stephens will look like a jerk if other people find out."

I didn't need to finish. Clem caught on right away. He said. "I hear you . . . and then we go down the shitter, with twenty million riding on this thing." He was staring at me. He said, "So what do we do?"

I said, "You've got no choice. You either fire me or put me on leave, but either way you keep me away from Pike Mountain and the vote."

Clem's jaw fell.

I said, "I mean it, John. It's the smart thing to do. This way, if anything gets in the paper, nobody'll be embarrassed. The vote'll hold up."

Clem was still staring at me. Then he looked at Borchiver, and after a moment, Borchiver nodded, almost imperceptibly, and said, "I guess I was just looking for a way around that, Will."

There was a silence. Then Clem said quietly, "All right, Will, you're on leave. Al, from now on, you handle the vote."

On the way down in the elevator Clem shot me an odd look. What I'd done was a little self-serving, since I planned to quit anyway, but I felt I'd made the right call for him, my own interests aside—and I figured I owed him that much. He asked me how I felt about this, and I said there was really no reason for me to be at the center of events, now that the votes were set.

He nodded thoughtfully. Then he said, "This could all turn around tomorrow, Will."

I told him I knew that, but I wasn't taking the cops lightly. He said, "Where do they take it from here? All they've got is a motive of sorts."

I nodded, and didn't offer anything, and as we got off the elevator he said he had a favor to ask of me.

He drew me aside. "Listen, Will . . . I told you Greg went out to see Cynthia. He plans to be back at the office by four. He knows what happened. . . . He said he'd like to see you."

"Why don't I call him?"

"Come on, Will. Sam and him were pretty close."

"But with all this . . ."

We went back and forth for a while. Clem said, "Just take him out for a beer. He's pretty torn up, he wants to know what happened. They'd known each other a long time, Will."

Finally, I agreed. Clem said he'd be in touch.

I collected my car from the valet and drove west on Wilshire. And as I sat at an intersection at Santa Monica, I sighed, thinking, I'd only been a few days from getting away from all this—from Clem Resources, from the council, from Gilmore, for that matter, and now I'd landed in the middle of this shit. The light changed and I drove on. A story came on the radio about a South Side gang doing us all a big favor by maintaining some sort of truce, and it seemed ironic to me that I'd wound up as the focus of police attention, with all the murder and mayhem that went on in this city.

Ironic, and a little weird . . . I was still grappling with the timing of the thing. The night after I'd punched him, and I was the guy who found him? The thought crossed my mind—did someone have a reason to kill him? But then, I hadn't told anybody I was going to see him—and the only person who might have had an inkling was Clem, but he didn't need this.

I turned south on Century Park East and pulled into the basement lot of the building. Then I took the elevator upstairs and made my way to Greg's office. I wasn't sure who else at the company knew I'd found Gilmore, but Greg's secretary gave me a strange look as I approached his office, so I figured she knew. She said he was in, but when I knocked on his door, there was no answer. The secretary looked at me as if conflicted, but she indicated I should go in.

I knocked again and went in. Greg was sitting at his desk, facing out the window, and there was a bottle on the desk in front of him, a third empty. He swiveled his glance slowly toward me.

"Oh, hi, Will . . . Come on in."

His tie was askew, and his voice sounded hollow and defeated. I closed the door and walked over to him.

"You want a drink?" he said.

I said I'd pass.

"John told me what happened . . . some of it, anyway."

He reached into his desk and set up a second glass, and poured unsteadily. Then he poured himself another, almost in slow motion.

I said, "Greg . . . I want you to know—"

"Oh, for Christ's sake, Will . . . I know you're not that crazy."

He pushed the glass toward me, and as he did, he knocked over the bottle. The liquor spilled onto his desk, and he sat looking at it helplessly.

I picked up the bottle and said, "Come on. I'll drive you home. We can talk." He sat for a moment, not moving. Then I took his arm, and he got to his feet.

I walked with him to the elevator, supporting him a little. He could walk, but I wasn't taking any chances. He looked a wreck, and a couple of passing assistants averted their eyes. Downstairs, he got into my car all right, and once we were out of the parking garage and on Wilshire, heading west, I told him we were going for a drive, and I put all the windows down. I drove north, to Sunset, then west, then turned south along the Pacific Coast Highway, and half an hour later we were standing on the beach promenade in Santa Monica, and Greg was staring off at the ocean with the breeze in his face.

He was looking a little better, and after a while he turned to me and said, "I'm still numb, Will."

He faced the ocean again, and I asked him how it was, in Montecito.

"About the hardest damn thing I ever had to do." His glance swiveled toward me, and he said, "I had to tell her, Will. About you and him."

I frowned. "Why?"

"Because the cops brought up your name to her. She wanted to know what it was all about." He looked a little disconcerted. "I had no choice, Will. What could I do, lie to her?"

I told him I understood. "So now she knows about him and Caroline?"

Greg shook his head slightly. "I played that down. I said you didn't like the way he was carrying on with her at the party."

"She'll probably figure it out."

There was a long silence.

Eventually, Greg said, "So what do you think happened . . . at the house?"

"I don't know . . . I guess it was a robbery."

He nodded slowly, then said, "John said you got a glimpse of the guy. Would you recognize him?"

"No, it was too dark."

"Where was he?"

"Back by the pool house. There's a lot of vine and shade back there." After a moment I said, "Do you know the house?"

He nodded. "When they rented the place, I told Sam I didn't care for the neighborhood." He sighed and leaned against the promenade rail. "I dunno, Will. You read about this stuff. . . ."

He turned and faced the ocean again, and I saw him brush his sleeve across his eyes. He didn't say anything for a moment; then in a slightly choked voice, he said, "This was supposed to be the high point for him. For me, too."

I felt sorry for him. I said he should go to Alaska, definitely.

He managed a wan smile.

Then he told me about the first project he and Gilmore had worked on, and he got a little wistful. And somehow this led to a story about a friend of his who'd been killed in a car wreck when he was still a student at engineering school in Washington. He said this was the second time in his life he'd lost a close friend. He was gazing at the ocean, and I just stood there listening, letting him talk it out.

He talked for a long time, and I didn't want to interrupt. Eventually, he said he was ready, and we went back to the car and I drove him to his apartment. On the way he brought up the subject of me and the cops. He said it was just classic they'd grab on to something like this.

I dropped him at his apartment just off Westwood, and I continued on home, nudging the rented Honda through the rush-hour traffic, feeling the weight of it all. I stopped a few blocks from the house, bought some cigarettes and a few magazines, then drove on, thinking maybe I'd take Caroline out to dinner—just to get out of the house. But as I pulled into the driveway, a brown Montego pulled in behind me. At first I thought the driver was just making a turn. Then I saw Lowndes and Tremaine get out. My stomach fluttered as they walked toward me.

Lowndes stood in front of me, rocking on the balls of his feet. He asked if I could give them a few minutes. I looked from one to the other, and I had enough presence of mind to say I wasn't answering any more questions.

Lowndes said, "I hear you, Will. We just want you to hear what we've got to say."

They waited, and I didn't say anything for a while. Finally, I said, "Why the hell should I believe you?"

Tremaine shrugged and said, "It's true, Will."

Lowndes suggested we talk inside, and I was still looking at them and feeling apprehensive. I figured, shit, if they wanted to arrest me, they'd arrest me—I might as well hear what they had to say. So I said, "Okay," and they followed me into the house.

I led them into the living room, and they sat opposite me, and for a few moments I was aware only of the sound of my own breathing, and Katia's and Fran's voices from the backyard. I said, "So?"

Lowndes said, "You're in deep shit, Will. Maybe worse."

My heart sank, and again my stomach fluttered. Then I started to feel anger building, and with an effort at stoicism, I said, "You came here to tell me that?"

They didn't respond, and after a moment I said, "I told you how it happened."

Lowndes sighed. "You're consistent, Will, I'll say that."

"Are you here to arrest me? Because if you are, I'll call my attorney."

"No need for that yet, Will."

"Maybe I'll call anyway."

Tremaine said, "Feel free."

Lowndes's eyes had narrowed slightly. He got up and stood facing me. "We think you did it, Will. We think there might have been extenuating circumstances, but we still think you did it."

They were doing their best to unnerve me, and it was about all I could do right then not to blow my stack and tell them to fuck off, and the only reason I didn't was that in some corner of my mind I thought it might provoke them into arresting me. Instead, I said, "I don't care for this game."

Lowndes said, "Let me run something by you." He paused, then said, "We figured there might have been an argument—"

"There wasn't. At least not with me."

He looked at me slyly, then said, "It's one thing to bring along a gun . . . there's a lot of people walking around with guns. . . ."

I saw what he was up to. "Fuck," I said. "You think I'm gonna cop to this, just because it isn't murder one . . . forget it!"

"We figured it might be a factor, Will."

"Well, it isn't!"

Lowndes looked at Tremaine. Then he spread his hands on the back of the sofa. "You want to take a drive with us, Will? Think it over?"

"No."

I was trying to stay calm. Tremaine looked at Lowndes and said, "If he says he's not going, I guess he's not going."

Then Lowndes said, "Here's how we see it, Will. We think you and he talked awhile. Then maybe he said something that set you off—something about sticking it to your wife. . . . Maybe something snapped. . . . You tell us."

A quiet fury had built up inside me. I said, "You're a sick fuck, Lowndes." Then I lost it. I said, "Get the fuck out of here! I don't need to listen to this!"

Tremaine said, "I think Will wants us to leave."

Lowndes nodded slowly, and then, to my surprise and relief, they glanced at each other and headed for the door.

I stared after them, and I could feel my face boiling.

Ten minutes later, I was on the phone to the attorney, Stella Nichols. She was still at her office, and I made an appointment to see her at nine the following morning. She said that in the meantime I should talk to nobody, and that if the cops called again, I was to call her and not talk to them. Then she said she doubted they'd show up again with a warrant, but she gave me a twenty-four-hour number just in case.

When Caroline got home, panic was written all over me. She asked what was wrong, and I told her I'd had a visit from the cops. I told her what had happened, and she sat, shaking her head. She asked what I was going to do.

I told her I'd already spoken to an attorney. I said I planned to retain her in the morning.

Caroline was looking a little desperate. After a while she said it sounded like the only thing to do, even if nothing happened. Then she asked what had happened that afternoon at the Beverly Wilshire meeting, and I told her about telling Clem that he should either fire me or put me on leave. She seemed resigned to this. Then I told her what Borchiver had learned from the woman at the D.A.'s office, which now seemed like old news.

Then it was Caroline's turn to get angry. She cursed out the cops and said she felt like going over there and letting them hear what bullshit this was. By then she was in no mood to go out, and neither was I. We ate some leftovers and sat looking at each other miserably, and eventually, Caroline said she hoped I'd understand, but she was running on empty, after getting only a few hours' sleep the night before. She said she couldn't even think straight.

I understood. I felt as if someone had taken hold of me and wrung me out, and yet I knew I couldn't go to sleep. And so I sat up for hours, thinking about it all, and listening to the dry sycamore leaves blowing in the driveway.

9

Stella Nichols's office was on Wilshire and Beverly Drive, and around eight forty-five the next morning I pulled into the basement lot of her building, after driving around for twenty minutes in the rush hour. I'd left earlier than I needed to, rather than risk the cops' showing up first thing and arresting me before I'd even had a chance to talk to my attorney. I took the elevator upstairs and had a cup of coffee while I waited. Then a secretary came out and led me in to a large corner office, and Stella Nichols came out from behind her desk and shook hands.

She was a pleasant-looking woman of about forty, with short, gray hair. But Leonard Ahnemann had warned me that she was as hard as nails. We sat down, and I gave her the abbreviated version of what had happened. She nodded slowly. Then she said, bluntly, that I should definitely retain a lawyer. She explained the fee structure and asked if I wanted to retain her. I said, "Yes." Then I wrote out a retainer check for twenty thousand dollars.

She put the check in her desk drawer, leaned back, ran a hand through her hair, and said, "Okay. Let's go through the whole thing."

I told her the entire story, in detail, and she listened carefully and took notes. And at the end of the story, after I'd told her about the cops' most recent visit, she said, "My sense is they came fishing for a confession."

I was silent.

She said, "That's good. It must mean they don't have much of a case."

The remark made me uneasy. I said, "What could they have—aside from a motive?"

Stella shrugged. "Let's bear in mind that you're the one suspect they have. . . ." She was silent for a moment, then said, "Anything else you want to tell me right now?"

I wasn't sure if she was asking whether I did it, or not. I told her flat out, I didn't. Then I said, "I feel pretty dumb for talking to them."

She made a dismissive gesture. "Everyone does. I've known lawyers to do it. They ought to know better." She asked me who else I'd talked to about this, and I told her about the meeting with Clem and his people. She nodded slowly. Then she said, "No more talking, to anyone . . . you understand?"

I nodded.

She said, "Okay, give me a little background about you and your wife."

I gave it to her, and I told her about Caroline's affair with Gilmore, and when I'd finished she said that as soon as we were done with this, she would call Caroline and advise her not to talk to the police under any circumstances. "Now tell me what you told the police."

I tried to remember everything I'd said. I said I'd told them about punching Gilmore, and that it was in response to seeing him with his hands on Caroline—I said I hadn't mentioned the affair. She said, "Good." Then I told her I'd uttered several adamant denials that I'd killed him, and that I'd described where I'd gone in the house and what I'd touched. I said they'd asked me how far behind the perp I was, and I'd told them about half a minute. Then I told her I'd signed a consent form letting them take my clothes and car.

She said, "Did *they* say anything that could imply they had it in for you?"

I said they'd made a couple of sly references to my having friends downtown, before they'd started taping. They'd said nothing damning on tape as far as I could recall.

She made a note on her yellow pad. "Who else went into the house, aside from the detectives?"

"The sergeant who first showed up, the paramedics, and the coroner."

"Who went in first?"

"The sergeant."

"Do you know his name?"

"Vern somebody . . ."

"Did any other uniformed cops go in?"

"Not that I saw."

"All right. Draw me a map of the place."

She turned the yellow pad toward me, and I sketched the floor plan of the house, the grounds, the pathways, where the body was, and where I'd seen the perp go over the wall. Then I turned the yellow pad back toward her, and she asked me to use the diagram to show her my movements, and I drew a few arrows. I told her I still couldn't figure out why the perp hadn't gone out the back door while I was coming in through the French window.

She said, "Rule number one. You don't think about anything that can't help you. That's the cops' job." Then she pointed to the diagram and said, "Did you get a good look at Gilmore?"

I nodded.

"How many bullet wounds?"

"One in the head, one in the base of the throat."

She made notes. Then she asked me about my professional relationship with Gilmore. I told her we'd never had any major disagreements. Eventually, I said, "So what do you think? What can they make of this?"

She looked up from her notes. "It sounds like they're suggesting you went over the wall to get rid of the gun. They've got your clothes, so they'll look for powder burns. . . . By the way, do you own a gun?"

I nodded.

"What kind?"

"A thirty-two Smith and Wesson."

"Do you shoot anywhere regularly?"

"No, the gun's never been fired."

She smiled faintly, then made a few more notes, and when she looked up, she said, "I think that's about it. Now it's their move."

I was a little taken aback. I guess in some way I'd expected her to take a more active role. Ridiculous though it was, I felt she could persuade the forces of law to see that I was a reasonable person who would never commit the crime I was suspected of. I told her so, a little wistfully, and she smiled slightly. "I know. It's a waiting game.

That's the hard part. They'll be talking with the D.A. If they decide to go ahead, they'll probably want blood and hair samples."

"What do I do?"

"You call me. I tell 'em to get a subpoena."

"No cooperation?"

"You saw how far that got you."

I asked her what I should do if I were arrested, and she handed me her card. "Night or day," she said, "And take your rights seriously. Not another word."

She stood up and said. "I know. It's hard. But try to go about your life normally."

We shook hands, and I left her office. The feelings of uncertainty and lethargy that were to dominate my life began almost as soon as I stepped into the elevator.

From then on—as I was to find out—it became increasingly difficult to maintain any degree of normalcy. It was hard even to fill the hours—in fact, I didn't even know what to do for the rest of that day, after I left Stella's office. Eventually, I drove to the beach and walked for hours, from Venice to Pacific Palisades and back, and when I got home, it was around six, and Caroline was already home.

She said she'd called me a couple of times, and she asked where I'd been, and I told her I'd walked on the beach all day after talking to the attorney. She said Stella had called her and told her not to talk to the police, which was just as well, she said, because that very afternoon the police had called her. This was another jolt. I asked her which detective had called. She said, "Lowndes." She had told him she had nothing to say, and I said I wished I'd been so tight-lipped.

Then she wanted to know all about the details of my meeting, and I told her about it. She asked if I had confidence in Stella, and I said, "Yeah . . . she seems thorough, conscientious." Caroline digested this, then said, "Sam's funeral's tomorrow."

I didn't say anything.

She said, "I'm not going, obviously." She looked awkward. "John's going, so are some other people from work."

I told her what Greg had told me.

She raised her shoulders slightly, and said, "All the more reason."

I wasn't sure if she actually wanted to go. I decided not to ask, and in the next breath she went back to talking about the police. Like me, she was asking, "So, what do *we* do next?" She was eager to take the reins, as any normal person would be, and only slowly did she begin to realize, as I already had, that there was nothing either of us could do—not a damn thing. As Stella said, it was now someone else's move.

And so began the period I think of as the dangling phase. A wait that was made even more burdensome by the fact that although I wanted it to end, I *didn't* want it to end with charges being filed against me. But as the days dragged on, even the dreaded possibility of an indictment began to seem more bearable than the interminable waiting. That was the worst of it, not knowing when, or if ever, charges would be filed.

At first, I made a concerted effort to distract myself, but no matter how hard I tried, it was always there, and I doubt an hour went by during those weeks when I didn't think about it, hanging over me. It was there when I woke up in the morning. It was there before I fell into restless sleep. It seemed to have a bearing on almost everything I did, ate, touched, saw.

At times, rage would set in. Not in front of other people so much, but when I was alone, in the car, just driving, killing time. Most of my life I'd regretted having a lack of leisure. And now that I had unlimited time, I was unable even to read a newspaper without growing dispirited. I would find myself paying close attention to the Metro section and to the outcome of criminal cases. More and more, I felt as if I were drifting apart from the mainstream of life. I was scurrying into corners, like a guarded animal, with little to do but eat and survive. And the worst of it was, I didn't even know if my fears were justified.

It was hard to get any information about what was going on

with the forces that had taken over my life. From time to time, I'd get some notice that machinery was quietly grinding, and although I fortified myself with the reminder that the police had nothing but a motive, Stella heard enough over the next few weeks to establish that the police and the D.A.'s office weren't sitting on this. She and I had several more meetings, and I wondered if maybe their inquiries were politically motivated—and whether the opposition to Pike Mountain within the council had gotten wind of this and was feeding the fires. I made a couple of calls, but I couldn't turn up anything to confirm it.

And so weeks went by. Nothing happened. And just as I was beginning to feel a little more assured a subpoena arrived. The police wanted hair samples, blood samples, fiber samples from our house. We complied, of course. Stella sent her investigator over to the house, a squat ex-cop named Ted Crawford, and he stood by, looking on as the police forensic team took little swatches from the rugs and from my clothes. It was unnerving, these guys tramping around the house, Fran not knowing what to make of it. Fortunately, Caroline was at work at the time, and Katia was at her preschool.

A few more days went by. More waiting. And when I got back from lunch one afternoon, there was a message on the machine from Stella. I called her back, and she told me she had just learned that the D.A. himself was looking into the case—probably in view of who I was. I asked what this could mean in terms of what the police had accomplished, and she said, "Well, they've made some kind of case."

I was baffled. I sensed she was a little concerned, too. I said, "How? What?" She asked me a couple of times if there was anything I'd neglected to tell her, but I couldn't think of anything. She told me to hang in—they'd either indict or they wouldn't, it always came down to that. And again, I said, "Based on what?"

She had no answer, and I spent the better part of that evening drowning myself in liquor.

For the most part, I'd been struggling to limit myself when it came to booze, in part out of deference to Caroline, and to Katia and Fran. No matter what the circumstances, I felt obligated to maintain a level of civility to those around me. And so when the urge to drink was at its most intense, I'd go out, or walk several blocks in a direction far from any bars, or find a reason to run some aimless errand. The hardest times were when Caroline wasn't around, such as when she went to San Francisco one weekday evening, for a meeting with Clem's underwriters on another resort project. That evening, faced with the temptation to imbibe, I cast around for an alternative and finally came up with something, even though I knew it wasn't wise.

I went downstairs, got in the car, and drove east, then turned north on Fairfax, and after several attacks of nerves, I headed for Gilmore's house on Courtney Avenue. By then my mind was made up. I squared the block on Courtney and saw nobody sitting in a parked car, and the second time I came around the block, I slowed and took a good look at Gilmore's house.

The driveway wasn't taped off anymore, but a police "Crime Scene" notice was still affixed to the front gate. I drove around the block again, and this time I stopped in front of the house on the far side of the street. A light had been left on, and from where I sat, I could see there was no way that anyone in the house could have seen who was at the front door. But other than that, I learned nothing I didn't know already, except that on this quiet street it would have been easy for the perp to slip out the front while I was around back. Then I decided maybe he'd come in the back way and felt more secure exiting that way, knowing his route.

I drove around the block to Nichols Canyon Road. It was a two-lane road, with traffic, and there was no way I could park. So I drove down the hill, parked on the far side of Hollywood, and walked back, checking the sidewalks and recesses, and the ditch alongside the road, looking for anything.

I had no idea how thorough the cops' search might have been, or how far it might have extended. But after half an hour I'd found nothing, and as I walked back to my car, the exercise seemed stupid and futile.

I drove home. That night I lay awake very late and went over everything that had happened. From the moment I rang the bell until I called the cops. I started to picture what might have happened between Gilmore and the intruder. . . . Then a thought occurred to me. There was one other thing—the fact that the music was on. Wouldn't an intruder have thought twice about coming in if he'd heard music? Finally, I swore off thinking about it. The perp was gone. Gilmore was dead. And from the way it looked, I was the only suspect.

If there was a silver lining in any of this, it was the state of my relations with Caroline. When all this began, my first thought was that it would send us over the precipice, but this had not been the case at all. In fact, a steady improvement seemed to have been occurring with us, and I wasn't sure what to make of this, or to what I should attribute it.

There were obvious reasons—some of it clearly had to do with Gilmore's abrupt elimination from the picture. But as time went on, I began to see that the improvement had less to do with the absence of any third party than with the change of circumstances between Caroline and me. To begin with, Caroline seemed unconcerned that I was home all day, doing nothing, and a number of times she stunned me with acts of generosity and consideration. It had been a while since she'd shown me anything like this.

I'd half-expected her to edge away from me, as people do from pariahs, but in fact, the situation seemed to have brought us closer. Maybe it was a case of "us" versus "them," but whatever it was, we were communicating and there had been no further mention of her feeling ambivalent about the marriage.

She was being supportive, and gradually, I began to realize that in all likelihood we would stay together—assuming I didn't end up serving a prison term. And I had to admit that as a couple facing a crisis, we seemed to be doing rather well. I was no peach during this time. I'd fall into funks, or I'd get distracted and find myself staring into space, not wanting to talk, but throughout it all, Caroline was pretty consistent with her support.

At night, when she came in, she would try to assess my state of mind, gauging whether I wanted to talk about it, and if she sensed I did, she wouldn't mind discussing it for the hundredth time. Sometimes she would get emotional about it. Sometimes I would. Once, early on, she sat on the sofa opposite me and said, "I'm starting to get really angry about this. I feel like my life's being fucked with." Then, to my surprise, she began to cry, and when I sat next to her, she said, "You don't know how guilty I feel about all this. . . ."

She was sitting with her feet curled up, and she looked very vulnerable. She said, "I blame myself."

I said, "Don't . . . you weren't the one who hit him."

"You know what I mean."

I sat looking at her. Then she took a tissue from her purse, wiped her eyes, and said, "It was a diversion, Will . . . that's all it was."

I nodded.

"It just happened . . . when we made that trip to Washington—"

She broke off and looked at her feet, and I could see she didn't want to get into it. Neither did I, but there was something I wanted to ask her.

Eventually, I said, "What was it for him?"

She looked at me. Then she shook her head slowly, and after a moment she said, "A little more intense."

"Go on."

"That's it. It was a little more intense."

"He was taking it seriously?"

She nodded. Then she looked at me and asked why I'd even bothered to ask her that. She said it wasn't like me to want to know.

I said I realized that.

"So, why?"

I told her I really didn't know.

This wasn't the time to get into it. I'd already forgiven her for the affair, in part, I'm sure, because she was being so supportive.

And in the meantime I'd done a lot of reexamining of our relationship, and both our parts in it.

That evening, as she was sitting in the living room, looking over some plans for Clem's new development, making a few deft strokes with her pencil, I had to remind myself, she *was* an artist, and she had the artistic temperament to go with it, even though her material side had come to the fore since she had been working for Clem.

But it was the passionate Caroline I had fallen for, the woman whose spontaneities always made her a little unpredictable. She was still a little secretive about her past—there were suggestions that she'd had a few wild experiences, but this was who she was. And since I'd chosen to marry her, I felt I had to live with the entire package—which included a lapse in fidelity when things had gotten rough between us.

Still, I wasn't entirely reassured. One night we went to a party of a girlfriend of Caroline's now married to a movie producer. The couple lived up on Benedict Canyon, and by the time we got there, the main rooms were packed. It took a while before we got drinks and began knocking elbows with everyone, and at first I had the feeling that knocking elbows was what Caroline had in mind. I saw her get hit on a couple of times, and after the recent experience, I was fighting a tendency to keep tabs on her. But she seemed a little apprehensive, too, and after a while she joined me, looked out across the party, and in what amounted to a gesture of reassurance, said, "I'm glad we're married, Will, you know that?"

Then she suggested that the social scientists should come up with some criteria that would allow single people to assess their chances of success in relationships. Maybe that's what the urban scene needed, she said, some correlative breakthrough on the relationship front that could project peoples' chances. . . .

She was getting a little drunk. But I let her run with the notion. We went off to the kitchen to grab a bite to eat, and after another hour, we were ready to slip away. Before we left, I went off to find a bathroom, and when I shoved a door open, a young woman wearing a feather boa was sitting on the can in the dark, her skirt around her knees.

I apologized, but she merely laughed. When she emerged, she said it had been the high point of her evening. I told Caroline the story. She loved it, and as we drove off, she said, "Suppose we'd met like that, how would we ever explain it?"

We got home around one and had a wild time in bed.

But these were rare moments of distraction in what was otherwise a travail. Brooding had become the norm for me, the basis of my condition, and I guess there was a certain comfort in it, because at times I found myself opting for it, rather than making the effort to put out for others. There was also a sense of security in nurturing my isolation, even if it was a false sense, for as long as I could perpetuate the illusion that I was isolated, there was less that could threaten me. To this end, I would indulge in the strangest fantasties, even going so far as to pretend that I wasn't in Los Angeles. It was important to avoid certain reminders, in order to make it through the day. And I guess I was in this frame of mind when Clem called one morning to remind me that the city council and the Riverside supervisors were due to vote the next day.

He and I had been in touch from time to time conferring about it, and everything had stayed on track. I'd made sure Premerlani was holding hands with a couple of council members, and I'd asked him to explain to others that my absence was due to exhaustion.

So far, nothing had leaked to the press about my being under investigation. I wasn't sure if this was due to caution on the cops' part or a lack of diligence on the part of the press, but the bottom line was that unless something happened in the next twenty-four hours, the Pike Mountain vote was about to sail through.

Clem said he thought I should be there.

I said I didn't want to be.

"Why not?" he said. "You worked as hard on this as anyone."

I told him I hadn't even considered attending.

"Come on, Will. I could use you there . . . just in case."

"In case of what? It's a done deal."

"Well, something could come up. If there's a last-minute hitch, and Al gets flustered, I'd just as soon you be there."

I said there was no reason for me to be there, and I started to argue against it. It was about the last place I wanted to be. But he hung on, encouraging me, saying it had to beat sitting around the house. It didn't, but I finally caved in.

And so, around two o'clock that Thursday afternoon, I drove downtown and headed toward city hall on North Spring. I was there a few minutes early, and when I got off the elevator at the council chamber on the third floor, I recognized a number of people from the press. I felt a little nervous, half-expecting them to converge on me and ask me questions about Gilmore, and it was almost a surprise, and certainly a relief, when nobody did.

Then I spotted Al Premerlani. He was talking to one of the members' aides, and he looked harried and sweaty, and when he'd finished talking and he was on his way to talk to another aide, he saw me.

"Oh, hi, Will."

He seemed a little worked up. I formed an image of myself several years ago when I was new to this. He started to run off at the mouth, and eventually I calmed him down and asked if there were any problems.

"No, no. It's fine. Guess what?"

"What?"

"Constanza changed his mind. He's for us."

He flashed a quick smile. Then he took a deep breath and asked, "How's it going by you?"

I said I'd been better. I told him I'd been keeping a low profile. Then he spotted Councilman Constanza's aide and went off to talk to her.

There was nothing for me to do there, and I figured I'd go sit in the chamber's spectator seats. But when I walked in, the council was debating whether methane gas detectors should be installed in houses with "California" basements, and rather than listen to that, I wandered out to get some coffee.

When I got back, the council had already voted on the methane issue, and the members were scattered around the chamber with their aides. I saw Romero look my way once, but I wasn't sure he'd seen me. Then, as I glanced around, people from Clem Resources walked in, Clem bringing up the rear, talking to Elaine Christensen, his financial vice president.

I saw Greg Stannert come in. But he moved up front, along with the others. Then the council members began shuffling back to their seats, and the debate on Pike Mountain began.

Stephens led off with a big speech about finding sensible solutions to problems that went beyond politics. He said he had believed all along that a solution to the garbage crisis could be found and he spoke of the key element in all this: an enterprising company, in Los Angeles County, which had taken the initiative in seeking a solution.

He mentioned John Clem by name, and there were a couple of flashes of cameras from the side rows as the press photographers took photos of the man of the hour. Stephens then said it was important that a company be fairly compensated for its efforts and enterprise, and he urged members to vote in favor of the added sanitation tax that would compensate Clem Resources.

With that, he sat down, and another councilman from the San Fernando Valley echoed his sentiments. Then Romero got up and made a favorable speech, but with a pro-government slant.

I looked toward the front and could see Greg sitting on the edge of his seat. I couldn't blame him. He'd put three years into this, and as chief engineer there was a time when he was constantly getting on or off a plane, to consult with some authority about particulate levels of atmospheric pollution at waste transfer stations, or some such.

Romero droned on for another five minutes, then sat down. A few members offered brief self-congratulatory remarks. Then Constanza got up and said he had some reservations about Pike Mountain and whether it afforded a solution that was long-term enough, but that present necessity made it appropriate for him to endorse the plan. After that, the dissenters voiced their objections, and five minutes later, the council voted ten to five in favor and agreed to add a surcharge to the sanitation bills of every resident of Los Angeles.

The chairman lowered his gavel. John Clem was beaming.

There were congratulations and embraces up front. As I was about to get up and go over there, I looked across the chamber and saw someone I didn't want to see. Cynthia Gilmore. I didn't know if she'd seen me, but right then I decided this was too weird for me, and it occurred to me that maybe this was why Caroline had offered to go to Riverside that day to baby-sit the simultaneous vote there. Maybe she knew, or had a hunch, that Cynthia would be here.

I looked over at Cynthia. She was sitting in a seat near the far wall, and she looked implacable. I knew Clem had been in touch with her a number of times. He'd told me about the conversations he'd had with her since the funeral, at which she had told him that she would take a passive role in the project, although Sam's interest in the partnership was now technically hers. Clem had insisted their interests were the same—move this thing forward toward a swift conclusion, and after a conversation or two with her attorney, she had agreed.

Clem had also told me that neither my name nor Caroline's had ever come up in his conversations with her. This was just fine with me, but I wasn't about to stay around to have to contend with her, face-to-face. I cut out and drove home.

Caroline got home around seven, in a talkative mood, given how everything had gone. She wanted to know the details of everyone's reactions in the aftermath, and I told her I had cut out early, and why.

She said, "Oh," and insisted it had never occurred to her that Cynthia might be there.

I gazed at her for a moment. "I keep wondering if Cynthia knew—about you and him."

She stared at me, then caught my implication. Her mouth opened slightly, and after a while she said, "Jesus, Will . . ."

She was looking at me like I was a little paranoid. I said, "It's just a thought. . . . Did he ever indicate to you that she might have known?"

"No."

I nodded, and didn't pursue it after that. But off and on, I thought about it over the next few weeks.

And finally, the boom fell. After weeks of waiting and agonizing. It was a Tuesday, and how else would the fates hand out their peculiar brand of recompense than by whacking me over the head twice within an hour?

First, my secretary phoned me to say I'd gotten a call from a Bernard Kurman. He'd left a message saying he wanted me to call him back.

I'd pretty much forgotten about Kurman with all the other stuff . . . assigning him less priority than I might otherwise have. Then Stella called with the main blow.

She wanted to see me, and from the tone of her voice, I knew it wasn't anything good. I asked her what it was, and she took a breath and said, "Just come on by, Will."

Half an hour later, I was sitting in her conference room, staring at a copy of an indictment with my name on it. I was shaking.

Crawford was there, and he gave me a couple of reassuring pats on the shoulder and said, "Don't worry, Will. They're a long way from sending you up yet." But I was staring at this piece of paper with my name on it amid all the legalese, and just the sight of the thing sent me into a panic.

Stella didn't have any more information, beyond what was in the document. She did have an assurance from the assistant D.A., Mark Hennessee, that the police would forgo arresting me and taking me to jail. The charges were set forth, and bail could be worked out prior to the arraignment or, if not, set at the arraignment itself.

Stella spent a few minutes trying to reassure me that there was no way I would spend any time in jail prior to trial. But all I could ask her was "What can they have?"

She kept saying she didn't know. Then she said that if past patterns held true, she would receive the discovery material within a few days. At that time she would have a chance to thoroughly examine their case, see if it was weak, and if so, request an immediate dismissal or at least a pretrial hearing, at which she could ask for dismissal.

I looked at her in dismay. "So what do we do?" I asked.

She patted my hand. "First, I want you to prepare yourself for this. Do you need to do things, before this makes the papers?"

I told her I'd been planning to quit my job—this seemed as good a time as any. Stella and Crawford exchanged looks. Then Stella said, "I don't think quitting is such a great idea, Will."

She explained that if the case came to trial, she'd rather have me gainfully employed than unemployed. I could see the sense in that. Then she said, "Unless it's something you feel you have to do."

In the back of my mind, I was thinking about Kurman's call. But I didn't say anything about that. I asked her when the indictment would be made public, and she said Hennessee would probably release it to the press in a day or two.

I thought, grimly, Well, that's one good reason not to call Kurman back. I could have my secretary, Jeanette, say that my lawyer had advised me not to talk to the press—about anything.

I told Stella, "No, I don't have to quit." It all hit me, as I said this, the sense of unreality, the feelings of desperation, and suddenly, I wanted to lash out at the cops, the assistant D.A., and all the fucking people who were infringing on my life for no good reason. Then I felt a desire to outwit them by simply running, and I think Stella saw something in my expression and sensed this impulse.

"Will," she said quietly, "you're going to get a lot of crazy ideas these next few days. Don't act on any of them. It won't do you any good."

I knew what she meant, but I already saw myself with Caroline and Katia grabbing a flight to Costa Rica, or some such enlightened country with no extradition treaty with the United States, and living there indefinitely, thumbing my nose at Uncle Sam and his fucked-up, misplaced system of justice. If Vesco could get away with it, so could I.

I confessed this in a bold sort of way to Crawford and Stella. Stella said, "Will . . . don't."

She told me I should call her anytime. Then Crawford told me to be careful driving home.

I continued to entertain the wild notions as I drove home. But reality set in again as I broke the news to Caroline. She was stunned, incredulous, and every bit as angry as I was. But she never made any mention about running. She alternated between fury and brooding, and every so often, as I got up and shifted about from chair to chair, she came and sat down next to me and tried to reassure me. After an hour or so, I called Clem, almost out of a need to do something. He took the news pretty calmly. Then I told him about Kurman calling me. He said, "Fuck him! He's the least of your problems, sounds like."

I said, "What about yours, John? We don't know what he knows."

"Fuck him. Let him call me if he wants."

I sensed he had the bit between his teeth, now that the Pike deal was done, and he was talking about weighing in on my behalf with some heavy political artillery and trashing this thing. Then he said, "I appreciate what you did for the deal, Will, taking yourself out of it, but I think it's time now to use all we've got."

He tossed out a number of names of people we both knew who might sit hard on the D.A. But even as he did, I knew it was probably too late for that. And I began to wish I'd taken his initial advice and let Borchiver call Stephens. I said I'd talk to my attorney about his suggestions, and I told him he might want to have Premerlani at the ready, because there would be a few calls from the press just as soon as the indictment became public. We hung up on this grim note, and I made a point of telling Caroline that we should leave the answering machine on to screen our calls. Now I began to feel that we'd adopted a bunker mentality.

That night, the fantasies really took over. More thoughts of flight. Feelings of desperate uncertainty. Feelings of shame, warranted or unwarranted. Maybe some part of me saw this as punishment—retribution from a power higher than the Los Angeles D.A.'s office—for all the bribes I'd paid. Still, it seemed bitterly ironic to be indicted for something I hadn't done.

I didn't sleep that night. After Caroline went to bed, I sat up, fighting the feelings of despair, and at the same time reminding myself that they couldn't have shit. Let 'em try and convict me on a paltry motive. I couldn't imagine any jury convicting based solely on that. Still, as Stella had suggested, they had to have something else, albeit circumstantial. And it was this, the missing ingredient, that kept me up nearly all night.

At some point Katia woke up, and I went in to check on her. My daughter, flaxen-haired, button-mouthed. I put the blanket back on her, and she went back to sleep. And I stood over her, thinking that I'd always wanted the best for her. But now, what a start for her, what a miserable start. And suddenly, I wanted to lash out at the whole world, not on my own behalf, but on hers.

The next day, Clem called and suggested that Caroline and I get out of town, take a vacation. It seemed like a brilliant idea—I couldn't imagine why neither of us had thought of it. Caroline said, "Let's do it," and I called Stella to see if she had any problem.

She said the arraignment date would be at least two weeks away, and an hour later, Caroline was packing and I was telling Fran all that was going on. I asked if she wanted to come with us, but she seemed hesitant. And eventually, I paid her to simply stay at the house and take care of the place while we were away. She looked very worried, and in trying to reassure her, I even reassured myself a bit.

That afternoon, we took a flight to Maui. We checked into the Kapalua Plantation Inn at three hundred dollars a night, and even managed to maintain a grim humor about the situation. As

Caroline said, "I'm sure there are better excuses for doing this." But even in Hawaii, we didn't escape it. Stella had our number, so did Clem, and the next morning they both called to say the indictment had been in the papers and on the TV news.

A couple of times during those weeks, I suspected I was about to be recognized. I wasn't—at least not that I was aware of. My picture, as it turned out, hadn't appeared in the papers. In fact, there didn't seem to be a photograph of me in general circulation. And so, the two weeks went by. Caroline and I dined together at night, and edged closer in many ways, and during the days, I spent hours with Katia, focusing on her, concentrating on her, finding every minute precious.

The weeks flew. Vacations generally do, but this one even more so. Getting on the plane home required a major effort, a struggle of will in the face of more practical instincts. But I got on it—with all the weariness of an army grunt with no belly for the battle, and five hours later, we landed in the land of the tail-finned burger stand. A place I'd always thought of as someone else's vision of hell—now, mine.

10

I was arraigned in Los Angeles Superior Court, on West Temple Street, a stone's throw from the council offices where I'd plied my trade, a fact not lost on one reporter whose story had appeared in the paper that morning. Stella and I stood at the bench, before Judge Rezek, a man of sixty, wearing bifocals, while a sprinkling of the curious looked on from the spectator rows, along with half a dozen reporters. Caroline had offered to be there, but Stella had maintained it wasn't necessary. The arraignment would be ten minutes at most. There was no need for a show of support. The trial would be another matter.

That morning, when we walked in, Stella had taken the assistant D.A., Mark Hennessee, aside and berated him for ten minutes before the judge came in. Then, she moved for an immediate dismissal on the ground that she had not been provided with adequate time to study discovery material—apparently, there had been some mix-up in its getting to her office. Judge Rezek scowled at Hennessee, who offered a long-winded explanation and occasionally glared at me, as if I'd had a hand in sabotaging it. Stella had already told me that there was no way Judge Rezek would dismiss.

Instead, he offered her a continuance or an early pretrial hearing. She accepted the latter, and the judge finally asked if she wanted a formal reading of the charge. She agreed to waive it, and I entered the plea of not guilty. The judge then asked both sides whether they were satisfied with the bail arrangement of fifty thousand dollars. Both sides were. That was it. He pounded his gavel and called the next case.

Ten minutes later, Crawford and I were scooting out of a side entrance to avoid the press. Crawford observed that I'd already managed to become something of a minor celebrity, which wasn't easy in L.A., where people had to work at it. I spent the rest of the day wandering aimlessly in the park. Stella had told me that she wanted me in her office at ten the following morning, by which time she would have read the discovery material. But around three, I called her anyway, only to learn that she was in court for a sentencing hearing. So I drove home, frustrated. Even now the justice system had managed to cheat me out of knowing what cards were stacked against me.

It was a glum evening. Caroline and I had both expected to be able to talk about the case. We were still clinging to the idea that a gross negligence or distorted coincidence had led to all this.

The next morning, when I arrived at Stella's office, Crawford came out to the reception area to get me. He said Stella was waiting for us in the conference room, and we walked in together. Stella was standing at the conference room table, with several legal pads and a cardboard box in front of her—the prosecution's long-awaited case. She asked me to sit down, and Crawford closed the door. The room fell quiet, as if insulated by the rows of law books.

Stella asked how I was, after yesterday. I said I still felt it was all unreal. At times anger would take hold of me, then give way to resignation. She seemed to understand. She then said she would like Ted to sit in on this because, as her investigator, it was important he be up to speed. I nodded, and she said that if there was anything I needed to tell her one-on-one, I was to say so.

I indicated the ominous cardboard box, and asked, "How's their case?"

Stella glanced at Crawford, then back to me, and said, "There're some surprises."

I felt my stomach pitch.

Stella took several envelopes from the box, and started to open one. She said, "Let's start with these."

She poured out a bundle of letters and several photos, which all landed upside down on the table, and as she turned them over, I saw that the photos were of Caroline—*all* of them.

I stared at them. What the hell were these? Then, in a low, quiet voice, Stella said, "These came from Gilmore's house."

I stared at the things. They were not your average three-by-fives from the local Fotomat. They were eight-by-ten black-and-whites—a bit like movie publicity stills—of Caroline walking, talking, gesturing in groups with other people. They were all taken at the Pike Mountain site, all but one—a picture of her smiling, in front of a government building in Washington, D.C.

I was reeling.

"Gilmore had these?"

Stella nodded. I picked up the photos and studied them, one by one. Amid the confusion, I was thinking they were flattering, artful even, accenting facets of Caroline's looks and gestures, as one might with photos of an actress, to emphasize range. Then Stella indicated the letters, and I felt major trepidations as I picked one up and started to read it. It was an elegiac poem—to Caroline—a kind of mystical rambling, such as an English student might write. I picked up another letter. It was another poem, written in the same tone, recalling passionate moments, and I couldn't help feeling some wild jealousy as I read it, then some scorn, thinking that Caroline, who loved to have provocative sexual talk whispered to her as she made love, would probably not have much time for these.

I looked up. Crawford and Stella were staring at me. I said, "What the fuck . . . ?"

Crawford cleared his throat. He said, "Do you know where the photos were taken, Will?"

"At Pike Mountain."

I was still a little dazed. Stella said, "Did Caroline ever say anything to you about these?"

"No."

There was a short silence. Then Crawford sorted through the photos, picked one out, and pointed to a blurred image in one corner of the picture. "See this—it looks like he took it from inside a building. That looks like a window frame got in the way."

Then he said, "My bet is, he was taking pictures of her with a long lens. Look at 'em."

I looked, and it was true. Caroline seemed utterly unself-conscious—unaware of a camera—in all of the pictures, except for the one taken in Washington.

Crawford held it up.

I said, "They were on a business trip together."

He glanced at Stella and indicated the others. Then he said, "I bet she has no idea these exist." He smiled at me. "Course, you may want to ask her."

His eye veered to the letters. He said, "There's no envelopes . . . no evidence these were ever sent or returned."

I stared at both of them. Then Stella asked me again if Caroline had ever alluded to anything like this.

"No . . . I mean, it never came up."

She nodded. "You should at least ask her."

I was still dumbfounded. I asked where these had been found, and Stella said, "In Gilmore's desk. At the house on Courtney."

"Did his wife know about them?"

Crawford merely shrugged, and I was about to ask them what it all meant in terms of the case when Stella reached into the box, took out a folded sheet of paper, and handed it to me.

She said, "Do you want to tell me what this is?"

I unfolded the paper, and the second I saw the list of names with the dollar amounts alongside them, my blood ran cold.

Stella was staring at me when I looked up.

After a moment she said, "Is it a contributions list, Will?"

I didn't say anything.

She said, "Will, I'm your attorney. . . ."

There was a silence.

"Yes," I said, reluctantly.

"*Illegal* contributions? On behalf of Clem Resources?"

I looked at both of them and nodded. Crawford said, "That wasn't so hard, was it, Will?"

Stella shot Crawford a look and asked me, "Why would Gilmore have this?"

I said I had no idea. I was reeling.

"Was he supposed to know about these?" Stella asked.

"No . . . these had nothing to do with Pike Mountain."

"So why would he have it?"

My mouth wavered.

"Could it have to do with this?"

She reached into the box and handed me a wad of computer

printout material . . . phone company records. Then she reached in the box again and handed me another piece of paper. She said, "This is a prosecutorial subpoena for Bernard Kurman. . . . According to these phone records, Gilmore was calling him."

I guess my mouth was flapping even before she indicated the contributions list again. She looked at me in a very deliberate way and said, "You know what I mean. . . . Do you think Gilmore was leaking information about you?"

It took only a moment for me to see the entire picture. I could feel myself sweating.

"Jesus Christ," I said softly. "It was him."

Stella cocked her head to one side. "You knew someone was speaking to Kurman about you?"

I was still in a daze. After a moment, I nodded.

"Why didn't you tell me?"

"I didn't connect it. I didn't think it could have anything to do with this."

The room was silent for a moment. Then I felt anger rising. Any sympathy I might have felt for Gilmore had vanished—that son of a bitch!

Crawford said, "Are you getting the picture, Will?"

I stared at him. Stella said, "No matter how we look at this, it looks like Gilmore wanted to hurt you. Presumably on account of his interest in Caroline." She paused; then she said, "It could lead a jury to think you had a reason to hurt him."

I stared at her. I couldn't believe it. So this was what the cops had.

Crawford smiled a tight smile and said, "Would you like a cup of coffee, Will?"

He looked at Stella, and Stella slowly nodded. Then Crawford got up and left the room.

Two minutes later, he was back. Stella, meantime, had stepped out to take a call. Crawford handed me my coffee and helped himself to one of my cigarettes, and when

Stella came back, she sat with her arms folded for several moments. Then we talked about what Gilmore had been up to.

I said it all began to add up: Caroline had told me it was a little more intense for him. His calls to Kurman had begun a week prior to the night of Clem's party. Was this his plan? To start the ground rolling out from under me? To go after Caroline? Did he plan to leave his wife? Again, the thought occurred to me. Did Cynthia Gilmore know?

I sat, considering this, asking myself, "How the hell did he get hold of this list?"

Stella said, "Will . . . ?"

I was miles away. I looked at her, and she rolled her pen back and forth on her legal pad for a moment. Then she said, "The police found a fiber from your jacket in the kitchen. It was next to a towel with powder traces on it."

I asked what this meant.

"I'm not too concerned about it. You told the police you *were* in the kitchen. They'll maintain, of course, that you wrapped your sleeve in a towel to keep off the powder burns, so it really doesn't do us any good that no powder burns were found on your jacket."

She hesitated. "But I am concerned about *this*." Again, she paused. "Did you smoke in Gilmore's house?"

"No . . . why?"

"Did you tell the police that?"

"Yes . . . they asked me."

"What did you tell them?"

"I told them I only smoked outside . . . on the patio."

"*When* did you smoke outside?"

"After the cops showed up."

Crawford and Stella exchanged looks. Stella said, "The police found a couple of your cigarette butts in an ashtray in the dining room. They knew they were yours because the saliva matched on the ones you left at the station. Unfortunately, they didn't need a warrant for those."

"What?"

My brain was swimming.

Stella waited a moment. "They'll argue that you and Gilmore talked. . . ."

I started to tremble.

Crawford said, "What Stella means, Will, is your story doesn't jibe with the physical evidence, at least as they'll present it. . . ."

I lurched out of my seat. "They're setting me up."

They were staring at me.

"For Christ's sake! . . . Can't you see?" I was unaware of anything else. The photos, the letters, the phone calls to Kurman. It took me a moment to get some kind of grip.

Stella looked at Crawford. Then she said quietly, "Are you sure you didn't smoke in that house, Will?"

"Positive!"

Crawford shook his head slowly. Then he dug in the box, took out a piece of paper, and studied it a moment. He handed it to me and said, "According to this, it was a forensic guy named Eastlake found those cigarette butts."

My mind was in a fog. Parts of me seemed to be breaking off, flying loose. My brain felt like it was cracking. Stella said quietly, "Let's take a break."

She got up and went back to her office. Crawford sat and looked at me, and eventually he got up, too. He rested a hand on my shoulder. Then he went out, and I was left alone, dizzy, scared, vaguely aware that my attorney and her investigator were conferring. Eventually, I couldn't sit any longer. I got up and started to pace.

I was still pacing when they came back in. They sat down and watched me. Then Stella said in a calm voice, "What are your thoughts, Will?"

I said, "You know damn well what I think."

I was more in control, but not much more. And when Stella started to say something, I said, sharply, "I didn't smoke in that house, Stella."

She looked at Crawford. "All right, Will. Let's pursue this. If it wasn't the cops put the cigarette butts in that ashtray, then it was someone else. Someone who killed him and wants to frame you."

I stared at her. "What makes you think it wasn't the cops?"

"I didn't say it wasn't. But it was a forensic guy who found the cigarette butts, and I think maybe we should look elsewhere." She was silent for a moment. Then she said, "Who else?"

I didn't respond.

She said, "From what you said, it was John Clem suggested that you and Gilmore talk."

"Yeah, but . . ." This made no sense. I said, "Forget Clem."

"Why?" Crawford asked.

"He had twenty million dollars riding on this deal. I'm the guy brokering it with the politicians—he's going to murder his partner and frame *me*? Why?"

Crawford didn't answer. After a moment I sat down at the table and said, "Where the hell was Cynthia Gilmore that night?"

Crawford said, "I hear you, Will."

Then he dug in the box, pulled out a copy of a police statement, and said, "She was at the Bel Air Hotel from seven-thirty on, having dinner with a girlfriend. Your call came in at eight-twenty." He put the statement back. Then he said, "Coroner estimates the time of death to be eight P.M. Besides, where would she get your cigarettes, Will?"

I was fishing wildly. "I guess anyone at the office could have gotten 'em."

Stella raised her pen. "But you didn't go to the office that day, Will. You worked at home. You said so. And if anyone got your cigarette butts, they got them that day. No one could have known in advance you were going to punch Gilmore."

I was thrown. I'd forgotten.

Stella said, "Who else would have access to your ashtray at home, Will? . . . Aside from Caroline."

I was staring at her. The message came through loud and clear. Then Crawford said, "Where was Caroline that day?"

It took a moment. I said, "That's absurd. Gimme a break."

"Well . . . where was she?"

"At the office. Meeting with Clem."

Crawford scratched his lip. He said, "Did you leave the house that day, Will?"

They were still looking at me, and finally I said, "For God's sake . . . Caroline! That's ridiculous. What would be her motive?"

Stella said, dryly, "You want to get into it, Will? I could give you a few reasons."

"Like what?"

"Gilmore let her down. He planned to dump her, after the dust flew between you two."

"Oh, for God's sake . . ." I was floundering, searching for words. Finally I said, "Who's really got a motive here?"

I realized what I'd said. Crawford laughed a little. Then he said, "Did you leave the house that day, Will?"

"I went to lunch."

They didn't say anything, and I said, "What if Cynthia found out that her husband was fucking Caroline?"

Crawford shrugged. "Still doesn't explain how she got your cigarettes, Will."

I couldn't offer any theory. Stella said, "Look, Will, let's go back to where we started. If it wasn't the cops planted those cigarettes, and if you didn't smoke in that house, then it was someone else." Her brow darkened, and she waved her pen at me and said, "So don't discuss this with *anyone* . . . and that includes Caroline."

I started to say something, but Crawford said, "She means it, Will. *Especially* not with Caroline."

I sat back in the chair, feeling like I was in some fugue state, feeling like I'd taken blows to every part of my body. Eventually, I said, "I hear you."

We were all silent for a long time. Then Stella said, "I suggest we take a step back from this, give it some thought." She turned to me, deliberately. "Will, I want you to ask Caroline about the photos and letters. Nothing else. Just that. And let me know what she says."

She stood up. Then she said, "Don't get down. This is still a circumstantial case."

Maybe it was. But the jigsaw, as I saw it, was a hell of a lot more complete than an hour ago.

11

I had a drink at the bar of a small bistro on Beverly, and as I sat there, some part of me began to shrivel. I felt as if I had committed the crime—clearly, many people already thought I had, since I'd been charged—and if I were convicted, it would merely become a judicial fact. Suddenly, I saw myself as one of those sad lifers, protesting his innocence to anyone who would listen. I almost had to remind myself I didn't do it!

I felt myself sweating. And the impulse was there again, to run. And yet I knew this wouldn't help. And it wouldn't help at all to start thinking this way again—it hadn't so far. Still, the hard part for me already was watching other people go about their daily lives. Even Caroline.

I would watch her go about the house, doing what she had to do, all the while maintaining her belief in my innocence. And I knew, yes, she would go on with her life, even if I were behind bars, and in those moments I would feel anger at her. I started to think again of what I'd talked about with Stella and Crawford. But it was absurd, especially what Stella had put forward as Caroline's possible motive for killing Gilmore—that Gilmore might have wanted to break it off! Caroline had no shortage of admirers, and she was far too practical to let her heart run away with her and commit a crime of violent passion. I sat there, reasoning that neither Crawford nor Stella knew her. Then I thought about Lowndes and Tremaine. Those sons of bitches. I could easily see these two setting me up, and no matter what Crawford had said about the forensic guy finding the cigarette butts, it still seemed feasible to me that Lowndes and Tremaine could have planted them there, just to make a case, especially since they were so damn convinced I did it.

I paid for my drink and walked out, through the aroma of warm duck salad and the perfumed niceties of the Beverly Hills lunchtime diners—hating everyone.

I collected my car and pulled out of the basement garage. I wasn't sure where to go. I sat at the curb, trying to sort through it all, and I decided I should at least tell Clem about Gilmore having that list. In the past few weeks, he, too, had received several calls from Kurman and, like me, had been refusing to return them.

I drove to a phone and called him. He was out to lunch, but Premerlani said he would be back—he had a meeting at three. I told him to say I was coming by, and that it was urgent. Then I got back in the car, drove to Wilshire, and nudged through the lunch-hour traffic, thinking again about what Gilmore had been up to. My brain was still spinning. Between the photos, the letters, the contributions list, and the cigarettes—cigarettes—as I stubbed out a cigarette in the car ashtray, I realized that this was one place from which someone might have gotten a few butts, assuming they could get in the car without leaving a trace of entry.

I was also thinking of Stella's inference—that Caroline was the only person who would have access to my ashtray at home—and for a while I took off on that, even knowing it was absurd. It made no sense. Why would Caroline frame me? What would she have to gain? If she really wanted to get me out of her life, she could tell me she was filing for divorce. It would be no more complicated than that. It seemed absurd to be even thinking about it. Gilmore's wife, on the other hand? That was not so ridiculous.

I made the turn onto Santa Monica and I started to think again about Gilmore and Caroline. She had probably led him on a bit. She was prettier than Cynthia, sexier certainly. Maybe Gilmore had a yearning for something he hadn't been getting in his marriage. Maybe that's what he'd been missing—just plain, good old honest sex. A lack of that, then the sudden experience of it, could certainly make a guy do weird things . . . like write elegiac poems, or try to sabotage a woman's husband. I could see him getting twisted over it, even risking the Pike Mountain deal, just to get me out of the way. Still, it wasn't Gilmore who had planted those cigarette butts, that was for sure.

I made a left onto Century Park East and drove down the ramp into the garage, to my parking space. Some graffiti was scribbled above my name—a nasty little surprise. I headed for the elevator, already slapping on the tough mask I'd adopted lately in the face of strange glances. Then who should I see getting out of a Mercedes coupe on the far side of the garage, but Cynthia Gilmore.

My attitude was a whole lot different than when I'd last seen her at the council chamber. I didn't know then about the cigarette butts. I guessed she was here to see Clem, about Gilmore's partnership interest, and I waited as she headed my way. She didn't see me at first. Then she came through the automatic glass doors of the garage, and when she saw me, she was clearly startled, and nervous.

I was a little nervous, too. I said, "Can we talk for a few minutes?"

"I don't think so, Will."

She started to walk by me, and I said quickly, "I didn't kill him, Cynthia, no matter what the cops think."

She hesitated and faced me. It was very tense, and yet, at the same time, I had the feeling that despite her bereavement, she was playing this for the theatrics.

She said, "Were you waiting for me?"

"No."

She looked away. Then she moved in front of the elevator, turned, and stared at me. She said, coolly, "I'm on my way to see Greg. If he's not back yet, we can talk in his office."

I wasn't sure why she'd agreed—she'd certainly delivered her lines with a righteous distaste. Maybe she just wanted to get away. The elevator arrived, and I sensed she didn't want to ride up with me, so I told her I'd left something in my car. I said I'd see her in a few minutes.

She got on the elevator, the doors closed, and I waited a minute, then took the next elevator upstairs, and as I stepped off, I received several strange looks. It had been weeks since I'd been in here.

I turned and went the opposite way from my office, and as I approached Greg's office, his secretary, Denise, turned pale, knowing who was already in there.

I said, "It's all right, Denise. She's expecting me." Then I knocked and went in.

Cynthia was standing at the window, arms folded. She turned and looked at me as I came in. Then she went back to looking out the window. She shook her head as if to indicate confusion and finally said, "I shouldn't even be talking to you."

I said, "I just wanted you to hear it from me."

"Why should *I* believe you? The police don't."

She looked at me in the same obdurate way, and I didn't know what else to say. I didn't even know for sure how much she knew about the affair, but I figured she must know all she needed to know—by now.

Then she said, "Why did you go to the house that night?"

"Because he asked me to."

"To talk about Caroline?"

"I guess. I assume you know—"

She interrupted. "From the sound of it, I was the last to know—"

She broke off and shook her head again. Then she said, "I can't believe I'm even talking to you. The police certainly don't want me to." Then she added, quietly, "You'd better go."

My perspective on this was changing by the moment. I was talking to a woman whose husband I'd been formally charged with murdering. I was even a little surprised that downstairs she hadn't screamed, or called for the police. So what did this mean—since we were actually talking—that she didn't believe I'd done it?

I realized I hadn't moved, then as I started to, Cynthia said, "I've thought about coming to see you. . . . I just wanted to look you in the eye."

I said she should have. Then I said, "Look . . . Cynthia . . . I took a swing at Sam because he was holding hands with Caroline. Not just holding hands—"

I stopped short and didn't elaborate. Then I said, "I was reacting to the shock. . . . I'm sure you can understand that. I'm not the type to kill anyone, I'd never reach the point where I'd think it was worth it."

She looked at me for a long time. Then she said, "So what did you hope to gain by going to the house?"

"Nothing . . . it was his idea."

She was studying me. Then she said slowly, "I know you. And

I know Caroline. I definitely think you'd think she'd be worth killing for."

I didn't like what she'd said, or the contempt with which she'd said it, and I could feel myself reacting. She looked away, which pissed me off, and after a moment I went for it. I said, "Doesn't it strike you as odd that the night after I hit him he gets killed . . . and I'm there?"

She was staring at me. She said, "What are you saying? That it wasn't a robbery? Wasn't that your version of events?"

I didn't answer for a moment. Then I said, "I guess I'm asking if he had any enemies."

"None, except maybe you . . . And I don't think it's your place to be asking me questions."

"Maybe it is."

She glared at me. "I suggest you leave."

But I was damned if I was going to leave without asking her what I wanted to ask. I said, "Did you know about the affair before Greg told you?"

Her eyes narrowed. She knew what I was implying. I saw anger build up in her. Then in a muted and even more hostile way she said, "I really think you should leave now."

I turned to the door, and as I did, it opened.

Greg walked in, and from his expression it was clear he'd been forewarned by his secretary.

He looked a little alarmed, and I said, "Hi." Then I continued on out, closing the door behind me.

I went to my office and sat quietly for a few minutes, thinking about her attitude. Then I glanced around, and it was strange, seeing the office exactly as I'd left it, weeks ago. I buzzed Premerlani, and he said Clem was back and was waiting to see me.

I walked down to his suite. I told him what had just happened. Then I told him about Gilmore having the list, and his look of sympathetic indulgence vanished. I said it was Gilmore who had been talking to Kurman.

His reaction was predictable. Shock. Disbelief. Then anger. He kept asking, "Why?" And I tried to explain it as best I could. Finally, I raised the question of how Gilmore might have gotten the list, and he looked a little sheepish.

He raised his hands, palms up.

"Where the fuck else would he get it, Will?"

I closed my eyes.

"You kept records?"

He kicked his lower desk drawer. "Jesus, Will . . . even I have to keep track!"

He wasn't angry at me. He was angry at himself. He said, "You know I let him use this place. . . . He was a partner. He had that lousy office on the floor below. He's gonna hold meetings with the EPA in there?"

He stuck his hands in his pockets and took a turn around the room. Then he said, "How was I to know he was gonna rummage through my files?"

I didn't say anything.

"Face it, Will. We both misjudged this guy."

He sat down and drummed the desk surface. After a while he asked me to run down the names on that list. I rolled them off, knowing he was considering the risks with each one, asking himself whether some kind of warning to the recipients was necessary. I told him I didn't think it was. The payments were in cash. It wasn't likely anyone would be stupid enough to deposit them in a bank account, given the federal regulations, which routinely examined all cash deposits above ten thousand dollars.

He said, "We're talking about politicians here."

"I know, but even they're not that stupid."

He shook his head and asked me if I thought Kurman could know anything else. I said I couldn't think of anything. He seemed to retreat into himself, and finally, he asked how things were going with me.

I said it was frustrating, scary, and weird as hell. He nodded slowly, then said, "Yeah . . . kind of puts this shit in perspective."

Then his secretary buzzed to say his three o'clock meeting had arrived. He got up and told me to "hang in" and we shook hands. I left, and for a moment I considered going to Caroline's office and talking to her. Then I thought better of it. It could wait until she got home.

It was nearly eight-thirty by the time she got back, and she wanted to know why I hadn't called her to let her know how things had gone with the lawyer—she said she'd left a couple of messages on the machine. I said I hadn't even checked the machine, and she recognized that things had not gone well.

She said, "Uh-oh."

I suggested she change first. This was going to take a while. She gave me a nervous glance, then went upstairs, and I poured myself a drink. When she came down, she said, "Is it true you went to the office today? Somebody said they saw you."

"I'll get to that."

She sat down, looked at me guardedly, and said, "So how did it go?"

"Did you know Gilmore had about two dozen photos of you?"

"What?"

Her reaction was one of utter bafflement. I was studying her closely, but she had no idea what I was talking about.

I said, "He wrote poems to you. Did you ever get any?"

Her jaw was slack.

"No . . ."

She stared at me, amazed.

"Well, he did. I guess he never sent 'em, but he wrote a few."

Her jaw was still wavering as she tried to form a question.

Then I said, "There's something else. Gilmore had a list of politicians I'd paid off. It was him who was talking to Kurman."

For a second, I thought she was going to drop her glass. She looked at me in stunned disbelief. "It was *him* . . . ?"

"Can you figure out why?"

I was trying to keep any note of hostility out of my voice.

"Pike Mountain was *his* project. . . . Why would he hurt his own project?"

"This was other stuff. He got the list from John's office."

She was reeling. She got up off the couch in a daze. Eventually, she said, "I think he took one photo of me, in Washington."

"From the way it looks, he took the others from his site office window."

Caroline blinked. I said, "All this stuff lends credence to the D.A.'s idea that I had a motive . . . or so Stella feels."

Caroline slumped down on the couch, and I sat looking at her for a minute. I said, "Look, I know this may be difficult, but we need to talk about what this affair . . . You said it was more intense for him."

"Yes . . ."

"Did you have any idea he might act like this?"

"Of course not."

She leaned back on the sofa and stared at the ceiling for a while. Then she said, "This is just too weird."

I said, "So?"

She cringed a little.

"This isn't any kinky exercise. . . . There are practical reasons."

"Like what?"

"Was he talking about leaving his wife?"

She hesitated. "Not really . . . It might have been implicit."

"But, he never talked about it?"

"No."

She looked at me for a long time. Then she averted her glance and said, "Have you read these poems?"

I nodded. "He was nuts about you, wasn't he?"

She squirmed, didn't say anything for a moment. Then she said, "It was the attention. Can you understand that?"

"Do you think Cynthia knew?"

"You asked me that before."

"I'm asking you again. He strikes me as the type who'd wear his heart on his sleeve . . . with the poems, and all."

"You keep bringing her up."

"Yeah, I told you why." After a while, I said, "I ran into her today."

"At the office?"

I nodded.

I told her what had happened. I said Cynthia was there to see Greg, and that I'd still like to know if she knew about the affair before Gilmore was killed.

Caroline knew what I meant. She said, "What about the guy going over the wall?"

"If it was a guy."

"You said she's got an alibi anyway."

I was silent for a while. Caroline shook her head and said she realized it was possible that Cynthia might have known, but she just didn't think it was likely.

"Because you two were careful?"

She shot me a look, and after that, the conversation grew more halting. I decided there would be other opportunities to talk about this, so I let it go at that, for that night anyway.

After we ate I went outside and sat in the yard. There were a few clouds in the night sky, and it looked as if nine months of life without rain was about to end. I sat under the umbrella and thought about everything that had occurred that day—then, from those wispy high clouds, a few drops of rain actually fell.

It stopped within minutes. And before I'd even noticed, the brick patio near our back door was dry again. I sat there, chewing over it all and thinking that in this town it couldn't even rain right.

12

There isn't much I can recall about my train of thought for the rest of that evening. I rambled about downstairs for a while. Caroline was upstairs, watching TV in the bedroom, and at one point I wanted to go up and talk to her some more, but I was hesitant to do so because I didn't want to be tempted to bring up the cigarette butts after Stella's solemn warning not to mention this.

I know at one point my thoughts veered back to Cynthia Gilmore, and I began to think about what I'd said earlier to Caroline, about Sam Gilmore being the kind of guy who might wear his heart on his sleeve. I guess some part of me believed that Cynthia might have suspected an affair. And if someone suspected an affair, they might well have taken the trouble to find out more. Then I thought about what Clem had said. We had all been fooled by Gilmore. But maybe not Cynthia. Maybe he'd been tipping his hand to her all along.

And so in the morning I drove north, along the Pacific Coast Highway, past the beachfront homes of Malibu, and out past Pepperdine. It was a pleasant drive—here, where the hills ran almost to the ocean, and the ugliness of modern California had been unable to encroach on natural beauty. Then I took the Ventura Freeway, which was an encroachment in itself, and as I drove, I thought about the evening Caroline and I had been to the Gilmores for dinner, and I wondered whether something had transpired that evening that had led to the affair.

I turned off the freeway in Montecito and checked the address. I remembered their place, it was up on a hillside—but I wasn't sure how to get there. I drove along a few lanes, where expensive homes were hidden by high hedges, but I didn't see the street, and after a while I pulled over and asked a couple of people if they knew it. They didn't. Then I saw a UPS truck up ahead, and I asked the driver for directions. He said it wasn't far—two lights, turn left, and up the hill. I got back in the car and drove on, and it was almost noon when I turned onto the Gilmores' street.

I drove by the house, continued on up the hill, and parked on the lane above it. From there I could look down at the house from beside a stand of pines.

An environmentally correct home, I'd have called it. Shade trees, no lawn—instead, a sort of extended rock garden with native grasses and plants. It was the kind of garden the *L.A. Times* magazine was always featuring to inspire water conservation. Then I walked down the lane a few yards, to get a better view, and I saw Cynthia Gilmore walk out of the house toward a hot tub.

Her hair was pulled back, and she began to do stretching exercises. As I looked on, I saw there was someone else moving about in the house. I couldn't make out who it was, or whether the person was male or female. He, or she, was behind a drape, and it could just as easily have been the maid. But the fact was, it was someone, and from the way Cynthia Gilmore was going about those exercises, as if following a program, I had the feeling she might be taking off a few pounds for someone.

My idea had been to come up here and follow her around awhile. But I saw now it wasn't going to be easy to park anywhere near her place without her seeing me. And I knew if I stayed here I was going to attract attention sooner or later. Even as I walked back to my car, a Westec security car drove by, and the driver gave me a second look. I guess I could have passed myself off as a prospective real estate buyer, but I could hardly maintain this posture by parking here half the day. Eventually, someone would wonder what the hell I was doing, and the last thing I needed right now was a run-in with cops—any cops. So I took a drive, but I couldn't find anywhere that was secluded enough so that I could spy on the Gilmore home, even with binoculars.

Around one o'clock, I drove back to her street and sat in the car for a few minutes with my head down, hoping she might go out for lunch. But she didn't emerge, and after twenty minutes, I opted for discretion and drove back to L.A., abandoning the idea for now. I decided that if I were to do this, evening might be a better time.

The drive back seemed longer, in the heat of the afternoon. As I approached Malibu, an accident on the Pacific Coast Highway slowed everything to a crawl. I turned off the coast road and took one of the canyon roads over to the Ventura Freeway again, and it was around four o'clock by the time I got home.

The house was quiet. Fran and Katia were at the playground. I checked the answering machine, but there were no messages. I was waiting for Katia to come back from the playground when the phone rang. I'd gotten into the habit of picking up the phone again, and hanging up if it was a reporter or some other asshole I didn't want to talk to. But I was always on the alert for these calls. So when I picked up, and a soft female voice I didn't recognize said, "Will," I damn near hung up.

I said, rather sharply, "Who is this?"

"It's Nadine . . ."

I was taken aback. I'd thought about her a couple of times, and I'd wondered what the hell she must have been making of what she read in the papers. I guess I should have expected her to call. Still, I was embarrassed at the prospect of having to talk about it, especially to her. My former girlfriend. Now a DEA agent.

I said, "Oh, hi . . ." I laughed and said, "Well . . . no need to catch up."

She didn't seem to know what to say. Then she said, "Do you mind me calling?"

"No . . ."

There was another silence, and after a while she said, "Will, I called because I wondered if you wanted to get together. I figured you might need someone to talk to."

It was just the way she said it. Straightforward. No bullshit. And something in me overcame the feelings of embarrassment. Nobody had wanted to "get together" with me lately. I wasn't even sure why Nadine would, and I had to remind myself that she wasn't the type to do this out of perverse curiosity.

I said, "Well, yeah . . . that would be nice." Then, suddenly, I realized I did want to see her. Badly. God knows, I needed to see a friend.

I blurted out, "Nadine, it's been a nightmare."

"I'm sure."

I said, "Yes . . . I would like to see you . . . when?"

"I'm home. Or tomorrow, around this time."

I said if she didn't mind, I'd drive over right then.

She said that was fine. Then I asked if she wanted me to come by her place, or if she would rather meet at a restaurant or a bar. She suggested a restaurant on Main in Venice, and before she hung up she apologized for not having called earlier.

Ten minutes later, I was driving west on Olympic.

Nadine came into the restaurant wearing a light blue dress, sandals, and silver earrings. Her hair looked much the same as when I'd last seen her downtown. I asked what she wanted to drink, and for a couple of minutes at least, we managed to avoid talking about anything having to do with cops, lawyers, or murder.

Then she asked me if I could talk about it, and I said things were complicated, but not so complicated that I couldn't tell her certain things. Then, once the waiter went away, she said, "Will, whatever you want to say . . . you don't have to worry."

I knew what she meant. I reached across the table and stroked her hand. And the contact set me thinking a little about our days together. I wasn't sure what she really thought of me now, and after our last conversation at the Hyatt bar downtown, I was tempted to ask if there were things she still wanted to say to me, about us splitting up, all those years ago. Then I decided that in my present circumstances it would be kind of imprudent to ask, so I didn't bring up anything. I began to tell her the story, starting with punching Gilmore.

I tried to skate over the reason for it. But Nadine said, "I guess I can assume why you hit him."

I didn't say anything. I just nodded. Then I continued with the story, editing out the parts I considered off-limits. When I'd finished, Nadine was silent for a long time. She gazed out the restaurant window at the traffic, then turned to me and said, "So why did he call you?"

"To talk about what had happened."

For the first time, I heard a cop's interrogational tone in her voice. My antennae went up. She was a DEA agent, after all.

I sat there thinking she was probably good at her job because she didn't come on strong—then she seemed to recognize that something was wrong, and she asked if there was a problem.

I said I wasn't supposed to talk to anyone.

"I know that."

I waited, but she didn't offer any assurance. She asked me what I thought might have happened at the house.

I told her.

Then she said, "So what do the cops have?"

Again, I hesitated. I said, "Nadine, I've been charged with murder."

She looked at me steadily, and after a moment she said, "That's why I wanted to see you."

I said, "What do you mean?"

She shook her head slightly, then said, "Will . . . I didn't want to get into this on the phone, but I kind of wondered why you didn't call me."

"You mean to ask for help?"

She nodded and played with a napkin for a moment. Then, in the calmest possible way, she said, "I know about lawyers' instructions to their clients, Will. But if you can't trust me, who can you trust?"

She studied me a moment. Then she said, "I'm going to say something. And I want you to think about it, rather than just react . . . okay?"

I said, "Okay."

"When are you going to start treating me like a big girl?"

She had called it. Right on the number. After a moment, I said, "I'm a patronizing son of a bitch, aren't I?"

She smiled. "Sometimes. I think you're still rooted way back in the past."

I knew why. For the longest time I'd seen her as a student, playing at making a living while I was operating in the real world. She was right. It all had to do with our past.

I said, "I'm sorry."

"That's all right. I just want you to recognize it."

There was a silence, and I sat there, feeling even more humbled, if that was possible.

She said, "Whatever you say goes no further, you know that. It's really up to you, Will."

I wanted to tell her everything, and finally, feeling some guilt that I was telling her, and not Caroline, I said, "There's a lot of other shit."

Then I told her the whole damn story. I told her about the photos, the letters, the bribes list. I even told her about the cigarettes. And when I'd finished, I felt I'd crossed a line by telling her, and there was no going back.

I felt nervous. I wondered if maybe I'd lost credibility by bringing up the cigarettes and implying that it might be the cops. I was about to ask her if she believed me when she said, "When do you think the cops might have done this?"

I said I didn't know. Then I said, "*After* they let me go from the station. By then they'd asked me if I'd smoked in the house, and I'd told them I hadn't."

She didn't respond right away, and I aimed a look at her. I said, "Don't tell me it never happens. . . ."

"I didn't say that."

"What, then?"

"Well, it's more common in situations when the cops know someone's dirty . . . as in drug cases."

I shrugged. "These guys seemed pretty convinced it was me."

Then I told her about the conversation with my lawyer, at which we'd discussed whether someone else could have planted the cigarettes, and I related Stella's theory about Caroline. I told her it was Clem who had suggested Gilmore straighten things out with me. Finally, I brought Cynthia Gilmore's name into it and told her about that. And when I'd run through all this, Nadine said, "Or none of the above."

I asked what she meant.

"Well, is there anyone who might have wanted to tie you up in knots for political reasons?"

I said I could think of several people. But would they go so far as to kill someone?

"A lot of people knew you slugged him."

"Yeah, but how would they know he and I were getting together?"

"Maybe someone did."

She was silent for a moment. Then she asked, "Does Caroline think you did it?"

The question surprised me.

"No . . ."

"Are you sure about that?"

"Yes . . . why are you asking this?"

I waited a moment, and she appeared to be on the verge of saying something else. Then she seemed to change her mind, and I said, "What's the question, Nadine?"

"Never mind."

"Come on . . . what?"

"I know you're going to take this the wrong way, but I'll say it anyway. I don't believe you did it, but I do believe you're capable of it."

My mouth fell open, and she went on, "I believe you could, under certain circumstances."

I stared at her, not knowing what to say. Finally, I said, "Gee. That's nice."

Without apology she said, "It's a professional judgment. They teach us that. The cops probably think you're capable of it, too."

I didn't say anything at first. Then I said, "The cops think I did it."

Nadine smiled briefly, then said, "That's why I asked if Caroline ever seemed to think you did it?"

"Never."

I was still staring at her, surprised by the tack the conversation had taken. Then I said, "What are you saying? That it's weird for Caroline not to have suspected me?"

"I don't know. I never met her."

She reached across the table and touched my hand. After what she'd just said, I wasn't sure how to react. Then she said, very tenderly, "Take it easy."

We were silent for a moment. Then I said, "I feel like I fucked up everything."

It just came out of me. I told her, "The worst of it is, I was going to quit the job. I tried to tell you that the last time we met."

"In a way you did." She smiled. "How's the screenplay?"

I said I hadn't even touched it.

She squeezed my hand and said, "It might never have worked with us . . . but I still have a soft spot for you."

"God, I can't imagine why."

She smiled again, and her nose wrinkled. "Up to a point." Then her expression grew serious. "So, is there any way you can think of that I can help?"

I knew of only one way. "Cynthia Gilmore," I said. "I'd like to know a little about her."

I told her what I'd been doing earlier that day. And she immediately advised me, in no uncertain terms, against doing anything like it again. "Will, get serious. The police and the D.A.'s office are."

I nodded. She said she'd see what she could do, and we walked out into the late-afternoon sunshine.

Ten minutes later, I was back on Olympic, crawling through the rush-hour traffic, pursued by the fog rolling in off the ocean, and I was glad I'd talked to her. I was getting sympathy at home, but somehow this was different—maybe because this was unconditional. And deep down inside me, I'll admit, no matter what I felt for Caroline, I realized I must have been an utter fool, years ago, to have turned my back and walked away from Nadine Jarmon.

13

The following morning, Greg Stannert called me. He sounded a little awkward at first. He said he had talked at length to Cynthia Gilmore and that she had told him she would not be coming by his office again after running into me. I said this sounded like theatrics. Greg said he felt he'd gone some way toward establishing one thing with her.

"What's that?"

"I got her to admit that it's easier for her to have someone to blame, rather than some nameless nobody."

"Even if it's not true?"

"It's progress, Will. At least she admitted it. I know Cynthia, she'll think about it."

I said I doubted we'd be sitting down for cozy dinners, and he said if he got another chance, he'd talk to her again.

I didn't know what to make of this. A part of me felt Cynthia Gilmore didn't believe it but that she couldn't resist the drama.

I spent most of the day thinking about the evidence against me and what a jury might make of it. At least I now felt I had an active role in this. Nadine was looking into Cynthia. Crawford was conducting his own investigation, and as Stella had said, we had only just begun trying to assemble our arguments and disassemble theirs. I considered once again taking up the discussion with Caroline about her affair with Gilmore, but when she got home that evening, I saw she was looking a little strained. Lately, I'd begun to recognize how it had been for her, and how it might get worse. If things turned out badly, she would have sole responsibility for Katia, and at that moment, rather than bring up the affair, I felt the need to reassure her.

I said, "Don't worry. This'll work out."

She looked at me as if I'd read her mind.

In the morning I went to Stella's office for another meeting. Crawford, it turned out, had checked out Cynthia Gilmore's story, and the night her husband was killed she was, indeed, at the Bel Air Hotel from seven-thirty on. The police had taken statements from both the maître d' and the waiter who had served her. Crawford ran through Cynthia's background. She was from Fresno. She had gone to Stanford on a scholarship. Her parents were middle-class—her father had been a loan officer at a bank until his retirement.

I said, "So where's she get off, with the airs and graces?"

"Probably learned 'em from Gilmore," Crawford said.

"Any boyfriends?" I asked.

Crawford shrugged. He'd run a check of her credit card billings, but he didn't see any unusual pattern.

Then I said, "I ran into her a few days ago."

Stella was making notes on a yellow pad at the time. She looked up and said, "What?"

I said, "I went over to see Clem. She showed up at the office."

Stella blinked. "So what happened?"

"I talked to her."

From Stella's expression, I knew I was about to hear it. I just didn't anticipate at what volume.

Crawford said, "Uh-oh," and he left the room.

I said meekly, "I ran into her in the parking lot, so we went up to Greg Stannert's office and talked. . . ."

"Are you out of your mind?"

Stella flew out of her seat. She stormed around the table and stood two feet from me. "What the fuck did you say to her?"

"I told her I didn't kill her husband."

"What else?"

"Well . . ."

I started into it. I said she had asked me why I went to see Gilmore that night.

"What did you tell her?"

"That he called me. I asked her if she didn't think it was weird someone killing him the night after I had a run-in with him . . . especially with me being there. . . ."

By this time Stella had slumped down in a chair, with her head slung back. I told her all of it, and when I started to say that I realized it was probably a mistake, she shouted, "Spare me!"

She got to her feet again. "What did I tell you when you first walked in here?"

I felt like a schoolkid being sent to the corner and told to wear a dunce's cap. I said, "All right, Stella, I hear you. I fucked up."

"No, you didn't hear me. And you *are* a fuck-up." She was livid. "You masquerade as someone halfway intelligent, but you're a screaming asshole!"

I said, "I was trying to get—"

That was as far as I got.

"I don't give a fuck what you were trying! You're trying to get yourself convicted." Her jaw trembled. "It's not enough that I employ an investigator. It's not enough that I'm sitting up half the night working on this case. You have to go talk to the guy's *wife*."

"I ran into her—"

"Did you walk away? Did you *not* talk to her?"

She was ladling out the sarcasm as Crawford came back in. She turned to him and said, "Correct me if I'm wrong. But wasn't it you who said, 'Will knows his way around the block'? Would you care to reconsider that opinion?"

Crawford avoided my glance, and without waiting for an answer, Stella said, "We're dealing with a jerk who wants to play amateur detective."

I sat in silence for a while. She was still glaring at me. I'd taken a few whippings in my time, but this one was princely. I knew the best policy was to sit and take it, let her vent until she ran out of gas, but Stella showed no signs of slacking up.

She paused to get her breath. Then she said, "I've almost got grounds for an insanity plea!"

I breathed hard. Finally, I said, "You might as well hear the rest of it." I saw Crawford cringe. Then I said, "I took a drive up to her place the other day."

Words failed Stella. She slumped into her chair.

Then I said, "I get the feeling Cynthia's keeping in shape for someone—"

Stella screamed at me. "Get her out of your head!" She leaped to her feet. "They're prosecuting *you*, not her! You dumb shit!"

Her cheeks were crimson. She leaned toward me and with unabated fury said, "Listen, Will, do you want me on this case or not, because right now I don't give a shit because I've got a fool for a client, and I don't care to represent fools because that way I lose. So you decide!"

I glanced at Crawford, but he merely shrugged and sipped his coffee. I said, "I'll stay away from her."

Stella was still glaring at me.

"You're damn right. . . . On second thought, that's not good enough. I want you out of here."

"What?"

"Go away for a week. Go up to the mountains, do whatever you have to do—but go and chill out."

I said I'd think about it. She said, "Uh-uh. I mean it, Will. This is part of the deal."

I could see she meant it, and I could also see the wisdom behind it. It was stupid what I'd done—I had to admit. Maybe beyond stupid.

Stella drove the point home. "You're fighting for your life, Will. This woman thinks you probably killed her husband. And you're talking to her?"

Again, I nodded. And that's when my active participation in my own defense came to an end.

That evening, I told Caroline what Stella had suggested. I didn't exactly tell her why. But Caroline had no objection to my going away. In fact, she supported it. And the next day, I packed a bag, took my car, and drove north on Interstate 5.

And with that day came a feeling akin to going into exile, and although this is hard to explain, on some level a part of me let go. I still had many nightmares over the next few months—many times I'd wake up in a tumultuous sweat, with the sheets tugged around my neck, as the terror of a conviction and prison life reared its ugly head. But in calmer moments, I began to accept that capable people were doing their best for me, and that it would probably benefit me to stay out of their way and let them get on with it.

Getting away helped. I took Stella's advice and rented a cabin up in Mammoth. After that first week I decided to rent the place for the season, and I began to go up there every other week or so, often taking Katia with me.

I had decided to spend as much time as possible with her, and once she got past not having the Disney videos to look at every night, she began to see it as a great adventure. We would take hikes together through the pine forests, and we'd spend our days looking at wildlife and plants, cooking by a campfire occasionally, and waking to a world far from the sounds of urban life. I even bought a book about the galaxy, and we spent evenings picking out stars and planets—now that we could actually see stars.

It was good for me. In a sense, getting away from the city equipped me for what I had to contend with while I was there: the inevitable snubs, the annoying phone calls, the isolation, the constant awareness that people were working determinedly to send me to prison. And it was while I was up in the mountains that I recognized that a part of me had already retreated within myself. I hadn't exactly lapsed into a Zen-like state—there were moments when my anger boiled to the surface. One such moment was when Katia's preschool principal suggested it might be better if Fran picked Katia up from school, because my presence was frightening to the other children. Being on the receiving end of that remark, I had to make a major effort at restraint. But a sense of acceptance would steal over me from time to time—or maybe it was resignation—even though I knew I wasn't about to give up. I knew that even if I was convicted I'd go on fighting. But when the weight wore me down to the point of exhaustion, I'd discover there was release, and that it lay within me, with what little I could control—rather than with all the forces I could not.

But none of this happened quickly. During those months of waiting I never thought of "time" as my friend. I was always aware that reductive forces were at work on me, chafing at me—some days worse than others, but the feeling was always there. Even my sleep patterns changed, and no amount of exercise could earn me more than a few hours of sleep at a time before I'd be jolted awake by some unconscious process. Sometimes I'd dread the nights. Other times it was the days that presented me with too many hours to fill. Most of the time, sheer embarrassment prevented me from seeking anybody's company outside my immediate family and my attorney, though there was some letup with this feeling as time wore on, and I'd find myself reacting gratefully to anybody who sought out an association with me.

One day, Greg Stannert called and asked how I was coping with it all. He didn't ask the question casually, and he seemed to have all day to spend on the phone with me. I wound up talking to him at length about how I felt. Eventually, he asked me if I'd like to take a drive out to Pike Mountain the next day. I said I would. I'd been housebound for a couple of days, and I was grateful for the offer. Greg was someone with whom I didn't need to go into all the painful details about what had occurred.

We drove out the next morning. There were a lot of long silences in the car, and I sensed Greg didn't want to steer the conversation in any way. Even when he talked about Pike Mountain, which had just gone into operation, I sensed he was muting his enthusiasm out of consideration for me. But as we drove up to the main gate that day, he couldn't entirely conceal the pride he felt, even as he acknowledged the number of depressing connotations this place now had for him.

While he took care of whatever business he was there to attend to, I walked to the edge of the pit. I stood looking down into that vast chasm, and I have to admit that at that moment, for the first and only time in all this, I saw the easy way out. I guess it says something about my state of mind and the extent to which an innocent man can be made to feel guilty by the overwhelming forces of opposition. The feeling passed. As I walked away from the pit I decided it was a spasm, and I was angry at myself for even entertaining it. But I guess the wildest, most irrational thoughts can be entertained when one's options are limited.

I rejoined Greg as he came out of a site office. He had one other person to see, and I sat in the car and read the paper until he was ready. Then we walked back to the edge of the pit and watched for a while as the cranes off-loaded baled debris from the tippers. The site had been in operation barely a month, and only on a small scale. But as Greg said, even when the operation was fully cranked up, you couldn't expect to notice any appreciable impact, so enormous was the capacity of that pit.

We left soon after that. On the way back we were silent for a long time, and eventually Greg admitted he was sort of running out of innocuous subjects to discuss. He quickly told me that if I didn't want to talk at all, he'd understand. He was really being considerate, and I apologized for being lousy company. I said I was grateful to him for simply asking me along for the ride.

After a while we edged into a conversation about Cynthia Gilmore's attitude. I let Greg do most of the talking, reminding myself of Stella's warning not to talk about the case. At one point I even had to tell Greg this. He nodded slowly and said he understood. Finally, I could not resist. I asked if he had spoken to Cynthia again since the last conversation he'd told me about. He said he had, but she had not brought up my name, and he'd decided to let things lie.

I let it go at that. I asked Greg if he was planning to stay on with Clem. He nodded slowly and said, "For now at least." Then he told me he had canceled his plans to go to Alaska, and when I asked why, he said he felt a sense of responsibility to deal with the site situation.

I figured he meant "with Gilmore gone." I told him I understood.

I had drinks one evening with Greg, and lunch with him and Clem a few months later, as the wait dragged on. And despite the reminders, there was always some small pleasure to be had in the break from a routine day. Pleasure, and some pain, too—pain at seeing other people with the freedom to get on with their lives. Greg was always easier to take than Clem. When I'd be confronted with Clem's ferocious energies, I was reminded of the stark contrast between the pace of his life and mine.

My routines were more or less the same, whether I was in the mountains or in Los Angeles. I'd spend hours with the paper. Meals were never rushed. Things that had never gotten done before, got done. Around the house, if something broke, a turn of a screwdriver, and it would operate again. I could always find time, ample time, for such minor chores.

At times, Caroline would look at me as if I were regressing, as if I were no longer the person she had known for five years. And yet, I believe, on some level she understood. She would fly up to Mammoth on Friday evenings to be with me, either bringing Katia or joining us, if Katia was already with me, and these reunions were always pleasant moments, seeing her step out of that turboprop at the local airfield, still in her city clothes, smiling as she walked toward the open Jeep.

We'd fix dinner. Caroline's city energies would gradually subside, and even with the trial hanging over us, we'd reach moments of just being. We'd make love, or get into serious games of gin rummy, tease each other about our efforts to adapt to rustic ways. Once Caroline even said she could see us living like this someday.

Still, I recognized an accommodation on her part. She was married to someone who had taken on invalid status, or something like it, and one weekend I told her she shouldn't hold back with any feelings of resentment she had. She nodded slowly, then admitted she had felt a few—especially when it had taken me a while to realize that she was going through this, too. She felt it was really important that I continue to share my feelings with her, rather than close myself off.

I tried to. I remember one night telling her how much it hurt when I envisioned the worst-case scenario and thought about Katia. I said at those moments I wanted to arm myself and rampage through the forces that were trying to deny her her father. Caroline began to cry, and when I said I was sorry for upsetting her, she said, "No . . . no . . . you have to tell me these things. I need you to share them with me."

More than anything, our priorities had reoriented themselves. We were closer. Our lovemaking had improved. There was one night when we talked about having another baby, if and when we got past this.

But there were other nights, too. Not-so-good nights. There was the night my parents called. I'd been keeping all this from them, but their local newspaper had finally discovered that the William K. Dunbar charged with murder in Los Angeles was in fact me. That was a real winner.

And then one Friday night, around ten, Caroline and I were dozing off when the phone rang. I picked it up, and it was Stella, and the news wasn't good. She said she had not had a chance to call me that day because she'd been in court, but in the meantime the judge had ruled on the admissibility of the photos and letters found at Gilmore's house. Stella had argued that there was no way I could have known of their existence, and that they were prejudicial and should not be admitted. But the judge had ruled against her. He had decided to admit them, which, as Stella said, was a blow, though not a fatal one.

While I was on the phone, Caroline had woken up and was paying attention. She already knew from my expression that this was not good news, and when I hung up and told her what had happened, she sank back into the pillows, wearing a despondent look.

I started to reach for the light, but she said, "No . . . wait a minute, Will. There's something I've been wanting to ask you for a long time."

I left the light on and looked at her, and she gazed at me. Then she said, "Is there something you haven't told me about this case?"

Later, when I asked her what had prompted the question, she said she had just intuited that I was holding something back. But in those brief seconds while I hesitated before answering, I tipped my hand. There was no point then in denying it.

I said, "There is . . . but I can't talk about it."

"What?"

Her expression was full of concern. Then she got out of bed, a little angry and adamant.

She said, "Will, I'm your wife . . . for God's sake."

After a few moments of hesitation, I told her. I said, "Someone's tried to frame me."

She stared at me, stunned. And I explained to her about the cigarettes, and why I hadn't told her about this before: because my attorney had asked me not to, and because of the inference about who could have gotten the cigarette butts, if it wasn't the cops. I told her I knew this was bound to upset her.

She sat looking at me for a long time as it all sank in. Then she lay facedown on the pillow and began to cry. And when she looked up at me, she looked pitiable rather than angry, and other than holding her, there wasn't much I could say or do at that point to make her feel any better.

14

My trial began on a gray January day, after two days of a downpour such as the city had not witnessed in years. A portent, I told Crawford—the gods venting their wrath at the forces of law and order for subjecting me to this injustice and humiliation. I was trying to keep a sense of humor, but I wasn't sure if Crawford noticed. He started to talk about mud slides—his home was in one of the canyons. Then he asked me to let the gods know they'd made their point.

For the week prior to trial, I'd spent a part of every day with him and Stella, and I'd received all sorts of instructions about how I should sit, what I should wear, who I should look at. Stella had met with Caroline, too, and counseled her in the same manner, about how to dress, and what manner to adopt in order to demonstrate support for me. I guess we were both well prepared. But the truth is, there is nothing that can fully prepare one for hearing one's name called as a defendant in a homicide case.

It is not simply that the dreaded moment has finally arrived, after all the waiting. It is the incongruity of the entire situation, seeing oneself as the central figure, the focal point in a drama in which one did not ask for a role. As I sat down at the defense table that day and heard the clerk reviewing my case number and mentioning my name, I found myself recalling my role in a school play and being filled with dread beforehand that my moment would come and I would not be able to recall a single line. I imagined the panic I would feel, the humiliation in front of all those faces in the audience staring at me. That is the only analogy I can make.

That day, I had a great many conflicting thoughts and feelings as the jury selection process began. Intense, burning hatred for the prosecutor, Hennessee, thin, fortyish, mean, sitting at the table in front of me. Feelings of hope as I caught the judge's eye. Gilbert Sobel was his name. He was a tall, angular figure with an intelligent, thoughtful face, and I imagined at that moment that he would allow no damage to be done to me while I was in his charge.

Then, a few moments later, when Stella was in sidebar with him, I saw him look at me again, and I don't know if it was the effect of the light or not, or merely the way he was peering between the heads, but his glance seemed piercing this time and cold as a hawk's. He seemed to be saying, "I am the judge, and in theory at least, you are commended to my charge, but I know you did it, son, and I don't plan to make it easy for you to get away with it."

Then the moment passed, and I was again looking at an eminent jurist, whom Stella had described as fair. And from then on, I did my best to look upon him without my usual cynicism for all people who held public office.

Then there were the jurors. My peers. People with whom I had not one thing in common. A train driver—a man who spent eight hours a day at the controls of the Blue Line—how would he feel toward a man who spent a good part of his workday at lunch or closeted with politicians? A hospital orderly, a bank clerk, a housewife who looked at me as if my presence, thirty feet away, could cause her to hyperventilate—she was excused, thank God. Even the young computer programmer, who was seated, seemed with his sly smile to suggest that nefarious deeds were not merely the purview of the blue-collar class, and that he'd been around long enough to know a thing or two about the minds of desperate men, such as me, perhaps.

Stella disagreed. She thought she recognized a skeptic, a man with a distaste for government. The selection process wore on, and once in a while Stella would kick my ankle whenever I seemed to be slumping in my seat. It was important, she said, to remember that during the voir dire the jurors formed their first impressions, and these might form the bases of later judgments—arguments and evidence notwithstanding. I sat up, and after a while I glanced around at the press row. The men and women who had been writing about me the past few months were sitting with their notepads on their laps, competing with each other for their mean details, like starlings fighting over so many scraps. I looked to my left, to Caroline, and she smiled bravely whenever I looked at her. It became a routine after a while—my searching look—the look of a man seeking solace in his darkest hour—seeking her smile, like a mating response.

At times, my mind would drift. I'd fasten on a detail—the walnut moldings on the jury box; the lower, rear part of Hennessee's suit, crushed, shiny, and worn; the metal frames of the court recorder's spectacles, which would catch my eye from time to time as they caught the light. Sometimes I'd zone out, and I'd get another swift kick from Stella. The jury selection ran two days, and to each batch of jurors Judge Sobel's instructions were the same: I was presumed to be innocent. It was the state's responsibility to prove that I was guilty, beyond a reasonable doubt. The jurors were to make their decision based solely on the evidence heard in this case, not on anything they might have read in the papers. On it went, the same routine, five times within the course of two days, with various jurors excused, for reasons sometimes all too obvious to me and at other times not obvious at all. Stella shared her reasons with me, and I began to understand something that had not dawned on me before: All prospective jurors lie, some more than others, but they all lie. They lie to the prosecutor, or to the defense, or to the judge, or for the hell of it, or because they're nervous, or to themselves. They lie by concealing prejudices and doubts, but either way, they lie. And these were the people who would sit in judgment over me.

Around two o'clock on the third afternoon, a jury was impaneled and Hennessee got up to make his opening statement. From the start, I realized he was a more than adequate orator. He glossed over the weakest part of his case—that the state could not actually produce an eyewitness to Sam Gilmore's murder—then he got to the meat of the issue. I was a man engorged with jealousy and rage: rage because of what Sam Gilmore was planning to do to me professionally; rage and jealousy because I had found out that Sam Gilmore was my wife's lover. Stella rose to object, and it was clear for the moment at least that I had a friend in the judge. Sobel was not about to let Hennessee go wandering all over the map.

In the sternest possible way, he told Hennessee to confine himself to what the evidence would be and to the witnesses who would be called. "You are not going to be allowed to draw inferences from evidence you intend to present, Mr. Hennessee, and I'm surprised I have to remind you of that."

Hennessee bowed his head slightly and moved across to his table for a moment before returning to the jury box rail. In the wake of the rebuke he appeared to have lost his rhythm, and his delivery became halting. Stella nudged me and offered the briefest of smiles. Then Hennessee seemed to hit his stride again. He reviewed the items of physical evidence that would be presented, and I could see he missed none of the basic points about the significance of each one. Then he brought up my state of mind. Several witnesses would be called, he said, who would testify to having seen me assault Sam Gilmore the night before the murder, at a political event no less, in front of many civic leaders. Other witnesses would testify that they had seen me exit ahead of my wife, who had attended to Mr. Gilmore before angrily following me.

"Mr. Gilmore was not a saint," Hennessee hastened to add. "And you may find some of the things he did to Mr. Dunbar reprehensible."

"Be careful, Mr. Hennessee," Judge Sobel warned.

Hennessee turned and indicated to the judge that he was aware he should not digress again. Then he turned back to the jury and said, "But he did not deserve to be murdered. No matter what his offenses toward Mr. Dunbar, he did not deserve that."

He then did what Stella had warned me he would do. He tried to undercut the argument of the defense in advance. Next to me I felt Stella stir. As Hennessee began to hit his stride again, she rose.

"Your Honor, I'd prefer to make my own opening statement, rather than have Mr. Hennessee predict what I might say."

There was some laughter in the courtroom. The judge issued a mild rebuke, advising Hennessee that he should avoid setting forth the more obvious arguments for the defense. Hennessee nodded and turned back to the jury. But he did not lose his rhythm this time.

"We will present evidence to show that Mr. Dunbar's account of what took place lacks all credibility." He looked from one juror to another. "Police officers who interrogated Mr. Dunbar will demonstrate to you that Mr. Dunbar's account of what took place that evening is totally at odds with the physical evidence at the crime scene."

He paused. "Why . . . members of the jury? Why are his statements totally at odds? Why does his account of what occurred conflict with the irrefutable physical evidence of a carefully preserved crime scene?"

He paused again.

"We ask you to look at this evidence, members of the jury, and ask yourselves this question: Did that man—William Kenneth Dunbar—go to Mr. Gilmore's house seeking satisfaction and revenge? Did he, in fact, commit this crime, then lie to the police to cover it up?"

He strode solemnly in front of the jury, looked over to me, then turned back to the jury.

"Look at the evidence we put before you, ladies and gentlemen. Look at that evidence, listen to the witnesses, look at the evidence again, and then ask yourselves that."

Then he walked back to his table.

I took a breath, and without even glancing around, I knew that every eye in the courtroom was directed at me.

Next to me, Stella stirred. I looked toward the jurors. Some were openly scrutinizing me, as if searching for criminal deviousness that might not have been apparent at first glance. I shook my head slightly and looked at Stella, and from her expression I sensed that at this moment I had adopted just the right attitude of sincere disbelief. Then the courtroom rustle died down, and the judge asked Stella if she was ready to make her opening statement. She said she was ready. She did not want the weight of Hennessee's words to sit.

She got up and walked to the jurors and didn't say a word until she was directly in front of them.

"Members of the jury," she said, "you don't know my client. And yet you have already heard some very damning things said about him by the prosecutor in this case, and you will be hearing more harsh things said about him by the police." She paused. "But you are the jury. You are the people who will decide whether he is guilty beyond a reasonable doubt or not guilty. So let me tell you a little about him, and I ask you to bear these facts in mind.

"He is a husband and a father. He is a man employed as a lobbyist by a major corporation in this city, and he has held his present job for the past eight years. He has never been charged with a crime before. That's right . . . you didn't know that until now, did you? All you knew about William Dunbar is what Mr. Hennessee said."

She looked at the jury and shrugged. Then she glanced over at Hennessee. "I don't know if Mr. Hennessee really believes what he said, but he contends that Mr. Dunbar murdered a man he was known to dislike. Why does he contend this? Consider this carefully, members of the jury. This is very important. There are no other suspects in this case, at least none the police can find."

She looked at me. "Except one." She turned back to the jury. "That's right . . . that's why he's here. Because he happened to be in the wrong place at the wrong time."

She shook her head in disgust and appeared almost distracted for a moment. Then she turned abruptly to the jurors.

"We will produce many witnesses who will attest to who Will Dunbar is. And when you've heard from these witnesses, I will ask you to ask yourselves some questions. I will ask you to put yourself in his shoes the evening he went to Mr. Gilmore's house, at Mr. Gilmore's request."

She paused and smiled at me. Then she turned back to the jury. "Members of the jury, you've heard Mr. Hennessee admit this is a circumstantial case, and it is. That's what Mr. Dunbar is caught in—a web of circumstances. And why is he caught in this web?

Not because he is a vengeful, jealous man, as Mr. Hennessee alleges, but because he is a decent man, a man with some courage."

She walked the length of the jury box. Then she said, "Let me ask you this. What would you have done if you were in Mr. Dunbar's shoes that night? Let me go one step further. What would you have done if, as Mr. Hennessee alleges, you had killed Mr. Gilmore? If you had, wouldn't you have left the house, gone home, showered, changed, disposed of the gun, and said nothing to anyone? Why not? There were no witnesses . . . isn't that what you'd have done—*if* you were guilty of this crime?"

The courtroom was pin-drop quiet. Stella continued, "But suppose you weren't guilty. Suppose you had come across the body of a man you were known to dislike—found him on the floor of his home, dead—what would you have done then? Wouldn't you hope you'd have had the courage to call the police, even knowing how this might look?"

She leaned closer to the jurors. "Because that's what William Dunbar did, members of the jury. He acted on his decent impulses in a moment of intense stress. . . . And for that courage and decency he is now paying the price."

Her glance swept the row of jurors. Then she looked over at me and returned to her seat without another word.

The courtroom began to stir. There was even a faint smattering of applause from one spectator row.

I looked at Caroline, and she smiled, and I smiled, too. And before I was really aware of it, Judge Sobel had called an early recess, and Crawford was escorting Caroline and me out by a side entrance and into a Town Car with tinted windows so we could elude the press. And as we were driven home that day, and drove straight into our garage, avoiding a reporter and photographer who were lurking at the end of our driveway, I could only think that things had gone wildly better than I'd expected.

Caroline was very encouraging throughout dinner, and only later, when Stella phoned me, after I had gushed my congratulations at the impact she'd made with her opening statement, did I settle down and begin to bear in mind again the things she had already told me.

I knew what the problem was. As Hennessee had said—and it had turned out to be the main thrust of his argument—my statements to the police lacked all credibility. Or as Stella had put it, "There isn't a lot of evidence against you, but what there is weighs heavy, and equally important, there's an absence of evidence that might help you."

I knew what she meant. If Sam Gilmore had been killed by an unknown intruder, where was the evidence of his visit? As far as we knew, there was none. He had left behind no fingerprints. There was nothing to suggest that an intruder had ever been in the house—any part of the house. Nothing of value had been taken. Nothing had been disturbed. There were no signs of a struggle. There were no threads of clothing other than a few threads of mine.

Nobody had come forward to say that they'd seen me waving frantically on Nichols Canyon Road, even though Crawford had canvassed every home on that street and up beyond, on Mulholland. And so the prosecution's argument was simple. If an intruder had not killed Sam Gilmore, then who had? Who else had a motive, besides me? Nobody, apparently—except possibly Cynthia Gilmore, and she had an alibi. And since I had lied to the police, as Hennessee would maintain, didn't this lend further weight to the argument that I was the killer?

It was, as Stella said, a case that would probably hinge on what the jury decided constituted "reasonable doubt." In other words, the jury might well believe that I did it, based on a lack of credible alternatives, but would they be prepared to convict on that basis? That, Stella said, was what made the outcome of cases like this, the most difficult to predict.

One thing was certain, she had said. The detectives would be going out of their way to convince the jury that they believed I'd done it. And never was this more apparent than the following morning, when Detective Lowndes took the stand.

From the very moment he was sworn in, he directed a look of scorn my way, for all the jurors to see, and five minutes into his direct examination, I'd received half a dozen such looks.

Hennessee took his time with Lowndes, reviewing the crime scene and the wounds to the body. Then he asked whose fingerprints had been found at the house. Lowndes said, "Mrs. Gilmore's, the housekeeper's, the deceased's, and *his*."

He jutted his chin derisively toward me, and Stella warned me to offer nothing by way of retaliation. I just had to sit there and take it.

Hennessee said, "You mean the defendant's?"

"Yes."

Lowndes looked at me as though he'd just squashed a snail.

"Isn't that a little unusual?" Hennessee asked.

Lowndes said that the housekeeper had cleaned that same morning. Stella objected, but Hennessee turned to the judge, insisting that the witness was testifying based on firsthand knowledge. Sobel overruled. Then Hennessee asked him where they had found my prints.

Lowndes consulted his notes. "On the open French window, the kitchen door, the rear screen door, the dining room light switch, the front doorbell, the phone, and the stereo."

"On the stereo?"

Hennessee raised an eyebrow. "Did Mr. Dunbar offer any reason why he touched the stereo?"

"Yes . . ." Lowndes answered with a sour smile. "He said he turned the music down."

"Down or up?"

"Down, he said. . . ."

There was a slight stir in the courtroom. The implication was clear. I'd turned the music up, according to Lowndes, to cover the sound of a gunshot.

Hennessee drifted back to his table, and I glanced at Caroline.

She was seated with Clem and Greg Stannert this morning, and they all offered quick, encouraging smiles.

Then Hennessee returned to the witness stand and plugged away.

"Detective, did Mr. Dunbar describe to you what occurred at the Gilmore residence?"

"Yes." Lowndes leaned back and looked directly at the jury. "He says he rang the front bell, got no answer, so he walked around the house and went in by the open French window—"

Hennessee stopped him there.

"Excuse me, Detective Lowndes . . . the window on which you found the defendant's fingerprints?"

"That's correct."

"Go on, Detective."

Lowndes consulted his notes.

"He said he called out to Gilmore. Then, he says, he heard the rear screen door open and went to see who it was. He says he tripped over the body. Then, he says, he ran out back and chased a guy going over the back wall."

Hennessee looked at me and shook his head slightly. "So, are we to believe that this intruder remained in the house *after* Mr. Dunbar rang the front doorbell? . . . Is that what we're to assume?"

"Objection, Your Honor. Calls for conclusion."

"Sustained."

Hennessee seemed unperturbed. He looked my way again; then he asked Lowndes, "Did Mr. Dunbar say how far he was behind this armed intruder when he gave chase?"

"Yes, sir. He said about half a minute."

"Half a minute? Thirty seconds?"

"That's what he said."

Hennessee let this sit with the jury a long time. Then he went back to his table.

Out of the corner of my eye I saw Stella glance at me. I guess she wanted to make sure I wasn't slumping in my chair. I wasn't, but I was starting to feel the weight of this testimony.

Hennessee returned to Lowndes, holding a plastic folder.

"Detective, I show you State Exhibit Three A, and ask if you recognize the contents of this plastic folder."

"Yes, sir."

Lowndes took the thing and studied it.

"These are fibers from the defendant's suit, the one he was wearing that evening."

"And where did you find these fibers?"

"On the rear wall of the property, in the dining room, and on the kitchen counter."

"What else was on the kitchen counter?"

"A towel with powder burns on it."

"Do you know what this towel was used for, Detective?"

"Yes."

"Would you tell us?"

"From the powder burns, I'd say it was used to muffle a gunshot, or to keep powder burns off someone's clothing—"

Stella rose to her feet, objecting furiously, and Sobel immediately sustained it.

"Jury will disregard what the witness last said."

Hennessee didn't seem to care. He had made his point. I saw him smiling slightly as he walked back to his seat.

He talked to another assistant D.A. for a minute; then he glanced across at me, picked up a small plastic evidence bag, and approached Lowndes, and I knew immediately what was coming. Hennessee was taking his time—to underscore that he was about to present a damning piece of evidence. He looked at me a second time, and Stella whispered, "Come on, big boy. Take your best shot."

"Detective Lowndes," Hennessee began, "I show you State Exhibit Five—two cigarette butts—and I ask if you've ever seen these before."

"Yes, sir, I have."

"Can you tell this court where these cigarette butts were found?"

"In the ashtray in the dining room of the Gilmore residence, on the night of Sam Gilmore's murder."

Hennessee paced a moment in front of Lowndes. Then he said, "Did you find these cigarette butts yourself, Detective Lowndes?"

"No, sir."

"Do you know who found them?"

"Yes, sir. They were found by a member of the forensic team—Cyrus Eastlake."

Lowndes glanced at me again. Then Hennessee approached Lowndes. "Detective . . . do you know who smoked these cigarettes?"

"Yes, sir . . . the defendant."

Hennessee took his time to make sure the jury was all ears. Then he asked, "How do you know that?"

"We ran tests on the saliva residue left on the filter. Since we had reason to consider Mr. Dunbar a suspect, we compared the results to the saliva residue on cigarette butts the defendant smoked at the Hollywood Division station while we were interrogating him. The two matched."

"I see. . . ."

Hennessee went back to his table and produced another plastic bag containing the cigarette butts I'd left at the station. He showed them to Lowndes, and Lowndes identified them for what they were. Then Hennessee told the judge he'd like the two state exhibits entered into evidence.

The judge so ordered. Hennessee returned to Lowndes.

"Now, Detective . . ." Hennessee took stock of the jury to make sure he had their undivided attention. "You just told us that Mr. Dunbar said he entered the house, turned down the stereo, called out Mr. Gilmore's name, and then stumbled across the body, isn't that correct?"

"That's correct."

"And according to the statement he gave to you, he then heard a rear screen door close, and after exiting via that screen door he chased an intruder, is that correct?"

"That's what he said."

"He also admits he called the police from the house, and that he walked out front to wait for the radio cars to arrive, is that correct?"

"That's correct."

Hennessee stepped closer to Lowndes, and again he looked at me. His brow furrowed slightly, and he said, "Did he, at any time, tell you that he had smoked in the house?"

"No, sir. He did not."

"He never told you he sat down and had a cigarette?"

"No, sir."

"During his interrogation did you ask him whether he had smoked in the house . . . at any time?"

"Yes. sir. I did."

"And what did he say?"

"He said he never smoked in the house . . . only outside, on the patio."

I saw the jurors exchanging looks. They understood the significance of this. Then Hennesseee said, "You personally saw him smoking on the patio?"

"Yes, sir. I asked him to wait there while I talked to the coroner, before we took him down to the station."

"But you did not allow him to smoke in the house?"

"No, sir."

"Did you allow him in the house at any time?"

"No, sir."

"Did any other officer . . . as far as you know?"

"No, sir."

"And yet these cigarette butts were found in the house?"

Stella was on her feet. "Asked and answered, Your Honor."

"Sustained."

Hennessee looked at me, shrugged, then turned back to Lowndes. "Detective, do you know how these cigarette butts came to be in the ashtray in the dining room, since Mr. Dunbar maintained he did not smoke in the house?"

"No, sir . . . I do not."

I could see the jurors glancing at each other. Then Hennessee looked along the entire row.

"No further questions."

There was a rustling in the courtroom for at least half a minute.

Judge Sobel seemed to be making some private note to himself. Then, finally, Hennessee looked over at Stella. "Your cross."

Hennessee sat down. There was another long rustle throughout the courtroom. I glanced at Clem, but he was looking at the jury. Caroline was chewing her lip. This would be the tough one, Stella had warned me, and I had to try to stay calm throughout it. But I could feel myself sweating. Next to me, Stella rose. She did not approach.

"Detective, did Mr. Dunbar tell you about all the items he touched in the house—the ones you mentioned?"

"Yes."

She walked around her table and made a little, matter-of-fact gesture with her hand. "He was quite candid about that, including about touching the stereo?"

"He told us—"

Stella smiled.

"He also told you he went through the kitchen, didn't he?"

"That's correct."

Lowndes stiffened a bit.

Stella smiled again. "Did he try to conceal *anything* from you . . . about where he'd been in the house?"

"I'm not sure I understand. . . ."

"Listen to the question carefully, Detective, and I'll repeat it. Did Mr. Dunbar attempt to conceal from you, at any time, where he went in the house or what he touched?"

There was a pause. "No."

"Thank you, Detective."

She walked halfway to Lowndes, so that she was directly in front of the jurors. Then she said, "Detective Lowndes, how long have you been a detective?"

"Eighteen years."

"Did you ever work burglary?"

"Yes."

"Did you ever hear of burglars wearing gloves?"

"Objection, Your Honor. Irrelevant."

Stella didn't even look at Hennessee. She swung to face the

judge. "It's certainly relevant, Your Honor. It goes to the heart of this case."

Judge Sobel thought for a moment; then he said, "I'll allow the question."

Stella turned back to Lowndes.

"It's not uncommon, is it, Detective, for burglars to wear gloves?"

"No . . ."

"And if burglars wear gloves, they generally don't leave fingerprints, do they?"

"Generally, no."

"Do burglars sometimes carry guns?"

Hennessee was out of his seat.

"I object, Your Honor, she's badgering."

Sobel sighed. "I think the jury understands your point, Counselor Nichols, please move on."

Stella studied the jury a moment, as if undecided whether to pursue this. Then she took a step toward Lowndes and said, "Detective, did you ever tell Mr. Dunbar not to smoke at the crime scene?"

I could see the question had caught Lowndes off guard. And in the brief silence, I saw him consider whether he should construct a quick lie.

"No," he said shortly.

"Did any other officer tell him not to smoke . . . as far as you recall?"

"No . . . not as far as I know. . . ."

Stella looked at the jury and nodded slowly. Then she aimed a look at Lowndes.

"Eighteen years on the force, and you forgot to tell Mr. Dunbar not to smoke at a crime scene. . . . Were you as conscientious about the other areas of your work, Detective?"

Hennessee objected, and Stella withdrew the question. She had nothing further, though she let the judge know she might want to recall Lowndes.

I was impressed by what she'd done, but it lost some of its impact during Hennessee's redirect. Hennessee got Lowndes to emphasize again that there was no evidence of a burglary. Nothing was missing from the house. Nothing had been disturbed. And when he'd finished, Stella had no further questions.

Lowndes was excused. The rest of the day was devoted to technical witnesses, who explained to the jurors the conclusiveness of fingerprint and saliva tests. And around four-thirty that afternoon, rather than put another witness on the stand, Judge Sobel ordered an adjournment.

The jury filed out, and I got to my feet and looked for a moment at Clem, Caroline, and Greg in the spectator rows. They were still maintaining their expressions of encouragement, but from those tight smiles I could see they were thinking that it had not been the best of days for the defense. I went over to them, and we talked in a group for a few moments, until Stella wanted to talk to me alone.

As I stood talking with her, I saw Nadine in the last spectator row.

We had spoken a couple of times the past week, and she had asked me how I might feel if she showed up in the courtroom. I'd said it wouldn't bother me, but right then it did, even though she was in my corner and offering to help in any way she could. It bothered me that I was reduced to the same state of indignity as many of the people she'd put away for dealing drugs the past five years, but what also bothered me was that her gaze was not directed at me but was focused intently on Caroline.

15

That evening, Caroline took the car home alone, and I went with Stella and Crawford back to Stella's office to review the testimony and to prepare for the next few days. Crawford was maintaining his usual optimism. I'd come to realize by this time that he took it upon himself to keep the client in good spirits, but as we took our seats in the conference room that evening, I sensed that Stella was a little down.

I asked for her candid assessment of the day, and she said she felt that Lowndes's obvious scorn of me might even have weighed in my favor—there were a couple of jurors she felt had a healthy mistrust of the police. But she admitted the testimony about the cigarettes had been damaging. She had to hand it to Hennessee. He had made the most of that.

I got a little down, too, then. I was holding the next day's witness list at the time, and as I glanced at the various names, a feeling of resignation swept over me. Stella seemed to sense this, and she warned me there would be moments like this, when I would feel all was lost. She told me to bear in mind that there were holes in the prosecutor's case, and that she would pounce all over these during her summation. I nodded, and I guess she wanted to occupy me, rather than have me sink any further, so she indicated the witness list and asked, "Who's up tomorrow?"

I gave her the names of the technical witnesses, including Cyrus Eastlake, the forensic man who had found the cigarettes. There were a host of witnesses to my punching Gilmore. She asked their names, and I read them off. Then I got to Tremaine and Bernard Kurman. Stella explained what Hennessee's strategy was: Fire one big gun—Lowndes; back up his testimony with the technical stuff; then emphasize motive with the eyewitnesses to the assault; then go to Tremaine, who would no doubt introduce the photos and letters. And finally, bring out Kurman.

She took the list herself and studied it. Then she asked Crawford, "What happened to Jess Mansell?"

It wasn't a name I'd heard before. I asked, "Who's he?"

"An invoice handler at the Pike Mountain site," Crawford said, "Apparently, Gilmore spoke to him just before he came into town that day."

Stella said, "So why's he not on here?"

Crawford shrugged and said, "They changed their minds, I guess."

Stella told him to find out why, and he said he'd look into it. Then she asked me, "What can I expect from Kurman?"

I said I didn't think Kurman would be too kind—he wasn't too fond of lobbyists.

Stella nodded slowly and said, "Well, I guess we'll see."

Then she told me to go home, get some sleep. She said she didn't want me looking tired in court. If I looked tired, I'd look defeated. That was the last thing she wanted.

I said good night and took a cab home. When I walked in that night, Caroline had a meal waiting for me. She sat opposite me while I ate and asked how I thought things had gone. I told her that Stella felt there were at least a couple of jurors who didn't like Lowndes. Caroline said she felt the same way, and I asked how it was for her, having to sit there all day with people staring at her. She said there was a part of her that could close herself off from all that.

We didn't get as depressed as we might have been. I think we were both trying to hold each other up. We sat up and talked for a long time, even though I'd been told to get an early night. And when we finally went to bed, I lay awake a long time, unable to turn my mind off. It didn't really matter. Since the trial had started, adrenaline had been flowing through me at a furious clip, and I knew I'd be fine on less sleep.

The following day, the rest of the technical witnesses appeared one after the other. Each gave an account of their area of expertise, and they talked about the evidence and how it had been handled, to underscore the care of handling and to undermine, in advance, any effort on Stella's part to discredit them.

Around three o'clock, Cyrus Eastlake, the forensic man, took the stand. He was a balding guy of thirty-five or so, unimposing. He stated his credentials and described how he had handled the cigarette butts. He had come across them in the dining room, picked them up with tweezers, and placed them in an evidence bag that was then sealed. Still, Hennessee kept him on the stand for a long time, capitalizing on the opportunity to remind the jurors once again of one of his strongest points of evidence: I had obviously lied to the cops. Clearly, I had smoked in the house. If I had smoked in the house, there was every chance I was talking to Gilmore at the time. Ergo . . .

Stella had no questions for Eastlake at this time. But again she told the judge she might wish to recall him.

That was day two.

Day three opened with the witnesses to my assault on Gilmore. That morning, before the jurors were brought in, there was a long sidebar at which Judge Sobel argued with Hennessee about how many witnesses to the assault he would be allowed to call. Once again, Sobel proved to be an ally. The judge wasn't about to waste the court's time hearing from a dozen witnesses who would all say the same thing.

Hennessee argued that his witnesses had all viewed the assault from a different point of view, but Sobel wasn't buying it. He dryly pointed out that I hadn't been charged with assault but with murder. "If these were witnesses to a homicide, Mr. Hennessee, I'm sure I would have a different opinion. However, they are not."

I guess he knew what Hennessee was up to. The man's idea was to drive home the motive through sheer weight of numbers. Finally, Sobel told Hennessee he could call three witnesses. That would be it.

In they came. First, a television actress whom Clem had invited to the party to impress the Riverside County people. The woman was clearly using the opportunity to gain publicity for herself, and in a freewheeling sort of way she described her surprise at seeing me suddenly punch Gilmore—"really hard," she said, "in the stomach." Then she offered some details about how Caroline had reacted, offering comfort, before Caroline finally left the terrace and followed me.

The next witness was a local assemblyman. He confined himself bluntly to what he had seen, but in a way his testimony carried more weight, because he appeared to be testifying reluctantly. The third witness was a waiter for the catering service. Like the actress, he seemed to relish his moment in the spotlight—and I suggested to Stella that she might want to ask whether he was, in fact, a part-time actor. Stella whispered, "Forget it." She wasn't about to ask a question she didn't know the answer to, and in her view, the sooner these people were off the stand, the better. They were gone by noon, leaving behind an impression of me as a man unable to refrain from violence.

Tremaine followed, and as a result, Hennessee scored double. He could as easily have had Lowndes testify earlier about the photos and letters, but there was more impact to be gained by introducing these *after* my attack on Gilmore was firmly planted in the jurors' minds. So after lunch that afternoon, Tremaine took the stand, and he reemphasized some of what Lowndes had already said, before Stella objected. Hennessee then put a large envelope in his hands and asked him to identify its contents.

Tremaine took out the photos and letters. He looked at the jurors and said, "These are photographs of the defendant's wife, Caroline Dunbar, and letters . . . poems, written to her by the deceased."

There was a stirring among the jurors and throughout the courtroom as a whole. I glanced at Caroline. She knew what was coming, and her expression tightened a little. Then Hennessee asked, "Can you tell us where these photos and letters were found, Detective?"

"In the deceased's desk, at his home, on Courtney Avenue."

"Judge, I'd like the witness to read one of these letters . . . er, poems."

Stella objected that the jurors could read them for themselves. But she didn't win that argument. And in a somber, earnest voice that lent some dignity to the content, Tremaine read one of the poems, which was entitled "Captured Moment" and made reference to Caroline in a tantalizing state of undress. I didn't know where to look during the reading. I knew I did not want to look at Caroline.

Hennessee then asked the judge if he could show the photos and letters to the jurors, and he was told he could pass them around. He walked over to the jurors, handed them the exhibits, then glanced back at the judge and said, "Thank you, Your Honor. Nothing further of this witness."

Sobel asked Stella to wait until the jurors had had an opportunity to examine the exhibits, and I sensed she could barely hold herself in check as the photos and letters made their way along the rows of jurors. Then, as the last of the jurors put the photos and letters down, she rose.

"Detective Tremaine!"

Her voice was loud. It got the jurors' attention. She marched toward him.

"Were these letters and photos found in a *locked* drawer?"

Tremaine said, "I believe so."

"Any reason my client should have known of their existence?"

Hennessee objected, and his objection was sustained. But Stella had made her point even before she rephrased the question.

"Detective, do you know if my client, or his wife, ever saw or received any of these photos or letters?"

Tremaine said he did not know.

Stella marched right up to him. "Don't letters sent usually wind up with the recipient?"

I glanced at Hennessee and saw him considering whether to object. He didn't. Tremaine said, "Yes, that's generally the case."

Stella then asked if he had found any evidence to indicate that these letters or photos had ever been mailed.

"No," Tremaine said, after a while, "we did not."

Stella laughed—a hard, scornful laugh that startled the jurors. "Detective, isn't it a fact that these letters are simply the pathetic, schoolboy ramblings of a lovesick—"

Suddenly, Hennessee was shouting his objections, but Stella kept going. ". . .the pathetic, schoolboy ramblings of a lovesick man? And can you give me one good reason why my client should have known of their existence?"

"Counselor Nichols!"

Judge Sobel was leaning down from the bench and glaring at her, furious. She fell silent and offered him a look of affected surprise. Sobel called her to the bench, and he let her know, loud enough so that everyone could hear, what he thought of her for flouting courtroom rules. He stopped short of making any contempt citation threats, and she returned to her table, unbowed, and went about registering her scorn another way.

"Detective, were these letters tied in any way—with a ribbon, maybe?"

"No, they were not."

"Really?"

She withdrew the remark. Then she asked for the photos to be brought to her desk, and Hennessee had to go round them up from the jurors and bring them over to her. She sat studying them for a minute. Then she went back to Tremaine and asked if he had studied the photos closely. He said he had, but when Stella asked him about the window frame in the corner of one photo, it was clear he had not noticed it.

Stella hammered away at him. Had he enlisted a photographic expert to establish how the photos had been taken?

No, he had not.

Had he ever noticed the apparent window frame?

No.

Stella piled up points, suggesting this was one more example of shoddy police work. In how many pictures was Caroline Dunbar actually looking at the camera?

"In one," Tremaine admitted.

The photos went back to the jurors for further examination, and throughout their perusals, Stella left Tremaine sitting on the stand. Only when the jurors had finished did she look at the judge. She said, "No further questions of this witness, Your Honor."

It was easily the best moment so far.

That evening Clem called me. He and Greg had been in court that day but stayed only a few hours, sitting next to Caroline. Still, it had been useful to Stella, to be able to identify Clem at one point, so the jury would know that my boss believed in me, despite the fact that I was charged with murdering his business partner.

He had called that evening for an update and I ran down how it had gone with Tremaine. I told him Kurman was due to take the stand the next morning. He said, "You'll see me there." He felt he should be on hand for press interviews, to rebut whatever Kurman might say. He also promised to make his outrage apparent during the testimony—"at least so the jury won't miss it."

Then he asked me how I was, and how the finances were holding up, given the cost of attorneys. He was really being very decent.

The following morning he was in court early, and he took a front row seat between Caroline and Greg. And when Bernard Kurman took the stand, looking unabashedly hostile, wearing a jacket with sagging shoulders, I could see Clem was in the direct line of sight of several jurors, who knew by then who he was.

Hennessee got up, and Stella whispered to me, "Here we go." This was the one testimony we were still in the dark about.

Hennessee asked Kurman for his name and profession. And then we got a surprise: Kurman, it turned out, did not know it was Sam Gilmore who had been calling him about me—at least not at the time he took the calls. Gilmore had been calling him anonymously.

Now it all made sense. Gilmore had found a way to undermine me without blowing Pike Mountain.

Hennessee then asked him when he had first received these anonymous calls, and Kurman said, "About a week before the murder."

"That prick," I muttered.

"And what was it this anonymous caller wanted to talk to you about?" Hennessee asked.

Kurman cleared his throat. "Information about illegal contributions made by Will Dunbar, on behalf of Clem Resources."

I could hear Clem groan with disgust, and when I looked at him, he was shaking his head. It wasn't a bad acting job.

Hennessee glanced around once, then asked Kurman, "Did the caller say why he phoned you with these allegations?"

"Yes, he did."

"What did he say?"

"He said he didn't like Will Dunbar. He didn't approve of his style of lobbying."

Hennessee raised an eyebrow.

"Even though Mr. Dunbar was lobbying for a project of his?"

Stella objected strongly, and Hennessee could find no way to get at it that way. He changed tactics. He introduced the phone bills as evidence, then asked Kurman if he had received the calls at the times indicated on the phone bills.

Kurman said he had.

Then Hennessee asked, "And when did you learn that it was Mr. Gilmore who had made these calls to you?"

"When your office notified me."

"Were you surprised?"

Again, Stella objected, but the judge overruled.

"Yes, I was surprised."

"Why?"

"Because I knew Mr. Dunbar was lobbying for the Pike Mountain project."

"And at any time, prior to the murder, did you try to call Mr. Dunbar about these allegations?"

"Yes, I did."

"And how did he respond?"

Kurman shrugged. "He never returned my calls."

Kurman managed to sound hurt—as if I'd stood him up for a date. I glanced at Clem again. I'd seen the jurors looking at him a couple of times, and I hoped he wasn't overdoing it.

Then Hennessee took Kurman through the specifics of the conversations, but it was obvious Gilmore had obtained nothing more than the list . . . which was a relief. Kurman could only repeat what Gilmore had told him, that I had paid bribes in certain amounts to the parties on the list, on specified dates. Still, there was no escaping the impact this was having on the jury. In their eyes now, this wasn't only a question of whether I was a jealous husband. They were asking themselves was I a sleaze. And if so, did I have more than one reason for killing Gilmore.

As soon as Hennessee was done, Stella went right after Kurman.

"Mr. Kurman, did this caller offer you any conclusive proof of bribes being paid?"

Kurman smiled sourly. "I guess that depends on what you mean by conclusive—"

Stella interrupted in an aggressive way.

"Well . . . let's put it this way, Mr. Kurman. Have you written a story yet about these so-called bribes?"

"Not yet."

"Why not?"

From the spectator seats Clem spoke in a stage whisper. "Because he has zip."

Kurman leaned back in his seat. He said, "A story such as this requires a second source."

Stella nodded. "Then I take it you haven't turned one up yet, Mr. Kurman?"

Kurman started to say something, and Stella demanded, "Yes or no?"

Sobel told Kurman to answer in the manner directed, and after a moment Kurman said, "No."

Stella returned to her table. After a glance at the jury, she looked at Kurman again and said, "You make a point of protecting your sources, don't you, Mr. Kurman? Even anonymous ones?"

"Yes."

"So Mr. Dunbar could not have learned from you who was talking to you?"

"That's correct."

"Because you didn't know yourself?"

"That's correct."

"Can you think of any way that Mr. Dunbar could have known the source of the information?"

It was to be Stella's last question. She was expecting a "no" answer. She was about to sit down. Then Kurman said, "Only if Gilmore told him that night."

For a moment I wasn't sure what was happening. I thought someone had opened the courtroom door. It felt as if a current of air had swept in. But it was Stella sweeping by me on her way to the judge, demanding a mistrial.

The judge sent the jury out. And his expression as he turned toward Kurman was one of unremitting anger.

"You, sir!" he began.

Then he berated Kurman for ten minutes about his response.

"You will confine yourself to yes or no answers unless otherwise directed, do you understand, Mr. Kurman?"

Kurman said he understood. Then the judge told him to step down from the witness box. He wanted to see both counsels in chambers.

They were gone for half an hour. Then they returned. There was to be no mistrial. The judge had agreed to instruct the jury in no uncertain terms that they were to disregard totally Mr. Kurman's last remark.

He did so. Then Kurman was called back. Stella put the question to him again, and he answered with a sullen no.

Stella had no further questions, and the judge told Kurman he was excused. Another sidebar conference followed, and from my seat I imagined they were still discussing what Kurman had said. Then Stella returned to me, shaking her head with dismay, and I was about to ask her how much harm she felt Kurman had done us when she laid a hand on my arm.

"Will . . . try not to react." She glanced over at Hennessee. "They're going to call Cynthia Gilmore."

I said, "What?"

"She's the first witness this afternoon."

Ten minutes later, I was standing in a courtroom stairwell with Greg Stannert, having buttonholed him in the corridor. He was telling me, "Will . . . I had no idea. . . . I haven't talked to her in two weeks. . . . She hasn't returned my calls." He was as baffled as I was.

I was stunned. The last I'd heard, she did not intend to testify, and there were several reasons for this. Some I'd learned from Greg, but mainly from Clem, who had met with Cynthia a while back and spent a day with her, after he had learned via Greg that the prosecution had sounded her out about testifying.

From what he had told me, he had gone into great detail with Cynthia about me and Caroline. He had drawn on the length of his association with both of us to drive the point home to Cynthia that there was no way I could have done it. He'd told her how calm I was the morning after the run-in, and he had emphasized that if he'd ever had any doubts about me, he'd have been the first one to want to see justice run its course. But he considered it an absolute travesty that I'd been charged.

At the end of this—at least as he had relayed it to me—she seemed convinced. Then he had urged her to call him anytime if she wanted to talk about it further, or to talk to Greg. And on a more practical level, he had also pointed out to her that her testifying might even jeopardize the expansion of Pike Mountain—which wasn't true—but as Clem said, "Sometimes the way to someone's head is through their pocket."

In the interim, I'd learned, Cynthia had spoken to Greg and told him she didn't intend to testify, because she didn't want to relive painful memories. Nor, according to Greg, did she really have anything specific to testify to, beyond describing her relationship with her husband. All this had been something of a relief to Stella, who had maintained that there was nothing worse for a defendant than having a grieving widow on the stand, whether she had anything pertinent to say or not. And so Cynthia Gilmore had not been an issue—at least not in terms of being a witness against me—until then.

So what had changed her mind?

Greg had no clue.

I kept asking him, "Was this her idea?"

He flailed his arms. "Will, what can I say?"

"How was she when you last spoke to her?"

"She was okay. I just assumed—"

He broke off. What could he say? He told me that if there was anything he could do for me, he'd do it. "If you need me to take the stand, I'll do it, Will."

I nodded. It slowly dawned on me to thank him, and at that point Crawford came and got me. Greg said he would try to talk to Cynthia before she was due in court, and Crawford told him where we would be having lunch. Greg went off, and Stella, Crawford, Caroline, and I had a miserable lunch, with the Kurman testimony still weighing on us—and now this.

When we returned, Greg had not been able to find Cynthia, and Stella had to assume that Hennessee was taking no chances and had stowed her safely somewhere. And so we trooped back into court none the wiser. The only clue we had about what might be in store was when Hennessee came back into the courtroom and looked toward Stella and me with a nasty gleam in his eye.

Five minutes later, with the jury seated, Hennessee's assistant escorted Cynthia into court. I felt all manner of queasiness steal over me as I looked at her. She was wearing a light gray suit, and as she was sworn in, her expression was pained, as if she did not want to be here at all.

The clerk asked her to state her name for the record, and she said, "Cynthia Margaret Gilmore."

Then Hennessee walked toward her.

"Mrs. Gilmore . . ."

His voice was gentle. He promised he would not keep her on the stand any longer than necessary, under the circumstances. He asked her, "How long were you married, Mrs. Gilmore?"

Cynthia looked directly at Hennessee and said, "Nine years."

Hennessee elicited some background, about where she and Gilmore had met, and under what circumstances. Then he obtained a few more details about properties they jointly owned. Then he said, "Mrs. Gilmore, I realize this is difficult for you. . . . But did there come a time during your marriage when you began to suspect your husband might be having an affair?"

Cynthia sat up, a little starchly. "This past year, I thought he might be having an affair. At the time I didn't know with whom. . . ."

"But you know now?"

"Yes."

As she answered, I felt Stella sink into her seat. Stella kept her face toward Cynthia, but she whispered, "She's going to cream us." She glanced at me as Hennessee went back to his table. Then she said, "I did warn you, Will."

Hennessee returned to Cynthia with the envelope of photographs and letters. He handed it to her, then asked her, "Do you recognize the woman in these pictures, Mrs. Gilmore?"

"Yes, I recognize her."

For the first time, Cynthia looked out into the courtroom.

"And do you see her in court today?" Hennessee asked.

"Yes . . . she's the defendant's wife . . . Caroline Dunbar."

Hennessee wanted Cynthia Gilmore to point out Caroline. He wanted the record to reflect that she was indeed indicating Caroline. Then he asked Cynthia about the number of occasions on which she had met Caroline, and whether her late husband was present on these occasions. Cynthia brought up the various times we'd been together, and she told them about inviting us to dinner at their house. I sensed the picture that was emerging was not about to escape the jury, and I could feel myself sweating.

Then Hennessee said, "Now, Mrs. Gilmore, did there come a time when you had a conversation with the defendant, *after* the murder of your husband?"

I felt a hollow feeling opening up inside me, and out of the corner of my eye, I saw Stella sink even farther.

"Yes, there was a conversation."

"Tell us about that?"

"Well . . ." Cynthia hesitated and shifted in the witness box.

Then she said, "It took place at the Clem Resources office. I went there because I wanted to discuss my late husband's partnership interest with Mr. Stannert—an associate and friend of my late husband's." Then she said, "I ran into Mr. Dunbar in the underground parking garage. He asked if he could talk to me, and I wasn't sure if he'd been waiting for me . . . but I agreed to talk to him, in Mr. Stannert's office."

"Go on, Mrs. Gilmore."

"Well, I . . ."

She hesitated. There was a palpable rustle in the courtroom. And suddenly I realized this had all been carefully rehearsed. Hennessee said, "Tell us what Mr. Dunbar said to you that day."

Cynthia looked at the jury, then back at Hennessee, then in a firmer tone, she said, "He wanted to talk to me about his wife's affair with my husband."

I could feel my ears ringing. "He also wanted to know if my husband had any enemies."

I could feel heat rising in my cheeks. I wanted to jump up and shout, "Tell them I denied killing him!"

Suddenly I was aware that Stella had hold of me by the suit cuff.

Hennessee said, "What else did he say, Mrs. Gilmore?"

She took a breath. "He suggested robbery might not have been the motive for my husband's death."

I was fuming. And only then, as Stella gripped my sleeve, did I see the effect this was having on the jury. They looked uneasy, several were avoiding looking at me, and I felt something turn in the pit of my stomach as I realized just how damaging this was.

Hennessee turned and looked at me. He asked her, "Was that all he said, Mrs. Gilmore?"

I waited, hoping, praying . . . but all she said was "Yes, that was it, pretty much."

"Thank you. No more questions."

I almost forced Stella to her feet, whispering fiercely, "Ask her whether I said I killed him. Ask her. . . ."

Stella half-rose, yanking free of me. Then she said, "No questions of this witness, Your Honor."

I could only stare at her, flabbergasted, making no secret of my dismay.

Stella wanted an immediate adjournment, and the judge granted one. In the corridor, I was still yammering at Stella, almost screaming at her, wanting to know why the hell she'd failed to ask a single question. In the midst of all this, Crawford was leaning over my shoulder, making an effort to calm me down, and finally Stella shouted, "Enough!"

She told Crawford to ride back to the office with me.

"We'll talk there," she snapped. "Once you've had a chance to cool off."

Then she shot me a look and marched off along the corridor, leaving me with the feeling of having been abandoned. I was still only vaguely aware how heated I'd gotten.

I turned and saw Caroline come out of the courtroom, and I didn't know what to say to her. Crawford went over to her and said a few reassuring words. Then I saw Clem and Greg emerge from the courtroom, both shaking their heads. Crawford came back to me and told me that Caroline knew where we were going. "We should go," he said, and he added that he would explain a few things on the way.

I walked over to Caroline and said something—I don't recall what—and as we left, I saw a couple of reporters approach Clem to discuss the Kurman testimony, which I'd almost forgotten about by then.

We rode the elevator downstairs, and when we were in the car, I turned to Crawford and said, "Why?"

Crawford sighed and said, "Are we calmer now?"

I sat in silence for a moment, trying to get a grip. I said, "I'm calmer. Why, Ted? Why no questions?"

"Stella had nothing to gain by asking anything."

"Cynthia Gilmore made it sound—"

"I know, I know."

I started to say something, but he talked over me. "Her husband was murdered, Will, and she wants her pound of flesh."

"She took things out of context!"

"Exactly."

I was still staring at him.

"Will, ferchrissakes . . . the woman's gonna believe what she wants to believe. What does Stella have to gain by asking her anything?"

I just sat there, shaking my head, not knowing what to make of it.

Stella was waiting for us in the conference room. She said to Crawford, "Is he calmer now?"

Crawford pronounced me sane, and Stella said, "The next time I tell you to shut your mouth because the jury's watching, do it."

I stood in silence in the face of the reprimand. She said, "Sit down." And once I was seated, she said, "The reason I didn't ask anything is because there was nothing to ask."

"Ted kind of explained . . ." I mumbled.

"She sandbagged us. You realize that?"

I said I realized.

Then Stella said, "No, you don't." She shook her head with a kind of weary patience and said, "She nailed us, Will! Aside from that enemies stuff!"

Again, she shook her head wearily, and said, "Will, don't you understand? Until now all they had were the photos, the letters. Nobody could actually attest to an affair. Who else could? Not Gilmore. . . ."

She was looking at me with exasperation. Then she said, "Don't you understand. They can't force you to testify, they can't force Caroline to—she's your wife! But Cynthia Gilmore got it in, Will. And in the worst light. You saw how that jury reacted!"

Finally, it hit me. And I didn't know what to say.

I sat down and lit a cigarette, and after a moment, Stella said,

"Give me one of those." She looked at Crawford and said, "I'm going to have to put Caroline on the stand. I can't let this sit!" She turned to me, "She's going to have to admit to the affair and tell the jury about your attitude that night, after you two got home."

I looked at Crawford. He looked uneasy. I guess I did, too. I knew what this would open up. It would give Hennessee every opportunity to go after Caroline about every detail of the affair. So for the next ten minutes, we went back and forth, going over the pros and cons. Stella herself changed her mind about half a dozen times. Then she went back to her original notion, insisting she had no choice.

There was a knock at the door. For a moment, Stella ignored it; then she indicated for Crawford to go see who it was. He got up and went to the door. It was the receptionist, with a manila envelope.

Crawford put it on the table next to me, and it took a few seconds before I realized it was for me. We'd already gone back to the discussion. Another minute went by before I picked up the thing. I'd been getting at least one request per day for interviews, and I assumed this was another. Then I opened the envelope, and for a moment I stared at the contents, thinking some reporter had sent me his press clips. Then I looked at the clips more closely, and my heart started to race.

A note with the stuff read, "This may help." Below it was the single letter *N*.

I was aware of Stella saying something. Then she saw the look in my eyes. She said, "What is that?"

I showed her the clippings. When she had read a couple of paragraphs, her mouth fell open. She showed them to Crawford, and I wasn't sure what to make of his reaction. He nodded slowly, then asked me, "Who sent these?"

I said, "An old friend."

It was a muted conversation when I called Nadine to thank her. Caroline was in the next room, and Nadine understood.

She said, "I just had a feeling."

I thanked her again profusely. I said, "You're really something."

She said she hoped it would help. Then she said she had to go, and we hung up. I went into the dining room, where Caroline was unwrapping some take-out food. She saw something in my expression and asked what was up.

I told her there was room for hope.

16

The following day the papers and the TV stations devoted a lot of coverage to my case, in part because of the strenuous denials issued by Clem about the bribes, as well as by the politicians whom Kurman had named. This was also the day the prosecution was due to rest its case. Stella had told me early that morning that she wasn't going to fool around with character witnesses. She wanted to get right to the meat of Hennessee's case, chop it up, and spit it back at him.

And so as soon as Hennessee rested, she told the judge she was ready to move ahead. And that evening, it was Caroline who went back to Stella's law office, so that Stella could brief her on her testimony.

When I arrived in court the next morning, I was feeling a little more confident. There was some spring to my step. I was still nervous, of course—by then I'd heard enough about juries to realize that if the Heavenly Host itself had showed up to testify on my behalf, the outcome would still have been unpredictable.

But I was fortified whenever I looked at my attorney. Stella appeared to have the bit between her teeth, and there was a spring in her step, too. A couple of times I saw Hennessee look at her in a nervous way. She had already bowled him over the night before, when she had told the judge she intended to recall Cyrus Eastlake, the forensic man, as her first witness. She had also notified Hennessee that she wanted Lowndes to be available for possible recall.

And so, at a few minutes after ten that morning, Judge Sobel walked in and held a sidebar conference before summoning the jury. Hennessee said the witnesses were in the building; then the jury was summoned. The clerk called Eastlake's name, and two minutes later, Eastlake walked into court, looking a little surprised at being called as the first witness for the defense. He took off his glasses and polished them as he waited to be sworn in. Then he was duly sworn, and he stated his name again for the record.

I glanced toward the spectator seats as Stella walked toward him. Caroline was not in court that morning. She had decided to arrive later, rather than wait outside the courtroom with witnesses hostile to me. Crawford had told me that once she arrived, he would step outside to keep her company.

"Mr. Eastlake . . ."

Stella's manner suggested she couldn't wait to get to him.

"You testified a few days ago that you found cigarette butts in the dining room of the Gilmore residence, on the night of Mr. Gilmore's murder, is that correct?"

"That is correct, ma'am."

Stella studied her notes a moment, and Eastlake adjusted his glasses. Then Stella approached.

"Mr. Eastlake, how many members of the forensic team were working at the Gilmore residence the night of the murder?"

"That night, there were three of us."

Stella asked for the unit members' names, then asked what time the forensic unit had arrived at the crime scene.

"It was around eleven forty-five P.M."

At this point Stella wanted a stipulation as to the time my phone call had been received by the police. Hennessee agreed to it. My phone call had been received at eight-twenty. Then Stella asked Eastlake if it was typical for a forensic unit to arrive at the scene of a homicide, approximately three hours after the police first arrived.

Eastlake said the timing was within the norm. The forensic units had to come from downtown. If the crime had occurred nearer to downtown, or if the body had been discovered during the day, their arrival might have been a little sooner.

"And at what time did you find the cigarette butts?" she asked him.

Stella already knew the answer to this question. Eastlake had already told us on direct.

"It was about an hour and a half after we arrived."

Stella looked at him, curious.

"Why so long?"

"Well, as I believe I explained . . ." He sounded a tad impatient. "The police photographer and the fingerprint unit were working in the dining room. We worked the other areas of the house first."

Stella went back to her table, picked up a copy of a log, and brought it to Eastlake.

"At what time did you complete your work, Mr. Eastlake, according to your log?"

Eastlake looked at the log, and said, "At three fifteen A.M."

Stella flashed him a polite smile.

"Thank you. Nothing further." Then she walked back to her seat.

Eastlake sat in the witness box a moment—then Judge Sobel told him he was excused. He looked a little mystified as he got up, and I could see him asking himself, What the hell was this all about? Why had he been dragged down here to say the same things he had already said on direct?

Stella waited until he had left the courtroom. Then she said, "Your Honor, at this time I'd like to recall Detective Lowndes."

There was a minute's wait while one of the court officers went out. Then Lowndes came in, giving me the same malevolent look he had given me the last time he took the stand. He was sworn in again and took his seat, and Stella whispered to me, "Don't count your chickens. I've still got to get this admitted."

She stood up and approached Lowndes.

"Detective Lowndes," she asked, "at what time did you release William Dunbar from your custody on the night of Sam Gilmore's murder?"

Lowndes thought about this a moment, and said, "It was around eleven-thirty P.M. or midnight."

Stella asked if he was sure about that, and Lowndes said he was fairly positive, give or take a few minutes.

"What did you do then?" Stella asked him.

"My partner and I went back to the Gilmore residence."

I felt my pulse quicken, and Stella paced a moment, looking thoughtful. Then she said, "Did you consider Mr. Dunbar a suspect at the time you released him?"

Lowndes smiled sourly. "Yes . . . he was a suspect."

Stella asked why, and for a moment Lowndes was caught off guard. He seemed to react as if she were trying to trap him.

Then he said, "Any witness to a homicide is automatically a suspect. And in the defendant's case, he told us during interrogation about hitting Mr. Gilmore."

He seemed satisfied with his own response.

Stella said, "I see." Again she paced. A few moments went by, and then she said, "You did ask him during the interrogation whether he had smoked in the house . . . isn't that correct?"

"Yes."

"And he told you he had not?"

"That's correct."

"You recall testifying to that, on direct?"

"Yes."

Stella came back to the table slowly, looked at me, and picked up a report. Then, without approaching, she asked, "Detective, did you once testify in a case brought against an Officer Raymond Guzzardi?"

Hennessee rose immediately to object. "This is irrelevant, Your Honor."

I was watching Hennessee, and from his expression I could see he had no idea where Stella was headed. Then I looked at Lowndes, and I could see he did. His jaw was a little slack.

Stella requested a sidebar, and Judge Sobel summoned them both to the bench. I strained to listen, and I heard Judge Sobel ask Stella where she was going with this.

She said, "To the very heart of this case, Your Honor."

Sobel said, "That's not enough, Counselor. Please explain."

She leaned toward him. "Your Honor, the outcome of this case may depend upon the credibility of this witness, police officer or not. I believe I have a right to raise questions about his credibility, including his record as an officer."

Sobel seemed momentarily conflicted. He looked to Hennessee, but right then, Hennessee had the look of a man who had just run out of ammunition. He didn't know where Stella was headed, and he could only repeat what he'd said when he rose to object—that such testimony was irrelevant.

Sobel scratched his chin and said, "Apparently, counsel for the defense doesn't think so." Again, he seemed to be giving Hennessee an opportunity.

But again, Hennessee was stumped. He had no basis for argument. Sobel asked Stella if she would care to elaborate, and Stella said her reasons for taking this line of inquiry would become apparent with a few questions.

Hennessee looked nervous. Then Sobel said, "All right, Counselor, I'll allow the witness to answer. But since you don't choose to elaborate, I don't know yet how far I'm prepared to let this line of inquiry go."

He told her to proceed, and as Hennessee went back to his seat, the judge told Lowndes he should answer the question. Stella said she would repeat the question, and in a loud, clear voice she asked Lowndes again, "Did you once testify in a criminal case brought against an Officer Guzzardi?"

There was a silence. Then Lowndes said, "Yes."

Stella walked back to her seat. "Officer Guzzardi was your partner at one time, isn't that correct?"

"Yes." Lowndes glared at her. Stella glanced toward Hennessee as if expecting him to object. Hennessee got to his feet, but the judge motioned for him to sit down.

Then Stella said to Lowndes, "You testified as a character witness? Isn't that so?"

There was another silence, then a muted "Yes."

Stella acted as if she didn't hear. She asked him to repeat.

Lowndes spoke up. "Yes."

Stella walked to the jury box rail. Then she said, "And what was Officer Guzzardi charged with . . . in this case?"

This time Hennessee objected, but Sobel overruled. I sensed he now wanted to hear the answer for himself.

Stella repeated the question. "What was your former partner charged with?"

Lowndes responded with a mumble. "Falsifying evidence."

Stella asked him to repeat the answer, and he did, and there was a murmur throughout the courtroom.

"What was the outcome of Officer Guzzardi's trial?" Stella asked innocently.

Again Lowndes hesitated and then said, "He was convicted."

I heard another ripple throughout the courtroom, and I felt like cheering.

"No further questions," Stella said.

She sat down next to me, and after a moment she whispered, "Reasonable doubt?"

Hennessee immediately launched into a redirect. He was winging it, but he managed to establish that Guzzardi had been Lowndes's partner for only six months. He established also that Guzzardi was a Vietnam veteran whose posttraumatic stress had been taken into account at his sentencing. He established also that Guzzardi had always conducted himself according to the book in Lowndes's presence. But no matter what Hennessee did, he couldn't prove that Lowndes had not lied on the stand in that case—even if it was to protect a distressed former partner. And as I glanced at the jurors during the redirect, I saw that Hennessee could not defuse the impact these disclosures had made.

When Hennessee was done, Stella had no further questions.

It was nearly noon, and Judge Sobel asked her if she would like an early lunch recess. She told him she would just as soon continue.

"Very well, Counselor, you may call your next witness."

"Thank you, Your Honor." She turned to the clerk. "The defense calls Caroline Dunbar."

This time it wasn't a *murmur* in the courtroom but a collective gasp. In front of me, Hennessee rocked back in his seat. He had not expected this. The rumble in the court kept escalating, and after a while Judge Sobel reached for his gavel.

Then the clerk took up the summons, and one of the court officers was dispatched to get Caroline. And while we waited, I asked Stella what impact she thought the testimony from Lowndes might have had.

"It certainly helps."

She nudged a shoulder toward the jury, and I saw several jurors talking earnestly among themselves. Then their faces wheeled as one as Caroline was escorted into the courtroom by one of the court officers.

She smiled at me as she walked by. She was wearing one of her best suits, with a lilac Hermes scarf knotted at the throat, and very little makeup. Stella got to her feet, and as Caroline took her seat, I saw she was following Stella's instructions to the letter. She sat straight in the jury box, and in taking the oath, she said, "I do," in a firm, clear voice. She looked at the jurors and then at me.

Stella approached, and the biographical questions began. Stella asked Caroline how old she was, how long we'd been married, how old our daughter was. She asked her where Katia went to school, and how long Caroline had worked at Clem Resources, and what she did there, and how Caroline and I had met. And as Caroline ran through the details, I saw one woman juror actually smiling, especially when Stella brought out the fact that we were an office romance.

This went on for several minutes. Then Stella asked Caroline if she was happily married. Caroline said she was. She also said that she had also learned a lot about being supportive since the indictment.

Stella returned to her table and picked up the envelope containing the photos and poetic letters that had been found in Gilmore's desk drawer. She returned with these and asked the judge for permission to show them to Caroline. Sobel nodded, and Stella handed Caroline the envelope and asked her to look at the pictures and letters carefully, and to take as long as she liked.

Caroline began looking through the pictures. She took her time, going one by one. Then she turned to reading the poems. And during this, the courtroom grew a little restless, but Caroline seemed unfazed. She read on, her face a mask, her expression impassive. Ten minutes went by. Then she looked up, handed the photos and letters back to Stella, and shook her head a little.

Stella asked if she had had enough time to examine all the contents. Caroline said she had. Then Stella asked, "Mrs. Dunbar . . . these photos and letters were examined by witnesses and jurors in this courtroom when you were present, but other than that, have you ever seen any of these photos or letters before today?"

"No," Caroline replied firmly, "I have not."

Stella indicated the envelope and said, "Before your husband was indicted in this case, did you know of their existence?"

"No, I did not."

"Did you ever receive photos or letters of any kind from Mr. Gilmore?"

"No."

Stella returned to her desk and put the envelope down. Then she asked, "Mrs. Dunbar, does it surprise you to read letters like these, written by Mr. Gilmore?"

"Yes, it does."

"Why is that?"

I knew the rehearsed answer. It was more or less along the following lines: "Because I had a very brief affair with Mr. Gilmore. It was never serious, and Mr. Gilmore knew that. It was a mistake, and I regret it, and I told my husband how sorry I was, on the night he found out about it."

Only Caroline didn't say that. She said, "Yes, I'm surprised. I'm very surprised."

Stella asked why.

"Because nothing like this ever happened between myself and Sam Gilmore."

There was a momentary silence in which one could hear a pin drop. Then a murmur of astonishment. It began to grow and grow, and the only reason I recovered in time to conceal my own amazement was because the jurors were focused entirely on Caroline.

Stella had her back to the jury, which was probably fortunate. I couldn't see her face either. She just continued to face Caroline for what seemed like an eternity. Then she turned and walked back to her seat, and in the course of that ten-second walk, she must have thought really fast on her feet, because as soon as she reached her table, she said, "No further questions."

She sat down.

The level of babble in the courtroom rose. I was looking at Caroline, and after a moment I did what Stella had urged me to do in anticipation of a different answer—I smiled bravely—suddenly realizing that even in these dramatically altered circumstances, it was the appropriate response. Caroline smiled back at me—a smile of sincere conviction—as if to say she had put an end to this nonsense, once and for all.

Then I glanced at the judge. To my surprise, he seemed nonplussed. Stella, too, managed to retain her cool in the wake of the perjury, though I didn't dare turn to look at her. But Hennessee was far from cool. Stella said, "Your cross," and Hennessee was on his feet storming toward Caroline, his face crimson.

"Mrs. Dunbar! Do you maintain, under oath, and before this court, that you never had an affair with Sam Gilmore?"

"That is correct."

She was gazing into his furious countenance, looking as calm as I'd ever seen her look.

"Do you know the penalty for perjury, Mrs. Dunbar?" Hennessee yelled.

Stella half-rose to object, then thought better of it, and in the interim, Caroline said, "Of course I do."

"Then can you explain to this court why your husband chose to punch Sam Gilmore the night of Mr. Clem's party?"

The question was a mistake. Stella had said it. "Never ask a witness a question you don't already know the answer to."

Caroline looked at the jurors first. Then she said, "Mr. Hennessee, for months my husband has been maintaining that he is an innocent man—"

"That wasn't what I asked," Hennessee blustered.

"I'm trying to answer. . . ." Caroline looked at the judge. "I've been waiting for this opportunity."

The judge interceded. He said, "Mr. Hennessee, if you wish to withdraw the question, you may. If not, I'd appreciate it if you'd let Mrs. Dunbar respond in her own way."

Hennessee did not withdraw it. He was too far gone. He uttered a loud, sardonic cackle, and with exaggerated disbelief, he said, "No . . . I'll hear what she has to say."

And that was an even bigger mistake.

Caroline actually smiled at the judge. Then, alternating her glance between judge and jury, she said, "Sam Gilmore made a lot of advances toward me. I didn't tell my husband because he worked with Sam, and that work was important. Sam was being a pest, but I thought I could handle it. And I did, at least until the night of that party . . . then Sam grabbed hold of me . . . and Will saw it. . . ."

She looked over at me. Hennessee was speechless. Out of the corner of my eye, I saw Stella and Crawford staring at her. Then Caroline said, "I know Will intended to apologize for what occurred—"

Hennessee cut her off. "No further questions!"

There was a long, strange silence in the courtroom. The jurors were all looking a little shell-shocked. Then the judge looked to Stella for any redirect, and Stella said she had none. Sobel nodded. Then he told Caroline she was excused.

She stepped down gracefully, smiled at me, and walked to the rear of the courtroom with a steady stride, pursued immediately by a couple of reporters.

17

People talk of moments when time seems to be suspended. That's how it was for me, that day in court.

Only when Caroline had left the courtroom did I begin to feel that time had resumed its inexorable progress, and even then, only at a glacial pace. At least until the judge ordered a recess. Then I looked at Stella and she looked at me, and eventually, I said, "This wasn't my idea."

Stella nodded. She'd seen my expression. She believed me.

When she and I walked out into the corridor, I expected to see Caroline fending off reporters. But Clem told me Caroline had already left, gone home. He told me he had lent her his car, and he didn't say anything beyond that. We gazed at each other. Clem just shook his head in amazement. Then Stella collected me, and we took the elevator downstairs, fended off a couple of reporters, and went to a nearby coffee shop.

For a while, we didn't say a word to each other. I ordered coffee, Stella asked for a salad, and when the waitress went away, Stella was still very quiet. Then she said, "I'm trying to adapt to what's occurred. . . . I want this case to go to the jury right away."

She paused. Then she said, "I don't want to give Hennessee any time to prove she lied."

I said I understood. Stella sighed and said, "She took a big risk, Will."

I didn't say anything.

"Why didn't she tell you at least?"

I thought about this, and after a while I said, "I guess that was the point—not telling *anyone*."

Stella's food arrived. She took a couple of bites, then shoved her plate aside. After another moment's thought, she said, "I'm going to call the character references in quick succession this afternoon. Then I'm going to rest."

And that's what happened. That afternoon, four witnesses took the stand—two old friends of Caroline's and mine, Al Premerlani, and a retired assemblyman I'd known for years, and all talked about me in glowing terms. Then, at four-thirty, Stella announced that the defense rested, again catching Hennessee by surprise. The judge called him and Stella to the bench, and Hennessee said, pointedly, that there might be some rebuttal testimony—and he asked for the following morning to prepare. The judge granted his request, then asked both counsels whether they needed time to prepare summations.

Stella said she was ready with hers, and if there wasn't any rebuttal testimony, she wanted the summations to begin immediately. A serious charge had hung over her client for a long time, she said, and after today's testimony, she was considering asking the court to dismiss the charge. Stella was sure Sobel wouldn't do that in any event, and so she was merely using the ploy to strengthen her hand in asking for summations to begin immediately. Hennessee balked, but Stella argued that the prosecution had had weeks to prepare its case, and there was no reason for Mr. Hennessee not to be ready with his summation. The judge agreed. His only concession was, he would give Hennessee until noon the next day to prepare any rebuttal.

By five o'clock I was on my way home. I still hadn't called Caroline. When the car pulled onto our street, there were a couple of reporters camped outside our house, and I told the driver to stop at the end of the driveway, rather than drive into the garage. As I got out, the reporters converged on me, with the look of men for whom perseverance had finally paid off. I kept it short and sweet. I said I was hoping the trial would come to a speedy conclusion, and they scribbled away. Then one of them asked if I'd care to predict the verdict. I said no.

I left them and went inside the house, which seemed oddly

quiet. Then I heard Katia's voice outside, and when I looked out the kitchen window, I saw Caroline out in the yard with Katia. I could see she already had a drink, and I poured myself one and went outside. Caroline heard the door open and turned. But she didn't offer anything . . . no smile . . . she just waited as I walked toward her.

I sat down under the umbrella and looked at her for a moment. Then I said, dryly, "Maybe you should have told me."

She didn't say anything. She studied me for a moment, then she said, "Maybe . . ."

I said, "You didn't think I could handle it?"

"No, I didn't think you'd go along with it."

I thought about this, then admitted she was probably right, and we sat in silence for a few moments. Eventually, she said, "They can't disprove what I said, Will."

"How do you know?"

"I know. . . ."

I was still worried. Especially after what Stella had said, about not wanting to give Hennessee time to disprove it. And after a moment I said, "Hennessee's probably scouring the city right now, looking for a witness."

"He won't find one."

She was silent for a moment, then said, "I remembered what you told the cops. You said you hit him because he was groping me. You didn't mention an affair."

She paused. "I don't know what you told Cynthia, but I'm sure she didn't tape it. So they can look all they want, but they won't find a witness."

She fell silent. I said, "Do you think the jury believed you?"

"What do you think?" Caroline smiled for the first time. "I wasn't about to let them send you to jail, Will. No way."

She looked over at Katia, who had just emerged from behind the garage on her three-wheeler. Then she just looked at me very steadily.

I said, "I'm still blown away. . . ."

She smiled again, then said, "It blew your lawyer away, too. But I figured, 'She's a big girl, she can handle it.'"

Then Katia came over and climbed on my knee, and when she went back to her bike, Caroline and I sat in silence. I was still looking for holes in her argument, but there were none, as far as I could tell. Who else would testify to the affair? Some bellhop, maybe? But what was the likelihood of that? And even then, how much weight would it carry? No, as far as I could see, there were no holes—assuming the jury believed Caroline.

If they did, then Gilmore's photos and letters went out the window—they would only serve to back up Caroline's assertion that he had been an obsessive pest. Cynthia's testimony would look like the bitterness of a recently bereaved woman who wanted to blame someone. The cigarette evidence had been called into question, if not discredited. And as I continued to think about this, I realized that if the jury believed Caroline, almost all the motive went out the window, too, and the prosecution's case with it.

After a while I said quietly, "I'm grateful. . . ."

Caroline smiled, then said it was getting a little chilly. She was almost ready to go inside. I asked her when she had decided to do this, and she said, "When Cynthia Gilmore did what she did. I was going to suggest to your lawyer then that I testify. But then you came home and said she planned to call me." She shrugged. "That's when I really thought about it. When it started to go badly."

She asked me how much longer the defense would last. I told her Stella had already rested.

She seemed a little surprised. Then she said brightly, "You see. Your lawyer thinks the jury believes me."

I didn't tell her what I imagined Stella really thought of her. I told her that unless Hennessee turned up a rebuttal witness, summations would begin tomorrow.

Caroline said, "Good," and got up, and I sat gazing after her as she went inside, wondering whether I'd ever known the woman I was married to.

There were no nasty surprises the next morning. Hennessee had no rebuttal, and his summation began shortly after noon. In the course of it, he looked and acted like a man who had suffered a huge defeat. His delivery was halting, and as he moved in front of the jury, he appeared at times to be engaged in a juggling act, worrying that at any moment he might drop some, if not all, of the balls.

He tried to persuade the jury of Lowndes's credibility. He did his best to imply that Caroline's testimony was an outright lie—the last desperate act of a loyal wife coming to the aid of her husband. But a couple of jurors looked away when he brought this up, and I began to feel a growing confidence.

Stella's summation was masterly. The prosecution had not come near to proving its case, she argued. Then she demonstrated the case's weaknesses, point by point, declaring that it was an outrage that I had ever been brought to trial in the first place.

A few circumstances had trapped me in a nightmare, she said. And the police had aided and abetted to win a conviction at any cost. This wasn't a case of reasonable doubt. It was a case of malfeasance on the part of the authorities. She hoped the jury would send a clear message to the police and the D.A.'s office, so that people trapped in similar circumstances would not be afraid to do the right thing.

She was giving the jury an ethics lecture as well as a case summary, and urging them to be part of a greater cause. And only at the end of her summation, when she had once again demonstrated her disgust that this case had ever been brought, did I realize that she had scarcely mentioned Caroline at all.

I looked around, and Caroline was sitting calmly in the front spectator row, with her hands folded in her lap.

The jury retired at 4:00 P.M., and I went downstairs with Caroline for some coffee. On the way we gave the press an opportunity for photographs, and after that nobody pestered us. Then a reporter came striding toward us, and it took a second before I realized he wasn't here to ask questions. The jury was coming in, he said. After thirty-five minutes.

Stella was waiting upstairs. Yet now I was feeling very nervous, despite my earlier confidence. It was the ritual as much as anything—the jury filing in; the judge taking his seat; the press anticipating; the spectator rows filling up. I looked around. Clem wasn't there, nor Greg, nor Nadine—most people had been taken by surprise by the speed of the decision. Then the judge called for quiet and asked the jury foreman if the jury had reached a verdict.

He rose, "Yes, we have, Your Honor."

Judge Sobel leaned toward him. "And how do you find the defendant," he said. "Guilty or not guilty, to the charge as set forth?"

"Not guilty, Your Honor."

The sound was like air rushing out of a balloon. An unforgettable sound. A vast exhalation in that windowless chamber. Suddenly, I felt people slapping me on the back. Then Caroline fell into my arms.

We stayed that way awhile, and when we unwound, Stella offered me her hand. So did Crawford. Then the judge told the jurors they were excused, and several of them stepped out of the jury box and came toward me and hugged me. At one point, I remember, I was fighting tears. I couldn't help it. It was over.

18

Or was it?

Maybe it would have been. Amid the relief, maybe it would have been, but for one encounter. Maybe it should have been anyway. But when you live an isolated and angry existence for months on end, something sets in—something that other people might consider to be perversity.

The fact was, during those months, I'd lived under a weight, and when the weight was finally lifted, I could scarcely believe it wasn't there. I was still reacting to it. I was like a businessman on the first day of retirement. I knew what I'd worked for, I knew what my reward was supposed to be, but I was still operating under the burden long held, and emotionally I was still wrapped up in the pain.

And the anger.

It happened that same day.

Stella suggested we hold a press conference at her office, and my first response was "You hold one if you like. I've got nothing more to say to those guys."

I meant it, too. I felt only slightly less hostile toward the media than I did toward Hennessee and Lowndes. But ultimately, Stella prevailed. If I didn't say a few words, she said, the reporters would continue to hound me. So I grudingly said, "Okay, I'll do it."

Caroline didn't want to be there. And so she went home, to prepare a celebratory dinner, for just the two of us, while I went to Stella's office with her and Crawford.

Half an hour later, the press swarmed in, and I said my piece. Stella said hers, and finally, the press was gone, and I was clutching a drink and looking at Stella, and in the sudden aftermath of the press's departure, she said, "Well, Will . . . Congratulations."

I thanked her solemnly, and I wanted to talk to her some more about it all. But then to my surprise, she stood up and said she had to go, and as she pulled her stuff together, she said dryly, "You should go, too. You have some people to thank."

I guess she meant Caroline, but in a way I felt it was a dismissal. And I really didn't know what to say in response. I wasn't sure what she thought of me—although I had a good idea what she thought of Caroline—and I wondered if that opinion had affected her view of me.

At that moment, I wanted to ask her, "Do you think I did it?" But as the words formed, I changed my mind. I don't know why. I guess I wasn't sure how I'd react if she said yes, and I still felt uneasy whenever I thought about what Caroline had done, even though my self-interest had overridden this.

Then Stella said she was going to take advantage of a rare free evening, for dinner out with her husband, and again I had the feeling she wanted me out of there. I guess I showed a reluctance to leave, because instead of waiting for me to leave, she left. I stood looking after her, wondering what she was really thinking. Then I went into the conference room to pick up the press clippings that Nadine had sent me. I was packing these into a briefcase when Crawford walked in.

He stood in the doorway, holding a drink, looking a tad unsteady and wearing a slightly sardonic expression. And I knew right away he'd had a few drinks—I'd seen him slinging them back even before the press got here. He came in, closed the door, and took a seat at the table.

I offered a subdued thanks, and he nodded slowly. But like Stella's, his attitude toward me seemed to have shifted, and I wasn't sure now where I stood with him. Then he put his feet up on the table and loosened his tie, and after a moment he said, "Well, you never can tell how these things'll turn out . . . can you, Will?"

I looked at him as I closed the briefcase. His words contained a hint of mockery, and I didn't care for his tone. Then he said, "She really came through for you, didn't she?"

I said, ironically, "Who, Ted?" I still wasn't sure what to make of his attitude.

After a moment, he said, "I don't mean Stella."

I asked him what the point was. And when he didn't say anything, I reminded him that Caroline's testimony wasn't my idea. Then he said, "I realize that, Will."

Again, he looked at me in the same ironic way. "Don't get me wrong," he said. "Stella's good. But not as good as Caroline."

He was studying me, and although his body was completely at rest, there was a faint aggressiveness in his eyes—the aggressiveness of a guy who had shored himself up with a few belts and was now ready to speak his mind.

Eventually, I said, "Does it bother you, what she did?"

"Course it doesn't fucking bother me."

He reached for his glass.

I said, "It sounds like it does."

He didn't say anything, and after a moment I said, "We both know she lied, Ted."

"Yeah. You and me both."

I heard the scorn in his voice, and I said, "So she lied. I still didn't kill him."

He shrugged. Then he uttered a laugh and said, "Doesn't matter to me if you did, Will. I get paid to do a job."

I looked at him steadily for a moment, and I said, "It does bother you."

He shrugged slightly. "Maybe . . . maybe not."

He didn't elaborate, and eventually I asked, "What's your beef, Ted? I told you all along I didn't kill the guy."

"Hey, I couldn't blame you if you did."

We stared at each other for a moment. Then he rocked forward and his lip curled. "Guy like that. Ain't no doubt in my mind he had it in for you."

I was silent a moment. I wasn't sure what to make of this. Why should he give a shit? I told him again, "I didn't kill him."

He got up and shook his head slightly, then smiled in a wistful sort of way, and finally said, "Will, maybe you oughta go on telling yourself that."

There was a silence. Then I said, "What the fuck's that supposed to mean?"

He smiled again. Then he drummed his fingers on the table for a while, and after a moment he sat down again and said, "I saw what Stella did to Lowndes, Will. And, yeah, sometimes shit like that happens . . . cops going overboard . . . but not in this case."

He sat looking at me in a knowing sort of way. And after a moment, I said. "What do you mean?"

"There was no plant. Not of any cigarette butts. Not by the cops anyway."

I could feel my ears ringing. And a moment went by before I asked him, "How do *you* know?"

He shrugged. "I'm an ex-cop, Will. Cops talk."

I saw how he was looking at me, and I realized he wanted me to know that he had cornered me, even if Hennessee and the jury hadn't. He smiled, and I was feeling angry, and finally I said, "So what do cops talk about?"

"Cops to ex-cops? When it don't matter anymore? Sometimes they tell each other the truth."

"And what is the truth?"

"You tell me, Will."

He laughed a little, and I was struggling to hold on to my patience, and finally I said, "Who did you talk to?"

He put a finger to his lips. And at that point I started to get really angry. What was this? Some idle game?

I said, "I'm not going to convince you, am I?"

"Like I said, doesn't matter to me."

I'd had enough. I said, "Fuck you. What am I supposed to say since you won't put your cards on the table?"

I picked up the briefcase and aimed a look at him, and after a moment, he got up, too. Then he said, "There's something else . . . since we're talking about this."

"What?" I said shortly.

"Jess Mansell . . . You remember him? The invoice handler out at the site?"

"What about him?"

"Changed his mind about testifying. Can't say I blame him. He works for Clem."

Suddenly, I felt off balance. I was troubled by all he'd been saying and the way he'd been saying it, but now he was alluding to something specific. I recovered a little and said, "You wanna spell it out, Ted? Or are you gonna run in circles with this as well?"

He laughed. And I wanted to grab hold of him, wring it out of him, and find out whether this was a game or not, and if he had talked to anyone. He seemed to sense what I had in mind. Then he said, "Maybe you can find out why Mansell changed his mind, Will. I couldn't."

I stared at him.

"I'm serious, Will. Why don't you do that? It might even convince me."

Then he downed his drink and started for the door, but when he reached it, he hesitated, and when he looked back at me, he said, very seriously, "Will, just in case you are innocent. It wasn't the cops who set you up."

I stared at him. I said, "Who did you talk to?"

He grinned. "His last name begins with an 'L' or a 'T.'"

He started to open the door, then said, "You know what I think? I think you and she figured out all along you could beat this. Clem, too. That's what I think."

He shrugged and opened the door. Then he said, "So long, Will," and he closed the door behind him.

I heard his sardonic whistle as he walked off. And suddenly, I felt crushed. I wasn't out of this. Not by a long shot. Two people who had stood by me now seemed to have doubts about my innocence.

The hollow feeling persisted when I got home. I was quiet during dinner, and when Caroline asked me what was wrong, I didn't know where to begin.

At first, I said it was the aftermath of the stress, and she was sympathetic. Then we talked for a while about the trial and all that had occurred, and eventually we went into the bedroom. She started to undress, and I realized she had planned this, too, as part of the celebration.

We did make love, but it clearly wasn't all she had expected. And as we lay in each other's arms afterward, she asked what was wrong.

I waited a while, then I said, "Somebody tried to frame me, Caroline, and I'm not sure if it was the cops."

She frowned. Then she rolled over and lay on her back and stared at the ceiling a long time. Eventually, she said, "Can I make a suggestion?"

"Sure."

"Why don't you go up to that cabin for a few days? You know you like it there. . . . I'll come up with Katia this weekend."

She stroked my cheek, and I said it didn't sound like a bad idea. Then she smiled and ran her hand across my stomach and said, "I don't want you being tense."

I lay thinking about her suggestion for a long time, then I said, "It's a weird feeling. Because if it wasn't the cops . . . then whoever it was is still out there."

But I could see right away that it bothered her. Me dwelling on it. After a while she said, "You won, Will."

I said I realized that. I also said I knew she would prefer it if I could put all this behind me.

She said, "I want what's best for you." Then she smiled and said, "I realize this may take a while."

I said, "Yeah, it could take a while."

She suggested again that I think about going to the cabin.

Eventually, she fell asleep with my arm around her. But when she first shifted in her sleep, I eased my arm free and got up. Then I went downstairs and lay on the sofa for a long time.

What was confusing to me was how quickly relief had given

way to anger—anger that wasn't able to find a focus. It veered between the cops and an unknown party, and after a while I realized that within the anger lay a deep desire for retribution. Someone had tried to frame me, and if it wasn't the cops—if they weren't lying to Crawford—then I damn well owed it to myself to find out who it was.

It was more than just a desire for revenge. I'd gotten a taste from Crawford of what my life would be like now, in relation to other people. There would still be people who'd think I'd done it and gotten away with it. So in a very real sense, I hadn't won.

Someone else had—whoever had done this to me. They may not have succeeded in framing me, but they had gotten away with killing Gilmore and succeeded in shifting the blame to me. For months, my life had been eaten away because of them.

So what was I supposed to do? Take refuge in scorn and cynicism? There was no magic potion that would make the pain go away, except maybe one. People I loved, admired, and respected would tell me to forget it, let it go, put it all behind me, but I knew it wouldn't be so fucking easy—not with that "person," or "persons," still out there.

And it was this, more than anything, that persuaded me at some point that night to act as if I were heeding Caroline's suggestion about going up to the cabin. Because I knew that way I'd have some freedom to maneuver.

19

In the morning, I was up early. By seven, I was driving east on Interstate 10, through the area known as the Inland Empire, an area little visited by the trendier crowd of west Los Angeles, and there's a good reason for that. In the entire United States, you'd be hard-pressed to find a place as depressing as the western half of Riverside County. Much of what has been built here is an eyesore. Mile after mile of cheap tract housing—cheap, by Los Angeles standards, although the prices people paid here for the privilege of commuting each day past the same scorching sameness would boggle the mind of someone who'd had the good sense to buy, say, in a suburb of Pittsburgh.

But once out past San Bernardino, one hits the resorts of Desert Hot Springs and Palm Springs, and out here the landscape is prettier. There is less housing, more open spaces, and in some lights, a certain beauty. At least for some people.

For myself, I am not, nor will I ever be, a lover of the desert. It just doesn't do it for me. It didn't that day, it doesn't now. Ultimately, I find myself repelled by the heat and the dryness. And that morning, as I drove, I was thinking what an act of faith it was to turn on a faucet anywhere in this part of the world. I was also thinking that it may be our destiny as humans to try to run all the rivers into the deserts, and that we might not fully understand the concept of emptiness until we were through trying. But what I wasn't thinking about that morning, as I drove east and settled in for the scenic views of the Little San Bernadino Mountains, was the possible consequences of what I was doing. There was really no way I could have foreseen these.

I wasn't even sure what I hoped to learn by driving out here. But the one name Crawford had given me was Jess Mansell, the invoice handler at the site who had changed his mind about testifying. It was a start, and there were no other distractions in my life right then. And as I drove by the Holiday Inn and the Mexican restaurant where I'd had lunch with Caroline, the Gilmores, and Greg, months back, I remembered that I still had to give Clem notice, and I was thinking about that as I turned off the freeway and drove north to the site.

I wasn't sure what people would make of my showing up. I imagined I'd be on the receiving end of a few strange glances. But when I pulled up at the gate that day, the guard at least had evidently never heard of me. I handed him my ID, and he offered me a cheery good morning, then told me he was having a little trouble with the gate.

As I waited, I glanced back at the rail tracks. I could see freight cars, with the dust blowing off them, and it was a little strange, seeing the site now in full operation. To my right, cranes were unloading baled trash from other freight cars, and beyond these, a bulldozer was moving piles of tailings from the old ore mine. Then the guard got the gate up and handed me back my ID. He asked who I was here to see, and I said I had half a dozen people to see, and I asked him who had the best coffee around here.

He said, "You might try Branson. He's got his own machine back there." Branson was the site manager.

I said, "Don't bother to call ahead, I've got a couple of other people to see first."

He said, "Okay, Mr. Dunbar. You have a nice day."

I drove on in and headed down the strip of tarmac between corrugated trailers and the site office buildings, and pulled into a dusty parking space.

I sat in the car awhile and waited. There were a couple of workers in blue overalls coming out of one building. Then a truck pulled up on the far side of the tarmac, and two other men got out. Nobody paid any attention to me, and after a moment I got out of the car and went into the building that housed Gilmore's old office.

There was a Plexiglas entranceway facing a couple of offices, but there was no receptionist sitting there—in fact, I didn't see anyone, and all the doors to the offices were closed, including the door of Gilmore's old office, which still had his name on it. I walked over to the door and tried it. It wasn't locked, and after a moment's hesitation, I stepped inside and closed the door.

I went to his desk and sat down. The place didn't seem to have been touched since his death. The geological maps were still on the walls. Then I felt queasy for a moment thinking that someone might have seen me walk in here. I got over it. So what if someone saw me? I still worked for this company. Even if somebody found me here, what could they accuse me of? Bad judgment. That was mild, compared to what I'd been accused of lately.

I stared at the computer on the desk, and then I opened a couple of drawers and looked through them. Everything in them seemed to be work-related—no private correspondence. And as I looked through the contents, I wondered if the police had even bothered to look for anything here. Then, in the lower left drawer, I came across a photo of Gilmore and his wife. Had it been relegated here after he developed his obsession for Caroline?

There was nothing else of interest. And after a while I got up and looked through the contents of various shelves. On the floor in front of one shelf was a cardboard box, and when I flipped it open, a pair of mud-caked work boots lay on top. My first thought was "dead man's shoes." I closed the box. Then I heard the door of the outer office open.

My heart thumped a little. After a while I moved to the door and edged it open, and I could hear a guy from an office across the hallway talking on the phone. From where I stood, I could see the nameplate on the "in" box outside his office.

Jess Mansell.

So they had offices across from each other. Why else would Gilmore be talking to an invoice handler just before he came into town that day—if it weren't for some work-related, physical proximity. I could hear Mansell talking on the phone, saying, "Yeah . . . okay . . . soon as it comes in, I'll call you," and I walked out of Gilmore's office and closed the door gently behind me. I stood at his door. He had his back to me as he talked on the phone, and he was wearing jeans and a checked shirt.

"No . . ." he said. "Sometimes we don't get those until the late delivery." Then he said, "Yeah . . . soon as it comes in, I'll call you."

With that he hung up, turned, and saw me, and it was clear from his expression that he knew who I was.

He continued to stare at me, and I stepped into his office and closed the door. He still had not uttered a word. Then he said, "What are you doing here?"

I looked at him steadily—early thirties, mustache, somewhat uneven teeth. I said, "I work for this company."

"What do you want?"

I said, "I want to talk to you . . . about Sam Gilmore."

"Why?"

I glanced around. He didn't say anything, and I figured I'd keep him off balance. I said, "Why'd you change your mind about testifying?"

He stared at me a moment, then blinked self-consciously.

"Who says I did?"

"My lawyer's investigator."

I could see him going on the defensive. He shifted in his seat, then said, "Why should you care? The jury acquitted, didn't they?"

For a second he avoided my glance, and I figured I'd try intimidating him. I said, "Don't fuck with me, Jess. I've been fucked with enough."

I moved toward him abruptly, and the sudden movement had the reaction I'd hoped for. It scared him a little. He said, "I didn't want to get involved. Clem told me it might help if I couldn't remember too well—that's all. . . ."

So it was Clem.

"If you couldn't remember what?" I said.

"About Sam saying he was going into town to meet with you guys."

"To meet with *me*?"

"No . . . just Clem, he said."

This was news. I was quiet for a moment. Then I said, "He was meeting with Clem about me?"

"Well . . . he didn't say that."

I was a little confused. I said, "So what did he say? How did my name figure into it?"

He hesitated. Then he said, "Well . . . I mean, after I read in the papers about what happened, I kind of assumed the meeting had to do with you."

I was baffled for a moment and a little annoyed. Then I said, "So you were going to testify to what? Some half-assed idea of your own?"

"No."

"What, then?"

He didn't answer right away, and I started to lose patience. I said, "What the fuck were you supposed to testify to?"

"Well . . . just the way Sam was, around here, that morning. The mood he was in. . . . He brought up your name once."

"About what?"

Again, he hesitated, and I leaned closer to him and said, "Why'd he bring up my name, Jess?"

He was staring at me. Then he said, "There was some Riverside County guy wanted to come see the site. Sam said, 'Tell him to call Will Dunbar—that's his fucking job. Maybe it'll give him something to do.'" He stared at me, then said, "Later, I heard about what happened . . . I mean I read the papers."

I backed up a moment. I was still a little confused. Then I said, "So what are you saying? Gilmore came out here, groused around, bad-mouthed me, then said he was going back into town to see Clem?"

"That's about it."

"Anything else?"

"No. He was off working most of the time. Got himself all muddied up."

I still couldn't figure it. This wasn't any big deal. Why the fuck would Clem care what this guy said?

I said, "And Clem asked you to forget about this?"

"Well, he just said it wasn't worth bringing up. I guess he was doing you a favor. So when the D.A.'s guy came out here, I told him it was hard to say if Sam was really mad at you, because I'd heard about what happened by then, and maybe I was reading too much into it."

He was wearing a slightly forlorn look, and I was starting to think that if I were a prosecutor, I wouldn't want this guy as a witness. He could blur all the edges.

He was still looking at me, as if to ask why I was leaning on him, and I was still trying to decide why Clem would care what this guy said, why he'd even be interested. Then I asked him, "How did Clem find out you knew anything?"

"I happened to mention something to Branson."

"And Branson told Clem?"

"I guess. . . ." He shrugged. "Clem was out here one day and asked to see me."

I stared at him. Why the hell had Clem never brought this up to me? Or did he not think it was worth it?

Then Mansell said, "Anyway, I didn't lie. Sam was in a bad mood all morning. It was worse when he got back from working. Damn near bit my head off when I asked him how he got all muddied up."

"Where was he working . . . here?"

"No . . . Morelos."

"Where's that?"

"About eight miles south of here. Out in the desert." He shrugged. "That's all I know."

I asked if he could remember anything else, and he said, "That's about it."

Then he wanted to know why I was asking him all this, and I said, "Never mind, Jess. And don't you tell anyone we talked."

His look was sullen and a little suspicious.

"Are we on the same page here?" I said.

"I hear you."

I wasn't sure I'd gotten through to him. He still looked uneasy, and after a moment, he said, "This is none of my business anyway."

I said, "You're damn right."

I left him then, went back into Gilmore's office, and closed the door, and I stood thinking for a moment. Then I opened that cardboard box and looked at those mud-caked boots again. I sat down for a long time, still thinking about it and wondering why Clem had cared about what Mansell said, and why Gilmore had been going into town to see Clem, and why Clem had never mentioned either of these things to me. Then my thoughts took a different tack, and I got up from the chair and went to a wall map and found "Morelos." It was ringed, as were many other desert communities, with various notations beside them: F.10-TSI-40, M.23-TSI-50, A.15-TSI-70. My.6-TSI-20. I had no idea what this stuff meant.

I gave up on it and went back to the desk. Then I took out the photo of Gilmore and his wife, and copied down the number of the phone on the desk. I figured it might be worth knowing who else Gilmore had called that morning, aside from me, and I knew one person who might be able to get me that information.

When I left the office, I made a point of looking in on Mansell on the way out. He was still looking a little concerned, and again I told him to say nothing about us having talked. Then I asked him if everything he'd told me was the truth, and he nodded slowly and said, "Yeah . . . but if this comes back on me, I'll deny it."

I told him it wouldn't, and when I left him, I was reasonably convinced that he would keep his mouth shut.

It was a little after ten as I drove south, and I kept watching for the turn to Morelos. After a while I figured I'd missed it, and I drove back looking for it. But there was only one turning, and it wasn't signposted, so I sat a while trying to decide if I should drive back and ask the guard at the gate if this was the road.

Then an old Ford Fairlane appeared on the road behind me. I waved the car down, and the driver looked like a descendant of some forty-niner. He was hard of hearing, and when I asked him if this was the road to Morelos, he didn't seem to understand. I tried various pronunciations, and when I found one that clicked, he pointed a gnarled finger along the road. I thanked him, and I got back in the car and drove on.

It was getting hot, and I cranked up the air-conditioning and turned on the wiper blades for a while to clean the dust off the windshield. As I drove, the blacktop, such as it was, began to merge with the desert alongside. Then the road began to dip a little, and after a while the surface broke up entirely, and I could have been heading into the heart of the Mojave. After another five miles or so, I rounded a bend, and in the distance I saw signs of habitation.

My thought was: What would have possessed anyone to actually live here? Out in the middle of nowhere? In the desert? I hadn't even seen a power line, or a phone line. Then I went down a short hill and saw power and phone lines feeding the community from the far side. So this was the back way in.

I slowed, and the car wheels skidded on the sandy surface, and up ahead I saw about fifty homes. There was one clapboard store and a junkyard containing a number of sand-blasted wrecks, and again, I thought, Who the hell would live here?

I pulled up outside the general store. And when I walked in, it was like stepping into someone's open pantry with a week's supply of groceries. The only thing that marked it as a store was the cigarettes on display. A door to the back room opened, and a woman of about forty wearing denim overalls stepped out. Her hair was stringy and unwashed.

I said, "Hi," and walked over to a refrigerator that was some relic from the fifties and took out a Coke. Then I indicated the refrigerator and said, "You got your money's worth out of this baby."

No smile. She was all warmth. I handed her a dollar. Then I walked over to the window and stood looking out as I drank my Coke, and after a moment, she said, "What brings you to these parts?"

I took a chance.

I said, "I'm supposed to meet a guy here . . . geologist. Works for the Pike Mountain site."

She didn't respond, and I walked over to her, took out the photo of Gilmore and Cynthia and showed it to her.

"This guy . . ."

"Oh, yeah. I seen him around. . . ." She handed me my change.

Then she said, "You might try down at the hollow, that's where I last seen him poking about."

"What's that?" I asked.

"Low patch of ground . . . far side of town. Fills up when we get rain. Sometimes when we don't."

I was staring at her. Then she said, "You're spilling your Coke, mister."

The bottle had frothed up and I hadn't noticed.

I got back in the car and drove a little beyond the far side of town, and then I saw it. It was off to the right, a low hollow flanked by rock outcrops. No dry bed ran into it, but the mud surface still looked a little damp from a recent rain.

I got out of the car and walked down a short slope toward the mud, and this looked like the stuff that had caked on Gilmore's boots. Then I looked over to the far side of the area, and there the soil seemed a little darker. I made a half-circle to where the darker patch of ground was. Then I knelt down and picked up some of the darker stuff. I ran it between my fingers. It was crumbly, and it felt—hard to describe, but it had an almost metallic texture.

I used my car keys and collected some samples of both. Then I got back in the car and drove back toward the freeway by the road that followed the power lines. As I drove, I wasn't sure what I was feeling.

I had a sense that this was all a little absurd. Gilmore had been in a foul mood to begin with, because of me, and I doubted that spending a morning in Morelos would improve his disposition. But why had Clem made a point of asking Mansell to forget about a few things, and more importantly, why had he never mentioned this to me?

It could be nothing. Clem was like any executive, and he often forgot to share things he felt he'd taken care of. But I was still bearing in mind that Gilmore had said he was going into town to see Clem, not me, and I was also bearing in mind that if it wasn't the cops who had tried to frame me, then someone else had.

20

I made it back to Los Angeles late that afternoon in time to drop off the soil samples at an agricultural test lab. And I promised the lab analyst front-row seats to a Lakers game, one of the few PR perks I still had through Clem, if he could analyze the stuff by the morning. His eyes lit up when I made the offer, and he said he'd put a rush on it. There was an earnestness about him, and in an odd way he reminded me a little of Gilmore.

That evening was an odd one. Earlier, I'd told myself that if I struck out entirely at Pike Mountain with Mansell, I'd do as Caroline had suggested—drive up to Mammoth and spend the week there. But now I needed to be back at that lab in the morning, and I didn't want to go home that night and have to explain to Caroline where I'd been and what I'd been up to, because I knew she'd only be critical and would tell me I should be clearing my head of all this. And so that evening I called her from a public phone in a quiet canyon in the Hollywood Hills, where there was no sound of traffic, and I told her I was up at the cabin. I said I was calling her from a phone booth nearby because the cabin phone hadn't been turned on yet.

She asked how I felt, and I said, "I'm relaxed," which was far from the truth. Then she told me that Clem and Greg had wanted to know when and where the acquittal celebration was going to be. I said I wasn't sure I was in a party mood yet, and she said she understood. Then she told me about taking the morning off and bringing Katia to her dance class, and as she talked on, I felt a little apprehensive that maybe some car alarm would start up nearby, so I tried to keep the conversation reasonably brief. Finally, Caroline said she had to go, Katia wanted a bedtime story. I said I'd touch base with her sometime the next day, and I hung up and found myself in the odd situation of being in the city where I lived and having to spend the night at a hotel.

I did one other thing. I called Nadine to thank her, but she wasn't home, which was a pity, because I'd have liked to have had dinner with her. Instead, I wound up eating at the coffee shop of a small hotel on Beverly, and I spent the evening watching movies on pay cable.

In the morning I called the sports ticket agent I dealt with, and told him I wanted to pick up Lakers tickets. I hadn't spoken to him in months, but he'd followed my trial, and when I dropped by his office, he was full of congratulations. I practically had to grab the tickets and run, or he'd have kept me there all morning, and it was nearly ten-thirty by the time I broke free and set off back over the hill, to the Valley and the lab. The lab analyst turned out to be a talker, too, and he wanted to go into detail about the Lakers' loss to the Jazz the previous evening. I handed him the tickets, and he gazed at them, a little awed, and said this would be a first for him. Then we went into the lab and he turned on a microscope, adjusted it, and picked up a couple of typed pages.

He said, "Okay, the first material you gave me . . . the clay . . ."

He started to read off its chemical composition, acidity, pH value, whatever, and after a while I stopped him.

I said, "It's plain old clay, right?"

He looked at me like I was a true Philistine, then said, "Well, there's no such thing as plain old clay. . . ."

"Is there anything weird about it?"

"Well . . ."

He started to tell me how clay was formed, and after a moment, I interrupted.

"What's the other stuff?" I asked.

He seemed a little rebuffed. Then he said, "Well, in some ways, it's more interesting. It's a wash material."

"What do you mean, wash material?"

"I mean it's been washed . . . to wherever it was."

I said, "You mean, naturally?"

His eyes brightened a little, as if we were now talking the same language.

"Well, there's limestone in there. But this looks more like sludge fines."

"What?"

"I'd say it's been hosed out of gravel somewhere along the line."

I felt my heart skip a beat. Then he indicated the microscope. "You want to see?"

I nodded, and I could feel my heart really thumping as I sat down next to him. He looked through the microscope and then invited me to look.

"You see that speck on the right side? It's glass." I looked up, and he said, "There are also metal slivers in there."

I was staring at him.

"Bacteria?" I asked finally.

"Oh, yeah . . . Off the charts."

He started to go into the bacterial content, and after a while I guess I started to shake a little. He noticed and asked me if I was all right. I said I'd had too much coffee. He started to lecture me about the dangers of caffeine, and I finally interrupted again and asked if I could take the lab reports with me.

He said, "Sure . . . you paid for them."

I guess he thought I was a pretty impatient, high-strung sort. I asked him a few more questions about the bacterial content, and he began to probe a little about what sort of project I was working on. I made up something, probably contradicting myself about half a dozen times. Finally I told him I had to run, and he pulled the stuff together for me.

Ten minutes later, I was heading south on the Hollywood Freeway, and I realized I'd broken out in a sweat.

I drove to the Bureau of Land Management then, in Riverside, and using my company credentials, I managed to get hold of a copy of the Environmental Impact Studies report for Pike Mountain that was on file there. I told the clerk he'd saved my life. I said I was on my way to a meeting with a county supervisor and I'd forgotten to bring mine with me. Then I spent an hour delving through the report, wading through details about other California landfills, and burrowing through more pages about cut-and-fill excavations and the disadvantages of these, then on to the advantages of Pike Mountain as a waste site. There was a long section about waste transfer stations, where waste could be screened for hazardous substances, and some of this I remembered having rewritten myself for press releases. Then, on page 95, I came across the breakdown of the geology of the Pike Mountain area, and its suitability as a waste site. I read through this, and then I read on through sections about slag piles—materials that could be used for daily landfill cover and landfill liner. Sludge fines. That's how it was described, and this could only mean one thing. This stuff must have washed underground to a place eight miles away—and along with it, waste material from the site.

I may not have been a scientific genius, but I knew what that meant. It meant that the water supply of that dumpy little town in the desert—which must have gotten its water from wells sunk in some kind of aquifer—had been contaminated.

I was sitting in a Thrifty parking lot as I read this, and I was so absorbed, I'd not noticed that the car was stifling. Finally, I rolled the windows down, and I sat staring out across the parking lot for a long time, thinking that Gilmore had to know about this. Had he learned about it that morning? The day I was supposed to meet him? I was asking myself all manner of half-finished questions, forming conclusions, and then having a hard time retaining a grip on them. Actually, I was so deep in thought at one point, it took a while before I realized that the horn tooting behind me was directed at me. Someone wanted to know if I was leaving or not.

I drove out and stopped at a phone to call Nadine. It was a little after 2:00 P.M., and she was still at lunch. I was told she would probably be back in about fifteen minutes. So I drove back to the drugstore and bought some aspirin—my head was pounding by then. After checking my watch half a dozen times in fifteen minutes, I called Nadine back. This time she answered. "Will!" She exclaimed.

She was bubbling. I hadn't spoken to her since the verdict. She said she'd gotten my message the night before, and then she just took off about how happy and relieved she was, and how dumb she felt for not having been in court when the verdict came in, but that like so many others, she'd never expected the jury to come in so quickly.

I said, "Who would?" Then I interrupted her and asked if she was free that evening.

She said, "Sure . . . can we have dinner?"

I said we could do that, but something important had come up, and I wanted to talk to her about it as soon as possible. I guess I made it sound as urgent as it was, and she asked what it was about. I told her I didn't want to get into it on the phone, and she sounded a little apprehensive.

She said, "Is everything okay?" And I wondered if she thought that maybe someone had found out about her tipping me to the stuff about Lowndes. I said this was nothing to worry about, but that it was really important. She said, "Okay." Then she told me she had a meeting with her supervising agent at four-thirty, which would probably last an hour, but she would be free after that. I told her to name a place—any place—somewhere downtown, if that was more convenient. She suggested a bar on Hill Street, and said she could meet me there at six. I said that was fine. Then she extracted another assurance from me that I was okay. I told her I was fine. Then we hung up and I drove back to town on Interstate 10 and killed a couple of hours wandering around the Griffith Observatory before making my way downtown.

At a few minutes to six, I was seated at the bar, and when Nadine walked in, she gave me a big hug, and I gave her more than a peck on the cheek—I was just really glad to see her and relieved to be able to confide this to someone I could trust. Then I suggested we take a quiet table, and she seemed a little flustered. I guess she wasn't sure what I had in mind. But she smiled as we walked across the room, and we took a booth together. The waiter came over, we ordered drinks, and once he went away, Nadine smoothed the lapel of her jacket, and said, a little dryly, "So was it all true? What Caroline said?"

I wasn't sure what to say. And finally I said, "I'd rather not get into that. Like I said . . . something's come up."

She said, "You made it sound so urgent."

She interlaced her fingers, then smiled again and said, "So how does it feel?"

I said I really hadn't had time to think about it, not since yesterday.

She asked why.

I hesitated. "Jesus . . . where to start?" I said.

Then I told her what Crawford had said—that it wasn't the cops who planted those cigarette butts. And as I ran through that part of the conversation and described Crawford's attitude, she sat looking at me, a little uneasy.

Then she sighed and said, "Well, here's how I feel. I never believed you did it. I didn't then, I don't now. And even if it's true, that it wasn't the cops, I don't feel too bad about what I did."

I saw what she was thinking. She was thinking this was the entire reason I wanted to talk to her. Then she said, "Anyway, Crawford only has Lowndes's word for it, at least that's what it sounds like."

I said, "I know, but this is only the preamble."

She said, "What do you mean?"

I reached into my pocket and took out the sheet of paper containing the soil analysis. "Here's what I wanted to show you. Take a look."

Nadine looked at it, puzzled, and I wasn't even sure why I'd handed it to her. I just wanted her to see something concrete, even though there was no way she could have made head or tail of those pH values and the other figures. I told her what it was—a soil analysis—and began to explain what I'd learned.

"The morning after I hit Gilmore," I said, "he went out to the Pike Mountain site and went off to work at a place called Morelos, about eight miles away. It's a little desert town, maybe thirty, forty homes."

Then I took out a plastic bag containing a sample of the contaminated soil and said, "I found this stuff out there, in the same place I think Gilmore was working. It's called sludge fines. They use it as liner material at the site. I think Gilmore turned it up in Morelos that morning—the same day he was killed."

She was staring at me, confused. Then she said, "I'm not sure what you're getting at."

I said, "Well, there're all sorts of studies been done to show that waste from that site wouldn't contaminate groundwater supplies. But I guess it has, since this stuff showed up in Morelos. There's water there. This stuff must have been carried from the site by some kind of aquifer."

I still wasn't sure if she fully understood.

"Nadine . . ." I said, "if this had become public, the Bureau of Land Management and the EPA would have been crawling all over Pike Mountain. They'd have probably put the project on hold, and the Riverside supervisors and the L.A. council would have had to delay their votes, and maybe some members would have changed their minds. But at best, there'd be compensation to pay here. Not to mention that while the project's on hold, there'd have been all kinds of interest costs being accrued."

"And you think Gilmore knew about this?"

"I think he may have found out about it the day I was to see him. I spoke to this guy who works in the office next door to Gilmore's. His name's Jess Mansell. Crawford put me on to him. This guy was supposed to testify against me, until he changed his mind."

I paused, "Well, in any event . . . Mansell told me that Gilmore was in a foul mood that morning. Mansell was supposed to testify that Gilmore brought up my name that day and made some crack about me—and he assumed Gilmore's foul mood had to do with my hitting him. But Mansell let a couple of other things drop. He says Gilmore's mood was even worse after he came back from work that morning. He also says that John Clem had a little chat with him and suggested he forget about testifying. And, he says, Clem also suggested that he forget about Gilmore's saying he was coming into town that day to see Clem."

Nadine was staring at me.

Then she said, "Jesus, Will . . . he's your friend."

She was looking at me a little startled. She stared at me a long time. Then she went right to the heart of it. "Are you saying Clem shut Gilmore up, because of this?"

I didn't say anything. In part, because I didn't want to.

Then Nadine said, "Without even talking to him?"

I felt an impulse to put forth a lot of qualifiers. But I didn't. I said, "Maybe Clem did talk to him. Maybe Gilmore wouldn't play ball."

I was silent a moment, then said, "If Gilmore found out about the pollution, what's he going to do?"

Nadine shook her head slightly. "I don't know."

"Well, it's Gilmore's project, as well as Clem's. But Gilmore's a geologist . . . he's Mr. Ecology . . . his rep's on the line here. . . . Suppose he tells Clem there's a pollution problem, and he wants to disclose it and put the project on hold. What's Clem gonna do?"

Nadine was still staring at me, but she didn't say anything. I said, "What's at stake here? Clem's got twenty million dollars invested. He's looking at revenues of fifty million a year."

Nadine looked at me wide-eyed.

I said, "Well? . . . Who's got the most to lose?"

Her mouth wavered a moment. Then she said, "And you think Clem would set you up?"

"He knew Gilmore and I were getting together to straighten things out. Hell, it was his idea." Then I shook my head and said, "Still, there's a problem."

"What?"

"Where did he get the cigarette butts?"

I started to explain that I'd worked at home that day. But Nadine reminded me that I'd already told her this when we'd met last, at that restaurant in Venice. Then she said, "You went out that day. Could Clem have gotten the cigarette butts from your car?"

I sat and thought about this. Nadine and I seemed to have exchanged roles. Now she was doing the extrapolating, and suddenly I felt as if I were falling into a state of denial.

I didn't want to believe it. I'd worked for Clem eight years. And yet I knew what his money could buy. I also knew that Clem had made use of a few shady characters in his time—I was thinking about a private investigator named Crenshaw who'd gotten the goods on a competitor for John Clem. Nadine took a sip of her drink, but she didn't say anything, and we sat for a while in a kind of hollow silence.

Then I said, "Clem's got millions invested in this thing. Now Gilmore's going to blow the whole deal . . . because of some crap town in the desert?"

I fell silent again. Then I said, "You know how little it costs to get rid of someone."

"But why frame you?"

I was silent, and she answered for me. "Because you're the perfect target."

I was feeling all manner of conflicting emotions. I was feeling some pain, too, because I still felt a loyalty to Clem, despite what I was saying. I didn't want to believe this. I'd have preferred it to be the cops. . . .

Then Nadine said, "He was in your corner throughout all this."

It was something I'd been thinking about all day. Again, I didn't say anything, and eventually, Nadine said, "You're having a hard time with this, aren't you?"

"Course I am."

"Why, Will? He's no saint. You know that."

"Neither am I, for that matter."

I looked at her, and she smiled faintly. Then she said, "I'll tell you one thing. Clem would be in your corner, even if he did set you up. You know why? Because it would be expected."

We faced each other in silence. And I sat thinking about Clem and all the money he had. That kind of money would cause anyone to doubt this. People had no trouble believing that a street dealer would kill for a few bucks, but they could never quite believe that rich people were capable of killing merely to become even richer. There was such respect for money.

I found myself staring at Nadine, and I was thinking that because she did what she did, maybe she had an understanding of this. She knew all about wealthy dealers who couldn't stop. And as I thought about this, I glanced off across the restaurant and saw a couple of guys looking at us. Nadine followed my glance.

"You know them?" I said.

"I work with them."

We were silent for a moment, and finally I said, "If this is true, how do I prove it, Nadine?"

I wasn't really asking her. I was just floating out a trial balloon. I'd already given the issue some thought.

She said, "You go to the D.A. with it."

I laughed. "I'm sure I'd get a wild reception there."

"How about your attorney?"

"What's she going to do?"

She conceded I had a point. We sat in silence again. Then Nadine looked at her watch and said, "So what do you want to do?"

I said, "You're a cop. You could help me take this a step further."

I took out the paper on which I'd scribbled Gilmore's office phone number. I told her what the number was, then said, "I'd like to know about all the calls he made that day. Can you get that?"

"Jesus, Will . . ."

I saw right away she didn't want to do it. She said, "Will, it's illegal. I need to file a requisition. These things go through channels. . . ."

She was staring at me.

I said, "Well, if you can't get it, I don't know who can."

She didn't say anything, and after a moment I said, "Let's take a walk and talk about it."

She got up slowly, and we walked out onto Hill Street. And as soon as we were outside, she turned to me.

"Will, why do you even want to do this? You're free as a bird."

"You know why. . . ."

"Why?"

I avoided her glance for a moment, then I said, "Because someone tried to frame me, Nadine, and if it was Clem, I want to know."

Then I looked at her and stuffed the piece of paper in her hand

and said, "See if Gilmore made a call to Clem that day. If he did, that's got to tell us something."

She was still staring at me. Then she said, "I could lose my job, Will. I could be indicted."

"Nobody will know."

"Whatever I get you . . . it wouldn't mean anything in court. It'd be inadmissible."

"It would mean something to me."

After a moment, she threw up her hands. "There's got to be some other way to go about this."

"Show me one," I said. "Your office covers that area, right?"

"Will . . ." She was still searching for reasons. She also looked a little angry, and in the midst of her uncertainty she looked at me as if I should be grateful for everything she'd already done. Then she said, "You had this in mind before we got together, didn't you?"

I said, "You're right." And then I admitted it wasn't fair. I was using her. I reached for the paper, took it back, and said I'd walk her to her car.

Then she said, "Wait a minute."

She held her hand out for the paper. I gave it to her, and she put it in her purse. Then she did something I did not expect. She kissed me.

I wasn't sure what to say to her. Should I ask her what the kiss meant, or whether she'd check up on the calls? She said she'd call me, and I quickly told her she shouldn't call me at home. I explained why—that I was supposed to be in Mammoth, recuperating—and Nadine shook her head, and said, "You lead some kind of life, Will."

I said, "I guess so."

Then I gave her the name of the hotel on Beverly where I'd stayed the night before, and she said, "Let me think about this." And she walked off.

21

That evening, I took root in a bar on Third and sat gazing at the liquor bottles, thinking about Clem and a whole lot of things. In some moments I'd be thinking that the darker side of my imagination had gotten the better of me; then I would have to remind myself that if Gilmore had tripped to a problem at the site, there was every reason to think he'd go into town to talk to Clem about it.

I was speculating, of course, about Gilmore's reaction to the discovery. For all I knew, he, too, might have wanted to sweep it under the rug. But the more I thought about it, I knew he wasn't the type. On the contrary, on this he'd want to be Mr. Clean—out of self-interest, as much as anything. And how would Clem react to that? I knew what Clem would say. "Fuck it. The vote's less than a week away. We'll worry about it after that." And I could picture Gilmore saying, "We'll worry about it now." And when I thought about this, my imagination took off. . . .

The truth was, I never knew where the limits lay with Clem. He was smarter than almost anyone I knew, and he was eminently capable of planning this, seeing an opportunity to lay it off on me. And the beauty of the thing was that nobody would be looking at the real reason Gilmore was killed. I realized it was intended that I should spot the "intruder." It was intended that I be a witness to a muffed "burglary." Given a choice between scenarios A and B, who would think to look at C?

Then, in the next moment, all these hypotheses would come crashing down, and I'd be seeing this again as the height of absurdity. So there was a problem at the site. Maybe Gilmore didn't even have a chance to get into it. And where did Clem get the cigarettes? Then I'd wind up thinking, Maybe it was the cops, after all.

Around ten, I left the bar and went to the hotel, and this time I called Caroline from there, still maintaining the pretext that I was in Mammoth. There were a couple of awkward moments when she started to talk about a cold front that was moving toward California, and she asked me how the heat was at the cabin. I said it was fine. Then she asked if she should bring up my skis for the weekend, and I told her that might be nice.

Then she told me Clem had said that I should be in no rush to get back. We also talked about my intention to resign, and that was a little awkward. I had all these feelings running, and here she was, raising the issue of how pained Clem was going to be by my anouncement that I wanted to quit. I bit the bullet and said I was going to feel some guilt about it, obviously, but I wasn't about to change my mind.

She said she understood, and we got past the slight note of contention brought on by the past argument.

I didn't sleep well that night. The hotel bed was hard, and around midnight I sat up and watched a movie. It was nearly two o'clock by the time I started to get drowsy, and after I dozed off for a few hours, an ambulance siren woke me, and I had trouble getting back to sleep again.

I was up around eight. After breakfast, I picked up my car and drove to Pan Pacific Park. I walked for a while, then I read a magazine in the park, and around noon I went back to the hotel, and there was a message for me from Nadine. I felt my pulse quicken as I picked up the phone to call her.

She answered.

I said, "It's Will."

She didn't say anything for a second, then said, "Can you be at my place around two?"

"Gilmore called Clem, didn't he?"

"Let's talk about it then."

"Come on, Nadine! . . . Don't keep me waiting."

There was another silence. Then she said, "No, Will . . . he didn't call Clem."

I felt crushed, rather than relieved. I'd come to expect it by then. But in the meantime, Nadine hadn't said anything else, and I was suddenly aware of that.

I said, "So who did he call?"

She took a breath. Then she said, "He made three calls, Will. One to you, one to his wife, one to *yours*. . . ."

"What?"

"Did Caroline ever tell you he called?"

I didn't even hear what she said next. And the next thing I was aware of, Nadine was saying, "Will . . . are you okay?"

I wasn't. I was in a daze. And I was shaking.

The next hour was a blur. When the initial shock wore off, I assured Nadine that I could drive over to her place. But saying it was one thing, doing it was another. I went home first, and I barely remember the drive after that—other than hearing the occasional blare of horns as my attention wandered.

Nadine was pulling in outside her apartment as I got there, and as I got out of the car, she saw me. Then she went to the trunk of her car and took out some files and said she was going to drop this stuff upstairs. She went inside and emerged a moment later. Very somberly, she said, "Let's go for a walk."

She didn't say anything else, and I trudged alongside her as we headed to the beach. After a while she said, "I was worried about you."

She looked at me and said, "You don't have to be the stoic in front of me, Will."

I nodded. What was I to say? I told her I'd been home.

She seemed surprised.

"To do what?" she asked.

"Just to look around."

I knew nobody would be there. Fran took Katia to a gym class on Thursdays.

Nadine didn't ask anything else for a while, and we walked in silence to the oceanfront and sat down on a bench. My legs still felt weak. She gave me a strange look and asked, "Do you have a handle on this?"

I didn't say anything, and she said, "I couldn't blame you if you didn't." She looked at me again and said, "What are you thinking?"

I said I didn't know what to think. I wasn't sure if the shock had worn off yet. Then I steeled myself and said, "If it is what we think . . . if it's true . . ."

I stopped there and tried to find a better way to say it, but I couldn't think of any other way. Finally I said, "I wonder if she just passed a message along to Clem."

I knew how lame this sounded. Nadine was looking at me, and after a while she said, "He spoke to her for fourteen minutes, Will."

There was a silence. I said, "To apologize, maybe?" Then I said, "Mansell said Gilmore was going into town to see Clem."

I looked at Nadine. She didn't say anything.

I said, "Maybe Clem called him."

"Maybe . . ."

Nadine looked off at the ocean for a moment. Then she said, "It really comes down to one thing." She swiveled her glance toward me. "Who got the cigarettes? We know you went out that day." She stared off at the ocean again. Then she said, "I'm just trying to follow the logic here, Will . . ."

I just sat there, thinking for a while, and eventually I said, "Do I have my head up my ass about all this?"

"You mean in terms of whether it was the cops?"

I nodded.

"I can see that's what you'd want to believe."

She looked at her feet, then at me, and said, "If it was she who got those cigarettes . . . why? . . . Why would she do it?"

"Money," I said.

"What?"

"That's the only reason there could be. Clem paid her."

"But she got you off, for God's sake."

Nadine sounded incredulous, and when I didn't respond, she said, "You mean, she'd put you through all this—for money?"

I looked at her for a moment. Then I said, "She knew I wanted to quit. We had a lot of arguments about it. Believe me, if she did it, it was for the money." I let out a derisive laugh. Then I said, "That's the motive, if you want to call it that."

Nadine got up and paced, and when she sat down again I told her a little about the way Caroline was with Clem—always wanting him to know they were of like mind, always wanting him to know there was nothing she couldn't pull off. I gave her a little history of our marriage.

She sat listening, and after I'd finished, she said, "Jesus, Will . . ."

I said it wasn't as bad as I'd made it sound.

"But we're talking about a murder conspiracy."

The words shook me. I nodded grimly. She asked if I thought Caroline was capable of that. I said in all honesty, I didn't know. But was she capable of forming an alliance with Clem? Yes.

I was trembling a little, and Nadine took my hand. Eventually, I said, "All she actually had to do was pick up some cigarette butts."

"But, Christ . . ."

"I know," I said miserably.

"I still can't believe she'd put you through this . . . no matter how much money there was. . . ."

"Fifty million a year for Clem," I said. "How much for her?"

She stared at me. Then she said, "Is that why you went home . . . to look around?"

I nodded.

"Did you find anything?"

I shook my head.

"No bank statements or anything?"

"Nothing."

Then I said, "She'd salt it somewhere, somehow. Draw on it in dribs and drabs . . . find ways to explain it." I turned to her. "She loves money, Nadine."

"She'd do this and still want to be with you?"

I didn't answer, and Nadine was quiet for a moment. Then she said, "It's really brilliant, I have to admit. They set you up. She gets you off. . . . She *knows* she can get you off."

Again, she sounded incredulous.

We were silent for a long time. After a few minutes I looked at her and said, "This is worse than the trial. . . ."

Nadine looked at me. Then tears filled her eyes, and suddenly I was in tears, too. Not over Caroline in that instant, but over the whole rotten world.

I swatted at the tears. Then I asked her, "Am I mad?"

She curled close against me and held me for a long time. Then she said, "What do you want to do, Will?"

I sat and thought about it, and half an hour went by, and I still didn't know. Nadine said, "You've got to find out, one way or the other. You can't live like this."

I was still holding her, and I was still feeling numb from the pain.

"Why didn't she tell me Gilmore called her?" I said eventually.

Nadine closed her eyes a moment. Then she looked at me and said, "You're right."

got up, went to a closet, and took out an object a little
an a transistor radio. She said, "This is a receiver." She
dial and showed me how to use it. Then she picked up the
and took the phone from its cradle. She unscrewed the cap
outhpiece, exposing the inner wires, and said, "Watch."
ed on as she inserted the microphone and showed me how
sure the thing didn't come adrift. Then she turned to the
ces of equipment, the two larger bugs, and showed me
e could be attached to the underside of a desk.
aid, "Make sure you put them where a knee isn't going to
st them."
ded. Then I asked her to take me through it one more
d she said, "Don't worry, Will, you'll get at least three
sons on how to use them, then we'll test them."
ave me a look, then got up, went to the kitchen, and came
h another beer for herself and a soda for me. She said, "I'm
you off. If you're going to do this, you're doing it cold
he gave me an odd look and said, "Where are you staying
after this?"
e hotel."
ed at her, and she said, "That wasn't an invitation. But if
to talk, you can come here."

At eleven-fifteen that night, I drove
Pico and turned north onto Century Park East. A briefcase
he passenger seat next to me. I parked in the basement lot
uilding next to the Clem Resources building and walked
n open plaza to the Clem building entrance. I knew the
ard in the lobby. His name was Henry Helton, and he'd
the same position behind the security monitors ever since
ed at Clem.
came in, he looked up and cracked a broad smile. Then he
r. Dunbar . . ." and he launched into a long congratulation
acquittal. I smiled and thanked him. Then he observed

Two hours
car outside a plain corrugated building
Nadine. It was dark already, and Nadin
an hour.

We'd driven here after I'd asked for
had resisted at first, not because she
because she recognized there was risk in
talked her into it. I said I had to know ab
the only way I knew to find out. Nadine
to come up with an alternative plan. But
thing, and given what was at stake for n
well refuse.

Finally, she emerged from the building
we drove back to her place, and when we
being in the same apartment where I'd sp
years ago. I looked around as she went i
couple of beers. She hadn't changed the de
help making comparisons, thinking how
changed ours in seven years.

Then she came out of the kitchen wit
to me on the couch. She opened a couple
to set pieces of electronic equipment on t
glanced at me in a meaningful way and
boxes.

After a while, I said, "I'm no whiz at
with the VCR."

She said, "Don't worry. I'll show you."

Again, she wanted to know if I had an
said, "No. Not now."

Then I asked where she'd gotten this
baleful look and said, "What stuff?" Then
So forget it."

She laid the pieces of equipment on the
and two larger devices that could be place

that I'd picked an odd time to come back to work, and I told him I was just here to pick up a few things.

I signed in and asked him, "Anyone still up there?"

"Not as far as I know."

"Clem's not burning the midnight oil, is he?"

"No, he left hours ago."

I chatted with him for another minute or so. Then I walked to the elevator, feeling a little nervous.

I rode up to the nineteenth floor, and as I stepped off the elevator, I glanced along the corridor . . . and dammit . . . there was one door open and a light still on. I took a breath and started forward, and as I edged toward the office, I recognized it as Greg Stannert's. I wasn't sure if the light had been left on inadvertently, but as I peered through the doorjamb, I saw Greg still at his desk, hunched over some diagrams.

I stood there, cursing silently to myself.

The problem was, even if I went to my own office and hid out until he left, there was every chance Helton would say something to him about my being here. Then he'd probably come back up, wanting to go have a drink or something. I glanced back toward Clem's office and knew I had to take a chance right then. I scooted back along the corridor.

Clem's office had a security code, but I knew the thing by heart. I punched it in, and when I opened the door, the mechanism gave off a loud click. I dove inside and closed the door, and took a moment to let my eyes adjust.

There was just enough ambient light from nearby office buildings for me to see without having to turn a light on. I set one bug directly under the seat of the chair opposite the desk—Nadine had told me it could pick up a normal conversation from anywhere in a room, even in an office the size of Clem's. Then I went to work on the phone. This took a little longer, maybe two minutes, and at one point I used my cigarette lighter to see, rather than turn a light on. Then, just as I had screwed back the phone mouthpiece, I heard Greg's voice outside. He had called out, "John!" He'd heard the click. And the next thing I knew, the door code outside was being punched.

I had no time to think of anything beyond grabbing the briefcase and diving behind the desk. The door clicked open, and a light went on. I heard nothing more. And after a couple of seconds, the light went off and the door closed.

After a moment, I got up and went to the door, realizing that even if Henry said nothing to Greg, he might see my name as he signed out. He'd know I was up here. I opened the door gently and peered out. And as I glanced down to Greg's office, I could hear him on the phone.

"Henry," I heard him say. "Greg Stannert on nineteen. Did someone just come up here?"

I started toward his office. Then I heard him say, "Will Dunbar! . . . No, it's okay, I thought I heard someone." And by the time he hung up, I was standing at his door.

I grinned and said, "I'm impressed by such devotion."

"Will!" He bounced out of his chair and strode toward me. "How the hell are you?"

"Pretty good."

"I was just calling downstairs. I thought I heard someone. I thought it was John."

I let this go. Then I tapped the briefcase and said, "I figured I'd sneak in under cover of dark, pick up some stuff."

He grinned. "Had enough of the limelight, huh? . . . So when are you coming back to work?"

"Monday, probably." I said I still hadn't spoken to John. Then I asked what was keeping him so late.

"Odds and ends . . . I'm trying to clear the decks. John's got some ideas on the boards." He grinned again. "So let's do lunch next week. You name it."

I told him, any day. I was on bankers' hours. He said he wished he could say the same. Then I told him not to work too late and I left, still feeling a little anxious, though I hoped he'd think his ears had deceived him, and that the sound he'd heard had not been the sound of Clem's door opening.

It was twelve-thirty by the time I got back to the hotel. I called Nadine and told her that everything had gone okay, although it hadn't exactly gone smoothly. I explained why, and she told me I was lucky. Then we hung up, and I thought of calling Caroline—for one reason only—I had said I'd call, and she would probably be expecting me to call. But I couldn't do it. I just couldn't do it. Even to maintain the pretext that I was still in Mammoth.

I was finding it torturous even to think about her. For the past several hours, I'd managed to push all thoughts about her to the back of my mind, while I concentrated on doing what I had to do—either prove or disprove what she might have done. But it was harder to shield myself from the magnitude of the thing as I lay there, and harder still to get to sleep, and I got very little sleep that night. Even less than the night before.

When I woke up to daylight everything seemed blurred. The events of the previous day seemed unreal, and as I lay in bed and looked at the small receiver Nadine had given me, I asked myself, Was I really doing this? Then I began to think it all through again, and I knew I had no choice. Eventually, I got up and spent a good twenty minutes in the shower.

I had some coffee downstairs and ordered an extra cup to go. Then I drove west through the late-morning rush hour, and around ten o'clock I pulled into the six-story parking lot opposite the Clem Resources building and drove up to the roof. Nadine had told me the receiver would work fine from there. It had a radius of about half a mile. There were no other cars on the fifth floor, and none up here, so I doubted anyone would come up. But if they did, I knew what I'd do. I'd act like some salesman catching up on his paperwork in a quiet spot.

It was about ten-thirty before I finally collected my nerve. I got out of the car and walked to the public phone next to the stairwell. With my heart thumping, I dialed Clem's direct number, having already worked out my plan. If he wasn't in, I'd at least find out when he was expected. And if he was in, I planned to feign an interruption and tell his secretary, Devonna, I'd call back.

Devonna picked up, and I said, "It's Will, Devonna," and I told her I needed to get together with John next week and I wanted to know which would be the best day.

She said, "Will, let me look at his book."

"Is he in this morning?"

"He's in the building, I'm not sure whose office he's in."

She started to mumble something about his being in Seattle on Tuesday. Then I told her, "Devonna . . . someone's at the door. Let me call you back."

"Oh, sure, Will."

I hung up and wiped the sweat off my palms, and I took a moment to compose myself. Then I dialed Caroline's number.

Her secretary answered and said, "Hold on, Will. I think her meeting's just breaking up."

I said I'd hold, and a good minute went by before Caroline picked up. Then she said, "Hey, stranger." She sounded very cheerful.

I couldn't believe how nervous I was. I managed to say, "How's it going?"

"Crazy . . . How's the mountain man?"

I took a breath and said, "He's back."

"What?"

She sounded surprised and a little disappointed, and I launched into the speech I'd been rehearsing all morning.

I said, "Something came up. I talked to Stella last night. She said Crawford found out Gilmore turned up a problem at the site the same day he was killed."

There was a short silence. Then Caroline said, "What?"

"Something to do with water."

There was another silence. Then she said, "Will, I thought the purpose in going away was to forget about all this."

I wasn't sure what to read into that, and I said, "I know. But she asked me to check in, so I did. And this sounded important, at least Crawford thinks it is."

"So what is it?"

"I dunno. He's supposed to call me back any minute. Why don't you cut out of there around lunchtime and I'll tell you about it. I should know by then."

She seemed to hesitate. Then she said, "Where are you?"

"At home. Where else?"

There was another silence. Then she said, "All right. What time?"

"Anytime. I'll go grab us a couple of sandwiches."

I didn't want her to call back and not find me there.

She said, "All right, I'll see you around one." Then she said, "I missed you."

I said, "I missed you, too," and I was surprised at how easy it was to say this.

I walked back to my car, lit a cigarette, turned the receiver on, and hooked a small tape recorder into it. Then I sipped some cold coffee and waited. My palms were sweating again, and for the longest time all I heard was the hiss of the tape. Then a sound came over the receiver, startling me. I heard a door opening, then closing. Silence. Then Clem's voice.

"What's up?"

His tone was subdued. I guess a second or two went by and I heard Caroline say, "Will knows about Sam's problem."

It was the strangest feeling. There was an odd satisfaction . . . like finding the answer to a complex equation whose solution should have been obvious. Then the void opened up, and I felt as if something in me had died.

I heard Clem say, "How the hell did he find out?"

Caroline said, "His investigator found out something."

There was another silence, and with shaking hands I lit another cigarette. Clem said, "Jesus Christ . . ."

Caroline said, "He wants me to come home. What do I do?"

I was wiping away tears, and I heard Clem say, "You do nothing. Act normally . . . act a little surprised. Go home, fuck his brains out, get his mind off it. There's nothing anyone can do now anyway. Just be careful."

I couldn't stand to listen to any more. I turned off the receiver and the recorder, and just sat there grappling with what I'd heard. I was aware that everything in my life was about to change, and I couldn't even begin to think about those changes. Suddenly, I was thinking of Katia. . . .

After a couple of minutes I started the car. Then I drove down the parking lot ramp and headed west on Olympic.

I almost had an accident as I went through a red light, and after that I forced myself to concentrate. I made it home. And as I came in, Fran was leaving for the park with Katia, and I was grateful for that at least.

I poured myself a drink and sat on the sofa in the living room, and when I looked at my watch, it was still only twelve twenty-five. Another half hour to wait. I didn't know what to do, except smoke cigarettes and drink. The minutes dragged, and after a while I got up and sat in the yard. Then I came back in, lay down on the sofa, and rewound the tape in the recorder, cuing it to the start of the conversation. I lay down again, asking myself whether there was any possible outcome from this that I could live with.

I was still lying there when I heard the sudden acceleration of Caroline's car in the driveway. I got up and went to the window, and as I watched her get out, I could see the faint look of concern on her face. Then I went back to the sofa, and she came in and smiled, tossed her purse down and her jacket, and said, "I can't believe you actually came back."

She walked over to the sofa and kissed me, and it took everything I had not to recoil. But I must have given off some negative reaction, because she said, "What's the matter?"

I didn't answer, and after a moment she said, "Is this about the other thing?"

I felt something form in my throat. I sat forward, moved a magazine aside, and pushed the "play" button on the tape recorder. A moment later, Caroline heard her own voice on the tape, and her face underwent a sea change. Her mouth opened, and the color seemed to drain from her face.

"Will knows about Sam's problem."

Then Clem's voice. "How the hell did he find out?"

"His investigator found out something."

"Jesus Christ . . ."

"He wants me to come home. What do I do?"

I turned off the recorder, and we sat on the sofa a few feet from each other. I hardly dared to look at her, and after a moment I said, in a strained voice, "Do you want to tell me why?"

There was a long silence. Then the color returned to her cheeks, and she said, with quiet amazement, "You bugged his office."

I said, "Do you want to tell me about Sam's problem?"

She said, "Not especially," and I didn't know what to make of the way she looked at me at that moment. I couldn't tell if it was a look of pain, nonchalance, or defiance.

Then her eyes fluttered between me and the tape recorder. She didn't say anything else.

After a moment I said, "A few people in a desert town were going to get sick. Gilmore told you. You told Clem. How much did Clem pay you to set me up?"

"What?"

The whites of her eyes grew huge. She just *stared* at me, and I was a little surprised by her demeanor. She seemed . . . almost angry.

Then she said in a strangled voice, "Is that what you think?"

I could feel something rumbling deep down inside me, and I knew I didn't want it to surface. I was trying to keep a lock on it, hold it down.

I said quietly, "You got him those cigarettes. What was it worth?"

Again, she stared at me. Then she closed her eyes for a moment. When she opened them, she met my glance, and she faced away from me to look out the window, her chin up stubbornly, and with that, I lost it.

I reached for her and yelled into her face, "Don't lie to me, Caroline! After what you put me through! What did Clem pay you?"

She tried to wrench away, yelling, "You don't understand!"

"What did he pay you?"

I shook her hard. She started to cry, and I didn't care.

"How much?" I yelled. "I want to know what it's worth to sell a husband down the river. . . . What's the going rate?"

"I didn't— You don't understand!"

"You're *damn* right."

"You don't!"

She was sobbing, trying to get her breath. Then she buried her face in her hands. She stayed that way for a while, and suddenly she looked up, exclaiming, "We didn't set you up! . . . John talked me into not bringing up the problem! You were going to quit. . . . He offered me some stock options. . . . We didn't even think they were going to charge you."

I stared at her. "What the fuck are you talking about?" I said.

"We didn't kill him! John didn't! I didn't! That's what you think, isn't it?"

There was a look of accusation on her face.

"You got him the cigarettes!"

"I didn't! Don't you understand? . . . We just went along with it. We thought that maybe it was *you*. . . . If not—" She broke off.

"What?"

She started to cry again, and I guess I felt the first real flicker of doubt right then. But I was still operating off what I'd learned and thinking this was some fantastic alibi. . . . What was she trying to tell me here, that it was a coincidence?

I said, "Bullshit! Gilmore told you about the problem."

"Yes!" She wiped at her eyes with her sleeve. "He was going to meet with John about it."

I felt myself grappling with something enormous and at the same time elusive. There were so many currents . . . anger, confusion, doubt.

She was sitting with her head down, still crying. Then she said, "I knew, even if they charged you, they would not be able to make it stick if I testified. I knew . . . but I never thought they would. . . ."

She looked up at me, tears streaming down her face.

I sat there, and I don't know when it started to sink in—I know it took a while to get beyond the *way* she was saying all this, and to think about what she was actually saying. At one point she put a hand on my shoulder, but I shook it off. I couldn't even think of being kind or sympathetic at that moment. I just sat there trying to reframe all that had gone on in the past few minutes. I'd gone from thinking of her as a co-conspirator in a murder—and worse—to this. Whatever *this* was.

I stared at her for a while. Then I got up and went to the window and gazed out at the dry leaves drifting up the driveway. And as I stood there, something happened. My thoughts seemed to perform a series of inverse gymnastics. The feeling was akin to watching a movie reel rewind. That's really what it was—a fast flicker in reverse.

It stopped. And I thought to myself, The cigarettes. And that was all it took.

I turned to Caroline. She was looking miserable, and I said, "Don't go back to the office today."

She nodded, slowly, and I knew she had no idea what to make of my sudden shift in attitude.

23

It was nearly three o'clock when I called Nadine. I called her from a public phone near the Cheviot Hills recreation center. She wasn't in her office, so I hung up and sat in the park awhile, then I got up and tried her again. This time she answered, and I said, "We were wrong."

She sounded baffled. "What do you mean?"

I said, "We were way off the mark."

There was a silence. Then she said, "I don't follow."

I didn't say anything. I didn't know where to begin. I said, "How soon can you get out of there?"

"Where are you?"

I told her, and she said, "I can meet you at my place in an hour."

She started to ask something, and I said I didn't want to say anything more just then. I wanted to bounce some things off her.

She said, "Okay, I'll be home around four." She asked if I was okay, and I said I was. Then I hung up and went and sat in the park again.

She was home by the time I got to her place. When I walked in, she gave me a look of studied caution, and as I sat down, she said, "Well?" I ran through everything that had occurred. I even played the tape. She didn't interrupt. Not once. And when I was through, she said, "What the hell is going on here?"

I got up and poured us both drinks. Then she said, "Do you believe her?"

I said, "Caroline may be a lot of things—stupid isn't one of them." She didn't say anything, so eventually I said, "I know she's not lying, Nadine."

"She could have told Clem. He could have set the thing up without her knowing."

"Where did he get the cigarettes?"

Nadine looked at the tape. "Will . . . she admits to knowing about the water problem!"

I nodded, and she rolled her eyes. Then I said, "Let's take a walk."

I drained my drink and stood up, and Nadine looked at me, shaking her head a little wearily. I picked up her jacket and handed it to her. Then the two of us left the apartment.

We walked the two blocks to the beach, and on the way she admitted she was utterly confused. "I still can't believe these two were just going to sit on this pollution business. . . ."

"Evidently . . ."

Her expression grew serious, and she said, "So where was Clem that day?"

I said I didn't know.

"If you gave that tape to the cops," she suggested, "they could check out what he did that day."

I didn't say anything.

Nadine hunched her shoulders in a resigned way. She knew how I felt about the cops. We walked on a few paces, and she said, "What if Clem knew about the water problem *before* that day? What if he was anticipating Gilmore's finding out and flipping out?"

I said, "He may be calculating, but I can't imagine him picking up my cigarette butts, anticipating he'd use them to frame me someday. Anyway, how could he know I was going to hit Gilmore?"

She conceded. She said, "I keep forgetting about that."

"Anyway, from the way it looks, Gilmore only got wind of the problem that morning."

After a moment I said, "Let's sit down."

I took her arm and more or less drew her down on the sand, and I guess there was an intensity to my manner at that moment because she looked at me curiously and said, "Will, are you holding something back?"

I said, "Not exactly. I've just been thinking about something."

She waited. Then I said, "Gilmore called Caroline, right? About the problem? He'd just found about it . . . ?"

She frowned. "Right."

"He called me earlier that morning about getting together. Then he went out to work. Then he came back, and called Caroline—which makes sense—if he couldn't reach Clem for any reason, he'd call her. No matter what happened the night before, she's still head of planning."

Nadine nodded, but she still looked confused.

"But Gilmore didn't call only Caroline that morning. He called *his wife.*"

Nadine's eyes narrowed a little.

I said, "If Gilmore was upset about the problem, don't you think he'd tell Cynthia about it?"

Nadine started to say something.

I said, "I know. She was at the Bel Air. . . ."

Nadine put a hand on my arm. Her mouth wavered a moment; then she said. "But she *knew* . . . is that what you're saying?"

I was squinting toward the ocean because the sun was in my eyes. Nadine came around in front of me. She said, "What are you thinking?"

I said, "Cynthia's the one other person who could have known about the water problem, aside from Caroline and Clem."

Nadine frowned. "Yeah, but why? Why try to frame you? What's the point? Even if she knew about Gilmore's affair with Caroline. . . ."

"I think she knew. I think Gilmore fessed up to her. I think he also told her he was seeing me that night."

Nadine shook her head, confused. She said, "Where did she get the cigarettes butts?" She was looking at me, a little exasperated. "And what does all this have to do with the water problem? Why should she give a shit?"

I said, "She'd give a shit. She's the partner's wife. Lots of money comes to the Gilmores if that deal goes through. She took a big interest in that project. All of a sudden, Gilmore's getting worked up over some ecological problem in the desert. How's Cynthia going to react to that?"

Nadine hesitated, then said, "The same way Clem might."

"Exactly."

She was still looking confused. After a moment I draped an arm across her shoulders.

I said, "I'm going to buy you dinner, and I'm going to tell you what I think happened. And when I've told you, I want you to think real hard because I'm going to suggest something."

She looked at me a little anxiously and said, "You're scaring me, Will."

I told her I seemed to be making a habit of it.

24

It was seven o'clock by the time I'd told Nadine what I believed had happened. We were eating at Hal's, in Venice, and when I'd run through it all, I told her what I had in mind. She got very nervous, and I decided to let her think about it—it was probably too late to do anything that evening anyway.

She sat quietly over her food, and once in a while she would raise an objection, and each time she did, I didn't challenge it. I just let her think about it. Then, over coffee, she brought up what we'd been talking about on the beach, and she said, "Do you really think we're right?"

I said, "I'd have bet on it the last time, but yes . . . this time, I think we're right."

Her face grew serious, and she said, "I don't know, Will. We extrapolated the last time."

I said, "If we're right, we're right. If we're wrong, we're wrong. What's to lose?"

But I could tell she was uncomfortable when I said this. And I sensed she was still looking for a way to present this to the D.A., neatly wrapped. I asked her if this was what she was thinking and she said yes, and I told her I'd already gone that route.

I said, "Where's the evidence? There is none."

She set her fork down abruptly. "There is something to lose, Will. Bluff's a dangerous game."

I said I couldn't think of any other way.

She didn't respond right away. Then she said, "So what do you do about Caroline?"

I said, "Does that mean we're on?"

"No."

She sighed and shook her head, then said, "I still think we need to talk." So we went through it all again. I laid out the arguments for this, she raised objections, and we ended up just where we'd been before.

Only this time I said, "We're still talking about it." And Nadine didn't say anything.

I said, "I'm going to call Caroline now."

Nadine didn't respond, and after a while I realized she wasn't going to. I knew it was going to be me who had to nudge this forward. After a moment I got up and went to the restaurant phone and dialed our number. Caroline answered just as the machine picked up.

There was a tense wait as we let the message run its course. Then she asked me where I was.

I said, "I'm in L.A."

"Are you coming home?"

I didn't answer her directly. I said, "I want you to do a couple of things."

She was quiet for a moment, then said, "Okay," in a resigned, compliant sort of way, as if she were looking for any way to make amends.

I said, "Have you told anyone about this? About you and me talking?"

She was quiet for a moment, then said, "No."

I said, "Is that the truth?"

"Yes."

She sounded faintly irritated, but I kept after her.

"You haven't called Clem? He hasn't called? You haven't spoken to him, or to anyone at the office?"

"I just told you . . . no."

"All right. Here's what I want you to do. Just do it, and don't ask why because this is really important."

She was quiet for a moment. Then she said, "Okay."

I said, "From now on, leave the machine on, and don't pick up. Don't talk to anyone."

I heard her sigh, and I got a little annoyed. I said, "I'm telling you, Caroline, this is fucking important. So just listen to me. . . ."

"All right. All right."

I took a breath. "I want you to go somewhere . . . for the weekend. Doesn't matter where. I want you to leave tonight. Drive up to Mammoth, go to Big Bear, or anyplace. Go see your sister in Phoenix if you like—but just do it. Take Katia, and if you don't want Fran along, give her the weekend off."

I heard her catch her breath. "And I don't ask why. Is that it?"

"That's it."

There was a long silence. Then she said, "I'm going to ask you one thing. . . . Will you be here Monday?"

"Yes."

"Can we talk then? I mean, are you saying you need the weekend to think about all this?"

I tried to be patient. I said, "Caroline, I'm asking you to do one simple thing . . . without asking why." Then my voice got a little sarcastic. "Do you think you can do that?"

"I guess. If it's that important."

"All right," I said.

There was another silence, and finally I said, "Go do it."

She said, "Will . . . I'm sorry."

I said, "So am I."

I heard her start to cry again. Then she said, "All right, I'll do it. . . . I can't talk anymore, not on the phone, not like this."

I extracted another solemn promise from her that she'd do what I asked. She said she would, then we hung up, and I returned to the restaurant table.

Nadine was looking steadily at me as I approached, and when I sat down, she said, "Well?"

I said, "Caroline's going away for the weekend. She hasn't talked to anyone, and she won't."

Nadine looked at me, a little skeptical. Then she sighed and said, "Well, I guess we're on."

I sipped my drink. Then I told her how grateful I was that she'd hung in with me through all this.

She said, "It isn't over yet."

We began to talk some more about what to do, and eventually we walked back to her place.

We continued talking when we got there. She asked if I'd mind if she got some sleep because she could think better in the morning. I said that was fine, and I got up to go to the hotel. She said, "You don't have to go."

I looked at her. I wasn't sure what was contained in the invitation. She said, "To tell you the truth, I'd just as soon you stay here. . . . I'm nervous about tomorrow."

I said, "Where do you want me to sleep?"

She lowered her eyes. "With me. I can handle it . . . if you can. We don't have to make love or anything."

Nor did we.

She went into the bedroom and got into an oversized T-shirt. Then I got into bed alongside her and put an arm around her. We kissed a couple of times, and once, after we had both resisted a passionate urge, she laughed and said, "I guess we're being grown-ups."

I said, "God help us."

For a few hours, I slept. Then I woke up, got up, and sat on the couch in the other room, and thought about it all, second-guessing myself a couple of times. Bluff was a dangerous game, as Nadine said, but something more powerful was driving me and enabling me to overcome any fear.

We were up around seven. Nadine headed for the shower. I read the paper while she showered and dressed, and when she came into the living room, she got very quiet. Finally I said, "Are you thinking of my safety in this?"

She was silent for a moment, and she nodded slowly. She said, "Will, I've been in on all kinds of operations, and I'll tell you . . . no matter how carefully you plan these things, something always goes a little haywire."

I thought about this. Then I said, "Stop worrying about me. This is my decision. You worry about you."

about to ring, and he stood there a moment and shook his head, flabbergasted. He handed me the report as I stepped back to let him in.

He said, "Jesus Christ, Will . . . I still don't believe this."

I said, "You will."

"Man . . ."

I said, "Come on in," and we started toward the living room. Then he asked me where the bathroom was, because I'd gotten him so damn worked up, he'd forgotten to go. I said there was one just off the kitchen, and I indicated the way. He went off, still shaking his head, and I stepped into the living room with the report and started to glance over it.

After a minute or so, he emerged, and I heard him walking back through the hallway. He called out, "Nice place, Will . . . How much space you got here?"

"Nearly four thousand feet."

From the living room, I saw him take a step back along the hallway and glance into the kitchen and the dining room. Then he walked back toward me and said, "All right, tell me. Before I bust a blood vessel."

I handed him the report and said, "Take a look."

It was open at page 95. He looked at it, puzzled, and said, "Site liner?"

I nodded and said quietly, "Sam turned up a problem at the site the day he was killed. Some pollution wound up at a place called Morelos."

He stared at me, baffled. Then he shook his head as if to clear it and said, "I don't get it."

I said, "Sam was coming back to town that day to get into it. Only he made a big mistake. . . . He called Cynthia first and told her about it. She told Clem. That's what got him killed."

"What?"

He was stunned. His mouth wavered for a moment. Then he said, "For God's sake!"

"You know the big interest she took in all this. She didn't want Sam getting all high-minded and screwing it up."

He seemed to be having a hard time digesting this. Then he said, "You mean that's why she took the stand against you?"

I said, "Maybe. But there is one thing that'll nail her. And Clem."

"What?"

"Her phone bill. It'll show she called Clem right after Sam called her from the site that day."

He was standing there, openmouthed. And I took the report back from him, tossed it down, and said, "We'll get into this. You need a drink . . . what'll it be?"

"Anything." He stood there looking dazed.

I walked over to the liquor cabinet. And as I poured the drinks, I said, "I bet Sam came clean about the affair. I bet he told her he was getting together with me that night. So they planted the cigarette butts, but they also staged this to look like a robbery—to me. That way there'd be two possibilities: it's me or it's the intruder. But nobody's looking at the real reason. . . ."

I heard a slight noise behind me. Then I turned, and he was holding a silenced nine-millimeter automatic on me. His face had been transformed into an expression of utter meanness.

"Nice try, Will," he said. "You got most of it right."

I looked at him in studied shock. After a moment, I said, "What the fuck is this?"

"Move away from there!"

I moved a few feet. Then he reached into his pocket, took out a set of handcuffs, and slid them across the hardwood floor toward me.

"Put those on."

I stared at the things.

"Son of a bitch," I said.

He smiled sourly. "You get it, Will? Can't have you finding out who Cynthia really called. Now put those on."

He leveled the gun and said, "I mean it, Will . . . unless you want it in the stomach. It hurts like hell there."

I picked up the handcuffs, and I said, "You were fucking her?"

He motioned with the gun again. "Yeah, I was fucking her. Gilmore was too busy playing around with you-know-who to notice." He glanced at the handcuffs I was holding. "I said put 'em on, Will."

I snapped one cuff on. Then I said, "What did you do? Cut a few corners on that site liner?"

He smiled sourly. "Very good, Will. Little too late, but very good."

"So what are you going to do?"

"Make it look like a suicide. You couldn't live with yourself. Guilty conscience . . . The cops can't stand you anyway."

I was still holding the other cuff. I said, "I figured out how you got the cigarette butts."

"Try me."

"The night I hit Gilmore. You and I were talking out on the grounds. I was smoking. When I left, you just went right back outside and picked them up."

He grinned. "Pretty good for an engineer, eh?"

"You'll never get away with it. Neither you, nor her."

He laughed.

"She and me got a lot in common, Will. About five million a year . . . Put that other cuff on and sit on the floor."

I snapped the cuff on. Then he said, "Sit down." And as he moved toward me, he said, "Sorry, Will, you're a loose end—"

"*Two* loose ends."

The voice behind him was calm. He froze.

"Drop the gun," Nadine said.

He just stared at me, with such a look of shock that his face didn't even register anger. I said, "We just needed it in your own words, Greg. It's all on tape."

I don't know what he intended, but he turned suddenly, and Nadine fired twice.

He absorbed the impact of the bullets and fell right in front of me, and I kicked the gun away from his hand. I watched the life ebb out of him as he lay on the floor.

Then Nadine started to shake.

I said, "Are you okay?"

She nodded, and after a moment I led her into the other room and dialed 911.

25

It was the cigarettes, ironically, that had finally tipped me, after it became clear it wasn't Caroline and Clem. It hit me when I was standing by the window in our house, running the film back, as it were, to the minute I hit Gilmore. Until then, I'd been thinking only in terms of someone obtaining the cigarette butts the following day. Then it had dawned on me. Since Cynthia Gilmore must have had a partner, and since she herself hadn't arrived at the party at that time, it had to be Greg.

There was no way to prove this, of course, other than the way we did. A calculated risk. Nadine and I had agreed that she would go on to the house ahead of me. We had also agreed that I would come in only at the last minute before Greg was due to arrive. If I did otherwise, she said, we would only set each other on edge. And so she went on ahead, and by the time I got there, she had already bugged the living room, and she was sitting in the hallway closet, listening and recording the conversation.

I was shit scared throughout it. I knew I had to walk a fine line, letting Greg know some of what I knew and at the same time letting him think that I thought it was all Cynthia and Clem, then dropping in that business about the phone calls, to lead him to believe he had no choice but to get rid of me. The big bet, of course, was whether he'd arrive with a gun, or at least with the idea that he might have to kill me. Nadine wasn't sure he would. But I told her, if this guy had the balls to kill Gilmore, I didn't think he would hesitate to kill me if he thought I was close to being on to him, especially if he thought he had the opportunity, since I was supposedly alone.

Like I said, it was a calculated risk, but there really was no other way to prove it. Still, I was shaking like a leaf when I turned my back on him and risked him shooting me right then. But I knew Greg wasn't stupid, far from it. I'd told Nadine we had to give him credit for being very calculating. And since he would have the opportunity to make it look like suicide, and close the book on the whole thing, I was gambling that this was what he'd do, take a minute or so to set things up, to make it look that way, giving me a chance to extract a line or two from him that would incriminate him.

When the police arrived, Nadine showed them her DEA badge and started to explain what had happened. They were having a little trouble grasping it, and when one guy got kind of short with her, I got angry and told him to shut his mouth and listen—I was still so tense. Finally, I decided to stay out of it. The cops were far more comfortable dealing with her than with me, and I could see she could handle it, even though she looked a little pale.

After a while I walked off toward the living room. Greg's blood was staining the hardwood floor, and for the first time the full implications of what had taken place hit me. Then I decided, I guess it had to be. I stared at him one more time, and then I walked out to the yard. I didn't feel too sorry for him.

At some point that afternoon, Detective Lowndes showed up. Nadine had called him, realizing that he could help her cut through some long-winded explanations she was going through with the other cops. I sat out in the yard and watched all the comings and goings, and at one point a cop wandered out and asked who the hell I was. I said I lived here, and I didn't move from the rattan chaise. The cop just shook his head and walked off. I got up at one point and caught a glimpse of Lowndes through the window talking to Nadine. He looked my way, and he gave me a strange look, but he didn't come out to talk to me or to apologize, and I felt I'd read him right all along.

Nadine gave him the tape, of course. And that was all that was really needed to take care of everything.

The Santa Barbara police arrested Cynthia Gilmore that evening. She was charged with conspiring to murder her husband, and she made a number of heated denials before finally confessing. It was Greg who had pulled the trigger, she said—which was true—it was him I'd seen going over the wall that night. Still, laying the shooting off on Greg didn't help Cynthia. There was really no way for her to avoid the fact that someone had to have told Greg I was meeting with Gilmore that night. And there was also the phone call she had made to Greg that day, after Sam had spoken to her.

From all I gathered later, Greg and Cynthia had been having an affair for some time. Cynthia was well aware Gilmore's attentions had wandered, and a number of things had sprung from that. In fact, she had found those letters to Caroline, and her bitterness toward Sam had reached such a level that she no longer harbored any desire to win him back. But what she was hanging in for were the profits from Pike Mountain, and in the meantime, she had found someone to scheme with, someone who would feed her bitterness.

From the sound of it, Greg was really a piece of work. A guy who saw opportunities all over the place to get a lot richer than he ever could from engineering. He'd been making money off kickbacks from the site subcontractors by letting them get away with work never done, and he'd split this with Cynthia, who was feathering her nest in anticipation of divorcing Sam. I learned also that there was a prenuptial agreement existing between the Gilmores, which stated that in the event of a divorce, Sam would hold on to the lion's share of the family money he'd inherited. But the piece of the pie Cynthia really wanted was half the proceeds from the Pike Mountain partnership, which were not covered by the prenup agreement. That's why she was always ragging on me about how the vote was going. But when Gilmore went into a flap about the pollution problem, she saw this money slipping through her hands, and that's when Greg realized they had no choice—or so Cynthia claimed in her confession. She said Greg knew he would be dead meat professionally when Sam found out the cause of the pollution, so he convinced Cynthia there was no other choice, and they took advantage of the opportunity I had handed them.

As I say, this all came out later. And I can't say for certain which of them was the instigator, because Greg wasn't around to contest what she said. I knew her attorney was trying to make a deal with the D.A., because her husband had been cheating on her, but it didn't help her much. The sentencing recommendation was twenty years to life, and I felt a certain satisfaction when I heard about that.

But I am getting a little ahead of myself.

My next contact with Caroline was on Sunday. She had heard the news on the car radio as she was driving to a grocery store in Mammoth that morning. She called me, and she sounded exactly as you'd have expected her to sound—disbelieving, awed, aghast. I told her not to come home. The police still had the yellow tape up.

I'd spent the previous night at Nadine's. I was alone in her apartment from nine until midnight, because she had to go downtown for the first of her debriefings with a police trauma unit. She looked drawn and pale when she got back, and she said she'd had a lot of explaining to do, and that a lot of what she'd said had not been favorably received, since she had gone against established procedure.

That night, she and I did make love. I guess it was inevitable, and under the circumstances I felt no guilt about it. Our bodies were next to each other, and Nadine wanted to, and that was fine by me.

Then in the morning she went downtown again to talk to her supervising agent, and I went back to the house.

The police had keys, and I talked to a couple of neighbors while the police finished up what they were doing. Then a cop came out of the house and said there was a phone call for me, and that's when I took the call from Caroline.

I drove up to Mammoth to see her the next morning. I wasn't sure how I felt about her, after what she'd done. She had been quite prepared to believe that I might have killed Gilmore, and she'd maintained a silence about the pollution problem. I'd asked myself a number of times whether this was naïveté or a convenient silence while she pocketed what Clem was offering her in terms of stock options, and in the end I'd decided I could at least see her reasoning. She was making the best of a bad situation, knowing she could probably get me off.

That night, she and I talked for hours, it seemed. I have no idea what time we finally went to sleep. But amid all our talk about trust, or lack of trust, about conflicts she'd felt, about mistakes she'd made, she did say one thing that night that made me realize, even then, that we were probably unsuited.

She had told me at one point that she had called Clem earlier that day, since he had no idea where she was. She said, "I told him you were coming up here. He wanted to know what you planned to do about the tape you made from his office."

I said, "What?"

"The tape you made in his office."

I started to say, "What about it?" Then I said, "Jesus Christ . . . you told him about it?"

She seemed a little unnerved by my tone. She said, "I felt I had to."

I just shook my head. I said, "Can't you learn . . . after all this?"

I don't think she had a clue what I meant. She said, "Well, Christ, Will . . . you can't blame John for wanting to know if you plan to use it in some way against him . . . or me, for that matter."

I stared at her. Did she have any concept of priorities, loyalties? I got up and went to the cabin door and stared off into the night for a while. Then I turned to her, trying to decide what to say, and eventually I said, "Clem's going to have to make a full disclosure about the pollution problem."

Her glance shifted a little. "Do you feel that's necessary?"

I shouted, "For God's sake, people in that town are going to get sick!"

She just looked at me and shook her head. And somehow I knew at that moment that we would part company.

Go ahead. Say it. Maybe I'd changed? A guy who'd once paid bribes?

I guess I had. Or maybe I'd always had some limits. But in any event, three months later, Caroline and I separated. It was at my instigation, and at one point Caroline said she could understand why I was bitter. I said I wasn't bitter—I really wasn't. I was just being realistic.

I don't know if she understood what I meant even then. But despite all the bonds, I just felt there was a huge gulf between us, and that it would only widen over time.

Since then it hasn't been easy. I can't call it a clean break because, of course, there is Katia. Caroline and I agreed to share custody, and we went through the legal arrangements for that, and in the meantime Caroline went on working for Clem, though I never set foot in the place again. But through Caroline, I let Clem know that I wouldn't make the tape public, provided he went public with the pollution problem.

He did eventually, and I laughed aloud when I read the story in the business section. Of all people, Councilman Romero was quoted as saying that a majority of the council felt it would be a step backward to close down Pike Mountain now that it was fully operational.

"We believe the long-term public interest is best served by continuing to operate," Romero said. "And I'm sure Sam Gilmore would have agreed."

Since leaving Caroline, I've been seeing Nadine off and on. She took a few weeks off—to see her parents, to visit a colleague she'd graduated with—and since she got back, she and I have continued to see each other, but it's hard to say where this will lead. Sometimes I feel we're like two wartime buddies who discover in peacetime that maybe they didn't have as much in common as they thought they did. Part of the problem, I'm sure, is that I don't really know what I want to do next, although I do know I'd like to leave Los Angeles, sooner rather than later.

I've heard people say that it is possible to be ostracized in this town as nowhere else, and I guess that's true in my case. After my initial brush with celebrity, nobody really wanted anything to do with me. And yet, in a way, I believe that what I did—when I set all this in motion by punching Gilmore—was not so much the beginning of my undoing, despite all that happened, but a first step in a new direction, a much better direction. It certainly got me out of the cesspool of politics.

It's also strange—but I remember that at the time I punched Gilmore, I sensed there would be consequences. I could never have imagined what these would be, but sometimes I laugh to myself and think, Woe unto him who stirs the waters, and reveals the dark currents that move below the surface of this city. That's how I think of Los Angeles. As a town that still tries to project a sunny serenity, despite its increasing bleakness—when in truth, it harbors a meanness that grips the souls of its citizenry.

This was never clearer to me than one morning, a month ago, when the phone rang in the apartment I've been renting, and I picked up to hear John Clem on the line. He said he realized it was probably a shock for me to hear from him, but he felt he had to call, even at the risk of my hanging up on him. He said he hoped I'd hear him out.

I said, okay. Then he said he wanted me to understand why he'd reacted the way he did when he learned from Caroline that I knew about Gilmore's problem. He said he was scared I'd go off half-cocked, bringing down everything, and cost him all he'd worked for.

Then he said, "Really, Will. Think about it. I'd have been in the shitter. . . . Maybe Caroline and I would have been looking at prison terms. . . ."

I said, "It didn't seem to bother you that I might be facing a prison term, for murder."

"Aw, come on . . . that was a different situation. We thought it was you."

"Really?" I said.

He started to search for words. Then he said he never actually thought I'd go to jail. That's why he talked Caroline into not bringing up the problem. Then he was silent for a moment. And I asked if he had anything more to say.

He said, "It's a dog-eat-dog world, Will. You know that. Look what we did in the past."

I said it was nothing I was particularly proud of, and there was a difference anyway. Nobody stood to get seriously hurt by me paying bribes.

"Hey, Will. That's my point. I stood to get hurt. Put yourself in my shoes. What would you have done?"

For some reason I just screamed at him. I just let loose. For a while I wasn't even aware that he'd hung up. I just gave vent to something that had been festering—for years. It was a primal scream. Then it died down, and in the aftermath I sat quietly and pictured John Clem shaking his head, then getting on with his day. And I realized, as Weiss had already told me, that there would probably be no resolution for certain things I felt.